DATE DUE

11/13/03	

MERIDIAN

144

MERIDIAN

144

MEG FILES

Meg Files

SOHO

*Northcoast Redwoods
Writers' Conference
2003*

Published by
Soho Press, Inc.
853 Broadway
New York, NY 10003

Library of Congress Cataloging-in-Publication Data
Files, Meg, 1946–
Meridian 144 / Meg Files.
p.   cm.
ISBN 0-939149-59-1
I. Title
PS3556.I426M47   1991
813'.54—dc20   91–16335
                                                          CIP

Manufactured in the United States
10 9 8 7 6 5 4 3 2 1

Book design and composition by
The Sarabande Press

For my mother
and for Jim and Steve

MERIDIAN

144

1

I was underwater that day. Malcolm Yarrow had taken me diving on the *Tokai Maru* in the harbor of Tanô Island. He'd brought me a black-and-white bikini from his trip to Bali, and he wanted to photograph me near the sunken wreck. I was hovering near the wheelhouse, posing fifty feet below the surface, and Mal was aiming his Sea & Sea camera at me when everything suddenly flared bright yellow, as if sheet lightning had penetrated the water. As the light faded, the yellow camera in Mal's hands flashed at me, an involuntary sputter of light in the wake of the monstrous flash.

The sea held the luminescence for seconds and then faded to amber. I held the mouthpiece to my face in panic and stared at Mal. He looked like a strange bug-eyed creature pinned to an enormous sheet of wrinkled amber foil. I began finning up and he grabbed my ankle and pointed down. I shrugged in slow motion.

I saw that Mal was crying behind his mask. He wrote on his slate and held it out to me: FIREBALL. He tipped his head back and cleared his mask. I started up toward the yellow foil surface.

Mal had my ankle again and pulled me down. I kicked hard and tried to crawl for the surface. The sea was a vast bag of jelly and I could not breathe. I had to puncture it and emerge into the air. Malcolm towed me down to the wreck. He held me and, body to body, we stared over each other's shoulder. A school of parrot fish darted frantically into a porthole of the wreck. I shivered uncontrollably against Malcolm.

He reached for his gauge and compared its readings with mine.

Mal's read 2000 pounds of pressure and I was down to 1800. Pointing at the bow of the wreck, canted upward, he swam away from me. I finned frantically after him, afraid now of the surface as I remembered a photograph of the huge dome of glowing water rising from Bikini Lagoon. Could the skin of the sea hold?

At the end of the bow gun, we were at forty feet. Malcolm floated with his arms out like featherless pinions. His skin looked like brass. He bent his arms and, with his hands at the sides of his mask, shook his head. Little opalescent fish pecked at the coral on the gun barrel. I might have loved him, I thought.

In broken-winged motion he wrote on his slate again and showed me the small printing beneath the large word already there: SHOCK WAVES.

I couldn't remember how to figure time underwater. My pressure gauge read 1500 psi, and I tried to slow my breathing. But suddenly aware that I was breathing underwater, I sucked in the air in rapid, shallow breaths. I might have another half hour, I thought, if I'd stop panting.

A school of pearly soldierfish dove at my leg, and I swatted at them in panic. From a pocket of his buoyancy compensator vest, Malcolm spun out a yellow nylon rope. He'd brought it to explore a deep hold of the wreck. He gestured me close to the gun barrel and pulled my arms and legs around it, then positioned himself opposite me on the now vertical barrel. Handing the length of rope back and forth, we wrapped it around ourselves and the barrel, three turns, and then Malcolm tied the two ends together. I thought of sailors lashing themselves to masts against the sirens' song. I reached down to make sure I could touch the knife strapped in its black plastic sheath to my calf.

Only once before in my life had I ever recognized that I would have to die. I did not believe in my own death. Surely I would not die hugging the gun barrel of a World War II wreck. Ships were sunk, but war brides waited in home villages and gave birth. Bodies were bulldozed into common graves, but the diaspora carried the common blood. None of us believed in the death of the world, not really.

Malcolm Yarrow was in the Air Force, a captain. "Let's get a dive in this week while we still can," he'd said. "The base is going on yellow alert. It probably doesn't mean a thing, of course." I choked now, laughing into the mouthpiece, snorting into the face mask. No, no, I shook my head at foolish Captain Yarrow. Malcolm was going to be embarrassed, I thought, humiliated. We'd never be able to dive together again or admire new bathing suits or order strange drinks at the Tree Bar or kiss again unless I handled him right. You just had that yellow alert on the brain, I'd say. You read your *Stars and Stripes* too avidly. This was just some accident.

The water shuddered. The gun barrel began vibrating. Sand shot up from the harbor floor. The wreck started to rock. Malcolm reached his arms around the barrel to hold my shoulders. I could barely see him through the silt. Broken fan coral and Coke bottles, coral rocks and tires flew around us. The *Tokai Maru* lurched, it was tipping. I knew it was going, and I struggled beneath the rope, shredding my thighs and bare belly on the coral encrustations on the gun. Whirlpools of debris and fish and sand pushed at the wreck and spun away. The ship fell sideways slowly, as if being sucked into quicksand. I pulled at my knife, remembered to thumb away the keeper, and yanked it out. I held my breath, just as I used to rounding the top of the double Ferris wheel, to keep my stomach still. I worked at the nylon cord in the shuddering water. The ship fell on its port side onto the scoured harbor floor just as I cut the cord through and kicked away.

I'd been on the island three weeks when Malcolm Yarrow visited the high school. His wing had adopted Matuning in the military's Sister Village Program, and he was recruiting students to help clear a field for baseball. I'd caught a glimpse of him in his dark blue pants and light blue shirt as he walked by my classroom with one of the school guards. Later, when the row of students next to the open louvers rose in their seats to look outside, distracted by voices, I'd seen him with the assistant principal, kicking at the red dirt. The afternoon sunshine glinted off the gold braid on his shoulders.

"All right, troops," I'd told the class, "nothing to get excited about." After school, I checked my mail slot in the office on my way out, and he followed me from the office to the parking lot.

"If you're not one of those haoles who only go for the natives," he said, "I'd like to take you out."

"I'm not one of anything," I said. "And I don't go out with racists."

After school the next afternoon, he was waiting at my car, an island heap I'd bought for three hundred dollars. "I tried to call you," he said.

"No phone," I said. "They've been scheduled to come install one three times so far."

"Now I'm sure you're new on island, or you wouldn't be so surprised. I figured you were, anyway."

Everyone said "on island" and "off island," omitting the article, just as if this were the only real place.

I put him off two more days and then, realizing that I liked finding him leaning against my rusted brown car when I left the building, I agreed to an all-day tour of the island on Saturday.

"Since you've only been here a month," he said, "I don't suppose you're a diver."

"Well, suppose again, regulator breath," I said. "I was certified years ago. In the middle of cornfield country. Can you believe that?"

I remembered the silly terror of jumping from the side of the swimming pool into ten feet of water and donning all my gear at the bottom. Wet hair stiffening in the cold after class, I'd driven home in the dark to Daniel. I was exhilarated. I remembered the

6

dark cold of the March open-water dive in a quarry. On our vacation in Florida, the diving was nothing like that in an over-chlorinated indoor pool in the winter, and nothing like the dense water of a rock quarry, bottomless as quarries always were. I followed Daniel in the Atlantic's clear blue water, down to the Christ of the Abyss. When a remora pursued me and attached itself to my bare belly, I'd panicked. Daniel had had his fun with female shark jokes after that.

"So what brought you all the way out here to our fair rock?" Malcolm asked.

"The job, what else?" I said. "The adventure."

He smiled and raised his eyebrows: tell me more, tell me the truth.

"I don't really know," I said. "It seemed safe."

"Safe?" he said. "Don't you read the news? Didn't you read that Baghdad has the bomb now after all? Don't you know what that means?"

"Well, but that's the Middle East," I said. "This is Tanô Island. The Pacific." I'd meant a different kind of safety, anyway. "I don't mean to be cavalier about it, but they've been squabbling forever. And we're way out here in the middle of the ocean."

"Right. With an Air Force base. With warheads. About as safe as Tel Aviv."

"But that's right," I said. "They'd go for Israel again; we'd be all right here." I didn't really read the news, not carefully, but we all knew that the danger was over.

"Oh, you innocent," Mal said. "Let me enlighten your pretty self."

"All right," I said. "So doomsday is upon us. Let's make merry in the meanwhile."

Malcolm took me diving every weekend. The best dive sites were accessible only from the base, and he belonged to a club that gave him use of a boat. He introduced me to the island with all the pleasure of a resident tourist. We drank coco-locos and tequila sunrises at the hotel's Tree Bar; we went diving on reefs and wrecks and came up to iced beer in a cooler; he got us invited to a native fiesta where we nervously ate octopus and kimchee and fruit bat; and, tropically stimulated, we made love on a beach with wet sandy towels under us. When he went on temporary duty off island, he stopped in Bali on the way back, just to buy me a new bikini, he said. "Did you know the bikini was named after Bikini Island?" he asked. "After all those tests, it was an island without a middle."

He described the beach masseuses on Bali and their shrieked pride in the erections they provoked. He described the shop where he'd bought my suit, and the Australian women who stripped to try on suits right in front of all the other shoppers. He teased me, but it didn't matter: I didn't think any exotica could overload my senses, and I knew I was compelling yet another man to love me. Coming to the island, I should have been safe— different and clean to myself—but the Malcolm Yarrows were many and I was still deficient. Malcolm bought me a black-and-white bikini and took me down to the wheelhouse of a wreck to model it, and the fireball turned the harbor to amber foil, and the first shock wave tipped the wreck.

After the shock wave had passed, the debris settled, the water stilled. I swam down for Mal, checking my gauges: just under 1000 pounds per square inch and fifty feet down. The barrel of the *Tokai Maru*'s bow gun lay on the harbor floor, maybe another twenty feet below me. Mal would know about staying underwater as long as possible, I thought. I'd use the air faster by going deeper, but Mal had been taken down with the gun. Another ten feet and I saw him vaguely through the sandy water. It was like seeing the defeated mutant in a grainy black-and-white movie. I let myself sink. I couldn't see his face. His purple arms and legs floated on either side of the gun barrel. He was crushed beneath it.

The mouthpiece of his regulator floated above one arm. I couldn't tell if the tank on his back had been crushed, too, and I didn't see his gauge, but the regulator was free flowing. I purged it and traded mouthpieces, floating above Malcolm. Old Coke bottles and cable and rusted mess trays settled. I thought, *Mal de mer*, and almost removed the mouthpiece to say it to him. I didn't think I was deep enough for narcosis, but a painful rapture passed through me. Malcolm. Malcolm.

I breathed the rest of Malcolm's air and then returned to my own. Blowing into the mouthpiece of my vest to inflate it slightly, I rose to twenty feet and tried to stay there until I was down to 700 psi. Then I ascended another ten feet, trying to see through the skin of the water as I waited. The surface looked pocked, as if by heavy black raindrops. Would a second or third shock wave follow, as with a tsunami? Leaving myself 500 pounds of air just in case, I emerged.

Hot gusts of wind were blowing large ashes across the harbor and into the water. The sky was dark yellow, whipped by orange. I turned my face from the coarse waves. I could see fires on the far side of the harbor, and as I turned to assess my distance from the other side, a fuel storage tank, halfway out to the breakwater, exploded. Malcolm had anchored our boat to the wreck of the *Tokai Maru*. It was gone.

I began stroking toward the breakwater, still breathing from the aluminum tank on my back, but the rough water and the bulky gear kept me swimming in place. I imagined radioactivity whipped toward me like dust devils. I knew nothing about fallout. Holding up the snorkel tube on my buoyancy compensator vest to let out the air, I sank a few feet and finned more easily toward the breakwater, surfacing now and then to check direction.

I swam underwater with my eyes closed, as if blindness would save energy and air. I held my breath, letting it out slowly before the next short inhalation. Near the breakwater the surface was very choppy, and currents yanked and released my body. Malcolm

Yarrow was at the bottom of the harbor. Through the metallic pull of my breathing, I pictured him on land again, awkward with the tank on his back and his new Power Plana fins in one hand, descending the rocks to the water. He had tried to balance enough to pull on the fins, then held the mask to his face with his spread hand and jumped straight-legged off the barge. Beneath the water, he'd devolved into a creature smooth and elegant. I wished I could stop my monstrous breathing. I thought of his purple limbs floating like tube sponges.

Finally, close to the breakwater, it became obvious I wouldn't be able to climb out as usual, crawling onto the boulders to the right of the concrete barge, one of many that had been dumped upside down to make part of the foundation when the breakwater was built after World War II. I would be battered against the coral and rocks.

Remembering that there were square hatches in the side of the huge, hollow, concrete block, I let myself sink, holding my arms out to push off from the barge when the currents threw me toward it. A few feet down, I swam with the rush of the water through one of the hatches. Inside, the water was usually still and cold and clear; now it was gray and silty. I swam to the shore side, where rocks had been dumped or had slid inside the barge. I made out a hatch high up the wall. Behind me, the water was dark blue swirled with orange, as if the currents were charged. I took off my fins and crawled up the rocks toward the hatch that opened to the air, and I wormed my way out.

Out on the rocks I sat for a minute, my mind frenetic like the water, my body numb. I didn't have much air left in the tank, and so I began climbing. I discarded my fins, snorkel, and weight belt; I still wore the mask, the knife, the tabi on my feet, and the gloves. Always I'd struggled quietly up the boulders before, not wanting Malcolm to think me a weak female who needed help. Now, beneath the dark yellow sky, even with the tank on my back, I climbed mindlessly, easily.

We'd left a pair of beach towels in a crevice next to the barge, and I tied one around my waist and wrapped the other around my shoulders under the tank. Would a wetsuit have helped against radiation? I thought I could feel fiery molecules lighting on my exposed skin.

Up on the road, the Scout sat exactly where we'd left it. Only the paint on the driver's side was scorched.

I retrieved the key Malcolm had hidden under the front left wheel. I opened the back end and pulled out a full tank, a 50 we'd meant to use on a second, shallow dive. Holding my breath, I changed tanks and, just as if it mattered that I return the rental gear, I lifted the empty tank into the Scout and climbed into the driver's seat, sitting awkwardly forward because of the tank on my back. I slid the seat back as far as it would go and automatically switched on the radio. The high, even tone of the emergency broadcast signal sounded, like a dead patient's heart monitor. I turned the dial, though the radio had been tuned to the island's only station. When I returned to "Hit Radio 100," KOKU, the emergency beep had died.

The shock waves hadn't badly shaken the breakwater's far end, but as I negotiated the rutted dirt and coral road, I passed a burning fuel tank and flaming tangantangan and an overturned Toyota.

Most of the buildings had been blown down and the boards and thatch and corrugated tin burned or scattered by the roiling winds. There were some black forms near the road, in the door-ways. I didn't let myself look at them, not closely. Not after the first few. But the dive shop was a small concrete structure and seemed almost unaffected. It was deserted. I stayed inside, afraid, afraid that my air supply would be stolen, afraid that I would be found. I tested all the tanks, even those beside the compressor, waiting to be refilled, and carried out every tank with any air in it. I slid the tanks under the rear porch to hide them and hoped the wooden platform wouldn't catch fire.

11

With no power I wouldn't be able to refill the tanks, even if I could figure out how to operate the compressor. I supposed that I wouldn't be able to pump gas, either. At least Malcolm's Scout was half-full.

I made a hiding place under the counter, laying down a stack of mattresses and using a life vest as a pillow. I wasn't sure what I was hiding from. I'd seen no one, no one but the dead. Wrapped in beach towels, wearing the tennis shoes I'd left in the Scout, I hid three caches of masks, snorkels, fins, dive gloves, underwater flashlights, buoyancy compensators, and knives among the rocks around the shop and down the slope to the beach. Then I removed everything else from the glass cases and the display tables and scattered it on the beach below the shop. An empty store couldn't be looted.

Using a dive knife, I pried a board from the floor behind the counter and dug a hole in the sandy dirt below. I lined the hole with a nylon gear bag. There I hid the can of hash and the can of chili I'd found on the shelf in the compressor room. I added the candy bars, for sale to provide quick energy for divers, and a dozen cans of Coke and Sprite from a cooler, as well as the six-pack of San Miguel from Mal's cooler. Outside, I buried the bowl of potato chips and the ripe bananas that had lain on a folding chair beside the compressor. I didn't want to be tempted by food that was probably contaminated.

And then, exhausted, overwhelmed, I lay down under the counter and drifted.

For the first two days, I lay under the counter with a tank beside me like a stiff baby. My legs and arms had been cut and abraded on the coral and rocks in the harbor, and I smeared myself with first-aid cream that I found in the glove compartment of Malcolm's Scout. I slept and I sipped Coke and I read books on tropical marine life, diving skills, and the sunken ships and planes wrecked in the other world wars. I heard occasional explosions as, I thought, ruptured gas lines and fuel storage tanks ignited. I crawled out to change tanks, lugging the tank beside me rather than wearing it on my back. Saving myself had drained me, and I was tired and empty, as if I'd spent an entire week in debauchery, as if I myself had decided to push the button and was now past weeping.

The wind settled to gusts full of soot, and the flare of fires died. Through the face mask I wore to avoid breathing through my nose, I watched the daytime sky darken with ashes and soot and low black clouds. The second whole day was dusk, and noon on the third day might have been midnight with a new moon. But there was no moon. Was this nuclear winter? The world's end? I didn't think the darkness could result from a stray bomb or two.

When I emerged, I saw that the jungle was filling up with soot like woods with snow. Much of the island seemed to have burned. The fires had died and the hills were black and stubbly. At night the sky roiled with black clouds. The sea was flat and oily. The dark sky and the soot suspended in the water rendered the sea dark gray. The shore was littered with fish, and dead fish floated in the water, as if some god had decided to harvest the entire crop by dynamiting the Mariana Trench.

On the black sand, with palm trees like wrought iron behind me, I sat and watched the sun set in the Philippine Sea. It settled beneath the black clouds into a gray band just above the horizon. For a few minutes, it sent an aurora of purple and green and orange streamers and flashes into the gray band. Then the sea absorbed it.

In the dusk I thought I could see shapes scattered on the beach, like bronze garden statues. They shed no reflections. They cast no shadows. They heeded no calls.

2

A year ago, Daniel called home late one afternoon and said, "Kitty, I'll be bringing a guest for dinner." I combed my hair, took a package of dinner rolls from the freezer, and put a cloth on the table. It was a weeknight and I had papers to grade.

Daniel's dinner guest slunk in on a leash. She was a Siberian husky, lost or abandoned, wearing a tag from Kankakee. Her owner's phone had been disconnected. She stayed for supper, but she didn't eat much. Daniel kept her at his side, trying to make the beautiful, timid dog his own.

Three months later, she gave birth on our bed. I scrubbed the mattress and finally flipped it over to hide the stains, and threw out the blanket and the sheets, but the bedroom always smelled like blood. Perhaps it wasn't the dog's fault. Daniel and I nicknamed the four pups and observed their mother nurse them, tolerate them, and finally shun them. We kept the prettiest little girl, watched her grow into something like a Siberian husky, tried to guess her paternity, and named her Cimarron.

I knew Daniel had left me when I found only that half-grown puppy and not her mother in the pen.

On the island, Cimarron was still in quarantine. I'd visited her daily, walking from the high school to the government animal facility during my lunch hour and driving from my apartment on weekends or getting Mal to stop. Dumb, he said: dumb to spend all that money, dumb to lock her in a cage for three months, dumb of the government to require all that time when the incubation period for rabies was only seven days, dumb to bring a thick-furred northern dog to a tropical island. He shook his head, humoring me: dumb to squander all that love on an animal. Cimarron was always frantic when I visited. She'd jump six feet to the top of her cage, bouncing as if her feet were on springs, until I opened the cage door and joined her inside.

Cimarron was still in quarantine. I was numb, the island's fires had faded, the land and the sky were black, the bodies in the road were bloating, and I'd nearly forgotten that Cimarron was still in quarantine. How long would it take for a caged dog to die? Had the quarantine building withstood the blasts and the fires? Something lurched in me, as I thought a pregnant woman must feel her child quicken, and I thought that now, as life returned with pins and needles to my sleeping body, I'd have to try to rescue the dog that Daniel had left me.

The Exxon station on Marine Drive hadn't burned. When I pulled up close and turned on a flashlight, I saw that the pumps' faces had been shattered. It might have been the shock wave, I thought. The handles on the sides of the pumps wouldn't move. The sign on the umbrella post between the pumps read NO PAY NO PUMPS. Wondering if I could figure out how to activate the pumps, I turned to the station office. The glass door and windows were smashed. The man behind the counter had been Chamorro, I thought. He lay on his back, shards of glass were embedded in his forehead and cheeks, and his body had swollen enough to pop the buttons on his flowered shirt.

Here and there, blackened palms rose from the burned land, like used pipe cleaners bent and stuck into the ashes. I drove with the headlights off, less out of fear than from a sense that light would be inappropriate. I drove slowly, with the windows closed and the doors locked, skirting or rolling over the debris—fallen palms, hunks of concrete, telephone poles draped with dead lines.

15

A bloated dog on the dirt shoulder of the road lay on its back with its thick, stiff legs straight up, like an old mahogany table, upside down before an estate sale.

Before, the island's roads had been packed with cars: new Japanese cars with tinted windows and rusted heaps like mine. When the junk cars finally burned out, they were left on roadsides or pushed into the jungle, and either way, tires were stolen and windows were smashed and soon vines crept over the bodies until some less-frequented roads seemed to pass through technological topiary gardens.

Now, most of the cars were off the road, as if the drivers had pulled over to watch the fireworks. Some had spun around and some had crashed into each other. Many had burned.

Near the high school, the shops and the rehabilitation center were blackened ruins, with hunks of bright melted plastic scattered around the remains of the Tick Tock store where the kids had bought radios and tape decks and electric guitars. One arch of the world's largest McDonald's had disappeared and the other, black and twisted, rested against a wall of the shop next to it. A sign hung vertically from the wall, still intact: MONGOLIAN BAR-B-Q.

I breathed my canned air and drove through the ashes in dead Malcolm's Scout. I wondered how the retarded workers in the rehabilitation center had died. I thought of them blinded by the flash, falling among the lawn mowers they were trying to repair, their bodies as burned and twisted as the arch. I drove toward my caged dog, weeping into my ridiculous face mask. I thought: Burnt offering. The whole little island floated like a bituminous leaf on the sea, a burnt offering on a blackened altar.

The animal quarantine facility was at the end of a World War II runway that had become a wide road without lanes. Much of the beaten-down jungle on either side had burned, with patches of ash-covered green showing. The concrete building and the chain-link fence around it were ashen but intact. As I started down from

16

the Scout to try the gate, I heard barking and thought abruptly: She's alive. Then I caught a flash of brown. I slammed the door and the dogs were upon the Scout as if it were a boar they could savage. They leapt on the hood, black lips pulled away from their yellow teeth, and dug at the windshield. They were boonie dogs, the half-wild scavengers that had roamed the island, dug in trash barrels, and bred until they all looked the same: medium-size, short-haired, generic brown dogs. A female snarling against the window had empty, loose teats hanging nearly to her feet. All of the dogs were scrawny, with mangy skin stretched over their skeletons.

Close to my own dog, surrounded by the only live creatures I'd seen, I began honking the horn. The dogs jumped back for a moment and then attacked again. For three days I'd been afraid to be found, but suddenly I wanted people, anyone who would save me from the pack of boonie dogs and from the ashes. Anyone. I held the horn until the constant blare seemed to drown, and then I punched out rhythms — dots and dashes, though I didn't know the code for SOS, the *beep-beep-beep beeeeeep* of Beethoven's Fifth, *shave and a haircut, two bits.*

I found myself pulling for breath. Sucking in a lungful, I switched the regulator to the extra 50 I'd brought, exhaled slowly as I turned the new air on, and then breathed. If there were ever a race for gear assembly, I'd be in contention. If there were ever an endurance test for survival among ashes, the pack of boonie dogs and I would be right up there.

The dogs jumped back when I started the Scout. I backed up carefully in the midst of the pack and pulled clear, wanting to escape the dogs, not run them over. They chased the Scout down the rutted runway until I pulled up beside a pair of cars that must have crashed head-on. One car had dark-tinted windows, closed, no good. But the other was a jacked-up Duster perched on huge truck tires, and an arm hung from the driver's window. I could see a red sleeve. The dogs leapt for the arm.

17

At the quarantine kennel I opened the gate, drove through, and got out of the Scout to shut myself in the yard. I took the car keys with me but left the doors unlocked. Beside the main building was a small trailer which had been air-conditioned for special pets. I began there, prepared to liberate anything alive.

If the cats and poodles in the trailer had survived the shock wave that had knocked over the cages and part of a wall, they'd all suffocated in the heat of the closed trailer. I closed the door against the stench, thinking of the boonie dogs leaping for the arm dangling out the Duster's window. I thought of an archaeologist someday discovering an aluminum crypt full of cat and dog mummies, each in a separate wire coffin neatly labeled with name and feeding instructions.

The front area inside the kennel housed the strays and the boonie puppies that needed homes. I'd walked between the rows of cages every day on my way to Cimarron. Some of the cages were empty, and many contained dead puppies and kittens, but two held live boonie dogs, one with its back leg in a splint. "I'll be back for you," I told them. They watched me silently.

No one was in the office. A note on the desk read: "Dad, I be back to hose out runs by 3:30. Dont worrie. Love, Your Favrit Son."

I started down the long concrete aisle between the cages for the quarantined dogs. The first cage held Lucy, a tan cocker spaniel, dead in the far corner of her cage. Next was Roofius, a dachshund, whose cage door had a countdown calendar tied to it. Roofius, with thirteen days to go, was dead. I'd seen dead people washing back and forth near the shore and dead people sitting in their cars and a dead man behind a gas station counter with shards of glass in his forehead and dead people, bloated or burned, strewn around ruins. I hadn't wept. I'd seen a baby wearing tiny gold earrings and blackened, half-melted Pampers. I hadn't wept.

But I stopped before each cage now and said farewell to each dog. I'd known them, and many of the owners, from my daily

18

visits to Cimarron. Newcomers, in their new bright island-wear, would discuss the island's corruption and violence and beauty and filth with me. We'd shake our heads, amazed, and then admire each other's dogs. Farewell, Lucy, I said around the regulator's mouthpiece. Goodbye, Roofius. Goodbye to Lollie and Pups, a pair of Cockapoos who shared a cage. I heard barking down the line. Still I stopped before each cage. Farewell, beautiful Sam.

In the next cage were Dobie Gillis, a Doberman, and his owner. The owner had been a young man with a curly blond beard. His belly and chest had been opened and emptied. Dobie Gillis lay with his head on his master's shin, watching me without moving.

The shepherd named Bear opened his eyes and then sat up when I stopped before his cage. A red-lettered sign said LIBERA-TION DAY!!! "Hello, Bear," I said. "Hello there, boy."

I found two more live ones before Cimarron. "Cimmie, Cimmie, Cimmie," I said. "My sweet, sweet Cimarron." She jumped once, straight to the top of the cage as if she had springs on her feet. "That's my girl," I said, "just like the old days, my sweet Cimmie pup." She put her paw in the empty water dish and rattled it against the concrete, and then lay back down. "Don't you know me in all this gear?" I asked her. "Now you just wait." I checked the few cages past Cimarron's and said farewell to the rest of the dead dogs.

I loaded two ten-pound bags of Purina into the back of the Scout, along with a half dozen cans of Alpo and a short choke leash and a long chain from the rack of items for sale in the office.

When I opened her cage door, Cimarron sat up and stared up at me. I crouched and she leapt at me, knocking me over so the tank clanged on the concrete floor and the mouthpiece was jarred out. I left it out. She licked my cheeks and my eyes and my mouth.

Before I took her to the Scout, I filled her bowl with the water in the hose. It was hot but she drank it frantically and then, on the second bowlful, drank with her familiar *shlup-shlup-shlup* pause *shlup-shlup* rhythm. Clumps of her black-and-gray hair were scattered in the cage and stuck to the fencing. Radiation made hair fall out, I thought. But she'd shed in the island's heat before, too; I hadn't seen the accumulation because her cage had been cleaned daily. I thought I remembered that concrete could protect against fallout.

Once I had my dog in the Scout, I emptied two plastic garbage pails of dry dog food in the yard and carried two buckets from faucet to faucet until I'd drained the pipes. I wasn't really afraid of the dogs, but I held a large dive knife when I opened the cages. Dobie Gillis lunged at his door, biting at the wire, and I passed him by. The rest of the dogs cringed, somewhere, I imagined, between the first panic of hunger, thirst, and abandonment and the frantic rage of starvation. I removed the mouthpiece to call them out.

I left the gate open after I drove out of the quarantine kennel's yard. There was no more quarantine. Now I was quarantined on the island.

In my wake, I heard the pack of boonie dogs in the kennel yard with the pets I'd freed, and with Cimarron sitting up beside me, snapping at the wind through the half-open window, I stepped on the gas and raced down the old runway past the jacked-up Duster that no longer had an arm hanging out the driver's window.

By the end of the first week, my air supply ran out. I had three full tanks stashed in my caches among the rocks by the beach, but I left them hidden. A few more hours wouldn't save me now, and I might need a sea escape later. The island was putrefying beneath the black sky, and the ocean's gray water was stagnant, the swells churning suspended debris and bodies to the surface. The shore was edged with gray foam. The air tasted brackish. There was nowhere to escape to.

I kept Cimarron tied beneath the dive-shop counter with me. When she needed to go out, I walked her behind the shop and a short way up the rocks among the trees. I'd eaten the chili and the hash; I'd drunk much of the Coke and Sprite, but I'd had to allow the dog to drink water I dipped from the barrels in which divers had rinsed their gear. The barrels had wooden covers and I hoped the water wasn't poisonous. Breathing through the regulator had kept me thirsty, but I wasn't hungry. I lay beneath the counter on a pile of deflated air mattresses, feeling hollow and lethargic, too stuporous ever to have belonged to a species clever and energetic enough to have obliterated itself.

As a child, I used to wake in the middle of the night and deliberately kick off my covers. "Mama, Daddy," I'd call, "Mama, Daddy, cover me up." Judy, my sister, tucked under her covers in the bed beside mine, never woke when I called them. Daddy never came to cover me up. But my mother always hurried to my bedside. She wore a satin bonnet to hold her hairdo. She smelled of Vicks. I remembered no nightmares. But I needed her at four A.M. She'd replace Judy's stuffed rabbit, Apricot, beside her, and then she'd turn to me and pull up my sheet and blankets. She'd tuck them around me and wait until I stopped shivering. She didn't kiss me. I was never an affectionate child, she told me later, though Judy, a year younger, hopped readily onto laps. She never asked me why I didn't pull up my own covers. I'd chant, "Mama, Daddy, Mama, Daddy, cover me up," and my mother was always there in the four A.M. dark.

My mother needed motion. Impulse or recoil—I was not sure it mattered. Perhaps her own mother's rejection of her had left her no possibility for peace.

One summer, coming home from college, she got off the bus and started walking toward the hotel. Halfway home, she spotted her mother, with the terrier on a leash, coming to meet her, and she set down her suitcase and ran to her mother, a fat woman herself in the way that petite women grew bosoms and turned square as they aged. The daughter was tall, round-faced, and pretty: an art major with all of her paintings awaiting, her brush

21

dipped in watercolors, in oils. And she was newly in love. The potential for love and art must have sent her running to her mother—and not as a pudgy child runs, thighs chafing and palms facing back, but as a pretty young woman in possession of her own height and big bones.

Her mother said: "I wasn't coming to meet you. I'm just walking the dog. Go pick up that suitcase."

My mother told me this sometime after I'd married Daniel. I didn't remember what made her recall it. Our talks spiraled and looped until we'd cocoon a topic, and then we'd unwind the silk and take another look at the chrysalis, turn it, and wrap and unwind again.

"I realized a while back that she really was coming to meet me," my mother said. "But she just couldn't say it. If she'd only said it."

How could I, a child battered by her moods, be the constant love she needed?

It was dangerous to be in the car with her when she became maddened. She'd snap off the radio viciously, swerve to the curb, and turn on us, slapping at Judy and me.

When she was coming at us once, in the living room, Judy picked up a chair and held it before her, lion-tamer style. "Down, Conga," she said. But her timing was off, and Mother jerked the chair from her and spanked her.

We all would cry afterwards. Judy and I would go to our room, and she would tease me about my "measles"—the red blotches on my forehead from crying—and we would write *I am sorry, Mama, I love you, Mama* notes and sail them down the hall to her.

Judy was an ever-cheerful mother. "Mom said to me once that I was a cold fish," Judy had told me. "I don't know if she actually said 'frigid,' but that word stuck in my mind. But I vowed I wouldn't treat my kids the way she did us. None of that up-and-down stuff, one minute you're her darling and the next you're out of her favor. Kids can't take sarcasm, either."

"There's such a thing as so much sweetness and light that you turn into a mannequin," I said.

"Say what you want," she said calmly. "You just take a good look at my kids. They always know where they stand with me. And they're well-adjusted, secure kids. They're *happy.*"

"Well said. I like to hear you getting defensive. That 'happy' sounded almost mad," I said. "But you're right. They're the most genuinely happy kids I've ever known. It's a good thing Daniel and I haven't had children. I'd probably have done a repeat of Mom."

Now, Judy was no mother at all. I thought of her straight body melting in a firestorm, puddling against Mitch and the kids. Here, Kitty, Kitty, Kitty, she used to taunt me. Kitty want its tuna din-din? Kitty want its sandbox? I'd hit her wildly and cry, and she'd point to my "measles." Her children weren't allowed to hit each other or tease. I thought of her melted body crystallizing finally into one of the giggling statues we'd been in the summer-evening games. She always drew teardrops on her *I am sorry, Mama* notes.

3

This morning I saw a lizard. Waking beneath the counter in the dive shop, instantly bereft though the dog lay against me with her hair sticking to my sweaty skin, I kept my eyes closed. And when I opened them, there was the gecko motionless on the wall of the counter. It was pale, nearly white like the paint on the wall. I watched the pulse in its throat. It must have been there for some time while I slept, for there were streaks down the wall and I could smell the acrid odor of gecko droppings.

People used to complain about the geckos, as they did about the cockroaches, because of the gray streaks left on whitewashed concrete walls even after cleaning, or because of the shudders caused by the little reptiles darting over the walls. But I'd liked them from the beginning, perhaps because their presence made me know I was someplace strange and new, starting fresh. They scurried and then suddenly stopped, as if confident that their suckered feet would keep them to walls and ceilings and windows, confident that the erratic dash was the correct way to convergence with insect or mate. When they abruptly stopped, the fever of the charge beat in their throats. It had felt cheerful to have them in the apartment: friendly, tiny cohabitants I could talk to harmlessly. And I'd read that once a house was deserted, the geckos left, too.

Cimarron knew I was awake, though I hadn't moved, and when she lifted her hind end to stretch, the gecko ran up the wall beside me. So close, he seemed to squirm more than run, moving the pair of legs on one side of the body toward each other, and then the other pair. That made three, Cimarron, me, and a gecko, along with a pack of boonie dogs and maybe a few pets, if they'd survived the pack. I'd hibernated for a week, breathing my safe air, and suddenly I felt guilty and charged, the way I'd felt at fifteen when I'd slept until noon on Saturday and Mom was downstairs cleaning house with angry thumps and bangs. I could stay hidden, and starve and sicken, offering myself up, though unburnt, but I'd never believed I'd have any other life, and so I stood and stretched, ready for convergence.

Seen from the air, Tanô was shaped like an elongated paramecium; the harbor on the west was its oral groove. North of the harbor were the long white beaches of any paradise. One stretch was lined with tourist hotels and a public park. The Air Force base had claimed the best of paradise, the northern end of the paramecium. Civilization had set up on the eastern back. Strung out along Marine Drive, which circumnavigated the island, were restaurants and massage parlors with a clump of government concrete structures on the inland side. Near the middle of the paramecium was the public high school, with the rehabilitation center and the animal quarantine facility across the road. Nearby, too, had been the Two Lovers' Apartments, where I'd stayed.

On the island, none of the local people would have asked where I "lived." Instead, they'd wanted to know where I "stayed." Even islanders who'd been born there never lived: they stayed.

The southern end of the island had offered much evidence of transience—hills swept every dry season with brush fires, remains of villages blown away and flooded by typhoons, scattered shacks of packing-crate wood and corrugated tin, shipping containers with doors and windows sawed out. The south had a wide bay, surrounded by hills and edged with a fine black-sand beach, where Magellan had landed in 1521. Every year the southern villages re-created the landing, with the Spanish in fading costumes and the

25

girls in grass skirts. Every year a brown Magellan, in napless velvet pantaloons, struck down seven Chamorros and christened the place the Island of Thieves.

And the southern end had its more recent history, too, as the territory of the Japanese camps and execution sites. The south had been picturesque still, the southern villagers believing they lived much as their ancestors had.

Malcolm Yarrow had given me the tour, pointing out the caged fighting cocks and the naked babies in front of thatched shacks, and he'd given me the lecture. "Oh yeah, they live the simple island life and love it," he said. "That's why their sanitation is so poor they die off from lytico. And somebody ought to tell them that the jungle and the sea might clean up a lot of their messes but nature doesn't know what to do with old cars or Pampers."

It was just an island, I'd thought, not the little world Malcolm was trying to make it, just a coral rock on Meridian 144 between the Mariana Trench and the Mariana Ridge.

My Chamorro dictionary had defined *Tanô* as *island, ground, home,* and *world.* I thought that the word must have lost its meanings to the islanders, just as names such as Taylor and Smith and Butcher had long been nothing but sounds. Now Tanô was the island-world again, the only ground, the last home.

I dreamed once that Daniel and I were diving, or somehow staying underwater without all the gear, and it was night. The ocean bottom was sandy and clear, and we flew like rays. Through the lens of the surface we could see the bright, watery moon. The water was an unripe green. We found a half-buried cannon and brushed the sand away. It was coral encrusted, and then smooth green copper where it had been buried. Suddenly a cannonball rushed out and hit Daniel, propelling him toward the brittle glass surface.

In the morning, I'd told Daniel about the dream. "Let's hear you interpret that one," he'd said.

"Oh, but you don't believe dreams mean anything," I'd said. "I don't," he'd said. "Not even cannons."

In the dream I'd fluttered after Daniel desperately, knowing I couldn't save him.

My mother had needed other people. She chattered away to me and Judy, to our father, to department store clerks, as if without us to bounce her words against, she'd have had no voice. She kept up a running chatter of what she was doing and why—the reasons for changing lanes as she drove, for throwing away an old measuring cup, for wearing black slacks. My mother never merely purchased a nightgown: she was buying it for her aunt, her mother's sister with whom she'd lived the summer she worked as a Rosie the Riveter, her aunt who was going to a hospital in Florida for colon surgery, and the aunt was the fussiest person to buy for and she'd probably send the gown back, but maybe she'd like this simple lavender, she had excellent taste but you couldn't please her, but you had to try anyway when she had been like a mother to you.

I used to leave her in stores, saying I'd meet her in the teen department. There she'd explain to the clerk why I needed plain blue pants to go with my sweaters, a yellow one and a light blue one and a real neat red-and-white ski-style pullover. And they'd look all right with my loafers; she didn't want to buy me new shoes, too. You know these teenagers. The clerk would nod, and I would cringe and preen.

At home, I could not stand her inane chatter. But after my homework was done, I'd hang around the kitchen where she was ironing or stand in her bedroom doorway until she noticed me, needing to be the one she sent her chatter against.

Daniel had no patience for the parsing, gleaning ways my mother had taught me. Oh, will you quit looking for the deep hidden meanings, he'd say. People just are the way they are, with no excuses. But I thought of my mother as a fat girl, holding her

27

mother's silk glove against her cheek at night. And I heard a current running beneath her chatter: See? You see? I'm just as normal, just as human as the next person.

After a week of breathing private air, I needed people. It seemed impossible that I alone had survived. I decided to tour the island, starting with the air base. With two large dive knives, a length of hose I'd taken from the outside faucet, and Cimarron, I started north in Mal's Scout, and then automatically turned onto the cross-island road and drove to the Two Lovers' Apartments.

Legend had it that a beautiful Chamorra, the chief's daughter, had fallen in love with a native boy, and to escape the match her father had arranged with the Spanish captain's son, the two lovers had tied their long black hair together and jumped off the highest cliff to the rocks and surf below. Besides the Two Lovers' Apartments, with a mosaic of the falling bodies on the end that faced the road, there had been a Two Lovers' Hotel, a Two Lovers' Gift Center, a Two Lovers' Laundry, and a Two Lovers' Fish and Pizza. The tour buses always took the Japanese honeymooners to Two Lovers' Point.

The Two Lovers' Apartments had disappeared. "Not exactly into thin air," I told the dog. The air was still smoky. All the cars, mine included, were gone, though a hand-painted wooden sign was still staked into the ground before a parking stall: PARK HERE, DUDE, AND I'LL SHOOT YOUR HEAD OFF. I saw a few blackened pieces of mosaic tile and two mismatched zori. I remembered the falling lovers fixed in the mosaic, as if they were a pair of shadows burned onto the end of the building by a nuclear flash. I wished that one wall, at least, had remained.

Nothing of mine was left. The spare life I'd assembled—a few dishes and one pan, a set of white sheets and two white towels— was gone. My books were gone and the mimeograph dittos I'd had ready to run off for Monday and Friday's vocabulary quizzes and the second period's paragraphs on "What I Wish" were gone. "This is stupid, Cimmie," I said. "Let's get out of here."

Returning on the cross-island road, I started watching for cars likely to have gasoline in their tanks. Many of the cars had burned and exploded. I stopped beside a new car, something gray and Japanese-made, with dark-tinted windows. I'd never had occasion to siphon gas before, and I didn't know whether I could reverse gravity and get the gas to flow upward to the Scout's tank. I wondered if the Scout took unleaded, and then I choked, with a sound I'd caught myself making repeatedly—a laugh at an ironic joke to no one but the dog and a sob stuck together in my throat. It didn't matter; the gray car's gas cap had a lock on it. I tried a knife tip in it, and then thought that if the keys were still in the ignition, the gas-cap key might be attached. But that would mean opening the door.

I drove on. Cimarron stuck her nose out the window, flapping and snapping at the air like a dog on vacation. Already the burned ground showed new green growth. A sign after the curve had been altered to read PISS WITH CARE. I choked.

At last, nearly out of gas, I turned around in the middle of the road and drove back to the new gray car. Tinted windows had been popular, though illegal. The police couldn't see if those inside were drinking beer or groping each other, if the driver was a child, if the people were present or absent, live or dead. I tried the driver's door, ready to slam it if it opened. It was locked. I circled the car twice and tried the passenger's door. I'd been keeping my distance from the dead. There must be distance between the living and the dead, I'd explained to the dog when she pulled against the leash. I hardly felt alive, but the dead and I had nothing to do with each other. I opened the car door a few inches and slammed it on the smell. Death was supposed to smell sickly sweet, but this was putrescence. I retched, and the taste of the bile that rose was a relief from the smell inside the new gray car.

Finally, though, I tied a rag bandit-style over my face, held my

29

nose, yanked open the door, and reached past the passenger for the keys. I couldn't tell how the people had died. Now they were lique-fying. This is the liquidation, I thought, come on out for the final liquidation of the species, and I choked. Now the driver and the passenger slid, uncongealed, in gobbets down the silver upholstery.

But I figured out how to insert the hose and suck on the end and curve the hose: I couldn't defy gravity with a straight tank-to-tank connection, but I could fool it with a hill that had a downward slope on the other side.

Back on Marine Drive, I drove north toward the base. Already the road was breaking up, and I slowed when a protruding chunk of tarmac sent Cimarron into the dash. The roads that had been World War II landing strips were better. The wit had been busy with the road signs here, too; I passed one with some of the letters painted out so that it read PEE LIMIT 35. I didn't recall those alterations from before, but they must have been there, for the signs were dusted with gray ash.

A mile from the gate to the base, there had been a string of girlie bars, placed to capture American serviceman and Japanese tourist both. The bars had been low wooden buildings, shacks glorified with purple and orange paint. Shorty's Hut, Booze 'n Stuffs, the Hafa Adai, Joey's, and the rest had been blown apart, as if the wind had entered peacefully and swollen, like a customer after five beers, until it grew feisty and broke the place up. The wall of jungle behind the cleared roadside was littered with splintered purple and orange boards. I poked around for cans of food but found only burst beer cans and broken glass.

Here, and along the next mile to the gate, nothing had burned. But already the jungle was breaking over the military's trimmed roadsides.

A sentry sat in the guardhouse. The gate had been rolled shut and padlocked. The land behind the gate was rampantly green. The sentry wore his cap. His head leaned against the window as if he were scrutinizing me. I honked, though I knew the sentry's wasted face was seeing nothing. The dark clouds over the base were smeared with dirty yellow. The dozen men around the guardhouse must have twitched and jerked themselves to death. The bodies were twisted and warped, and sheened with yellow and orange like mildew. When I saw a gas mask beside one body, I thought that the base must have been the target of chemical warfare, and I turned around and sped away.

During the Japanese occupation, the Chamorros sang "Oh Mr. Sam, Sam, my dear Uncle Sam, won't you please come back." Three years after Pearl Harbor, the U.S. recaptured the island. Later the military laid claim to a quarter of the land. Later the girlie bars and the massage parlors were strung along Marine Drive, named for the liberating Marines. Later lone servicemen were pulled into the boonies and gang-raped. Uncle Sam hunkered down on the north end of the island, and sunbathed on his long white beach, and shopped at his commissary, and groomed the jungle, all behind his fences. To the lower island, he sent down tendrils of democracy, election campaigns blared from truck beds, Spam, nearly enough governmental jobs for all those not on welfare, and money.

South of the Air Force base, I turned down the road that looped in front of the hotels. At the bottom of the slope, I couldn't go any farther in the Scout. The new wing of the Hilton, which had been under construction, was scattered with its scaffolding across the road. I parked, and with Cimarron on a leash, walked around the jumble of concrete and twisted rebar. The dog pulled toward a swollen brown arm sticking up from the wreckage as if in salute. "No, Cimarron, no," I whispered, just as I used to whisper when I was reading late and Daniel was asleep, just as if she were a pup cutting up in the living room.

The Hilton, the Dai Ichi, and most of the other hotels were gone. I could almost see the shock wave moving across the bay, the silent shudder of the hotels, and the dusty collapse. I could almost see the buffet brunches, linens, room keys, postcards, maids, gift-shop coconut heads, and tourists sucked in with the implosion. Most of the wreckage lay in anthill heaps. The beach had disappeared, and the shallow bay was full of concrete blocks, scaffolding, and a dirty yellow crane on its side.

The rear half of the Fujita Beach Hotel was still standing. I walked toward it, past the ruins of a Denny's Restaurant. Its banner was draped across the smashed concrete. DESSERTS IS ON US, the banner said. I couldn't see how it could have spread so neatly by accident. Most of the island's tourists had been Japanese, and I began to wonder if the sign was spread as some hotel survivor's ironic comment. In the restaurant's ruins I found broken dishes and a counter griddle that had been folded into a U-shape, but I found no food. Malcolm had taken me to the restaurant once for Sunday breakfast, and I'd noticed that the menu featured Spam-and-Eggs. I hated Spam and I couldn't find any cans in the ruins anyway.

"We wouldn't eat if we had it, would we?" I asked the dog.

The Fujita had been a minor hotel, small, yellow-tan concrete, two-story, cheap. The front half had sheared off like part of an iceberg falling into the ocean; I couldn't see any sign of it nearby.

The island had been silent since the wind had died, but abruptly the sky rumbled. It was the first time I'd heard thunder since I'd come to the island. I ran for the hotel and began trying doors to first-floor rooms. The seventh door opened, and I yanked the dog in with me. I heard a rattle across the room, and without moving I said, "This dog will kill you." Then I turned, and no one was in the room with me. The window above the air conditioner was partly open and rain spattered sporadically on the metal, as if the weather had forgotten how to operate properly.

I checked beneath the bed and in the closet, and then I dropped onto the unmade bed and tried to weep. The sobs were dry. I didn't know if someone had been in the room and crawled out the window before I could turn. How could anyone be afraid of me and my killer dog? I'd been no one's enemy but my mother's and my own for years. I remembered the stories of the American Marine who'd hidden on the island during the Japanese occupation, and the stories of the Japanese soldier who'd lived in a cave on the southern shore for twenty-seven years, never knowing the war was over. The U.S. and Japan had been allies for years now.

I leaned out the window. "Friends," I yelled. "Allies." Cimarron chased her tail furiously on the orange carpet. "*Konnichi wa*," I yelled out the window. I thought it meant good afternoon. It was the only Japanese besides *sayonara* that I knew.

A raindrop hit the air conditioner and I pulled back. The water was black. I felt as crazed as the dog. She's got the rips, Daniel and I would say whenever one of the dogs was overtaken by frantic charges. The rain would be contaminated, I thought. I felt as if the blood had beaded in my veins and arteries and begun jumping, as if I had the rips but couldn't chase my tail and race around the room. I felt as if the tears would be black if I could release them.

"Cimarron!" I said suddenly, shocked. She was humped up, all four feet together, defecating on the orange carpet. "I can't believe this," I said. "Why didn't you tell me you had to go?"

Still hunched, she looked over one shoulder at me, her eyes red-rimmed and guilty. I began crying again. It was crazy to cry over a dog's guilty eyes. It was crazy to be shocked at the dog's lapse when the world was gone. I lay on the bed. The sheets were yellowed and there was a stiff semen stain in the middle. It was crazy to cry about an unmade bed.

Cimarron jumped up and licked me tentatively. I pulled her down beside me and held her as I should hold some person, but the world was gone, and I hadn't been on a bed for an entire dead week. I fell asleep to the black rain.

I had them all again in the patterns of dreams: my mother laughingly trying to balance on a small rubber raft in some shallow sea, myself trying to hold the blue-and-yellow raft for her large body. My mother splashed into the water, not caring that her hair got wet. I had teased and combed her blond-gray hair.

In dreams, I had defunct sounds: neighbors arriving home after dark, the familiar *thunk* of the car door slamming closed at homecoming, the children running back out onto the wet grass in their pajamas.

In the summer dusk, we'd played statues. We were summer-brown, and the grass was mown and damp, and the peach tree shed overripe fruit which Judy mashed and spread in a mud crust to make peach-a pie, and the cut grass stuck to our bare legs when we fell. Donnie Reynolds took our hands, one by one, and spun us. Arms taut, we whirled: peach tree, green-shingled house, corner yard, street, willow tree, peach tree, house, corner, street, willow. When Donnie let go, we flew across the yard and let our bodies loosen until we fell, until the side yard was littered with toppled statues. We held the fallen poses. Then Donnie pinwheeled alone and finally fell, dizzy, in place.

The house was green-shingled on the bottom and sunflower-yellow up to the low roof. It was a new tract house with a breezeway. The yards and the streets were raw, with no sidewalks or curbs yet. The Reynoldses lived in a gray-and-pink-shingled house across the street, and there was an empty rutted lot beside it. Sally the deaf girl lived one block north with her aunt. Statues was Sally's favorite game. When Sally didn't play fair, her aunt told us, we should pantomime crying. Once when the new drains had been overwhelmed by a summer thunderstorm, we put on our ruffled cotton bathing suits and swam in the flood, and later we all had ear infections, even Sally the deaf girl.

In the summer dusk, the brown statues giggled and collapsed. Lightning bugs shone and vanished like incandescent candy corn tossed into the air. I found the jars I'd hidden behind the garage in the afternoon, knowing it would not be safe to go into the house for them at lightning-bug time. I would be seen and young-ladied.

I'd punched holes in the metal lids with a rock and a thick nail. We let the lightning bugs flash in our fists, like a flashlight shone through a cheek, and then stuffed them into the jars. They would be our secret lights when Judy and I sneaked out and met Donnie Reynolds and his sister Carol at midnight on the dot.

In the summer dusk, the mothers appeared in screened doorways and called us, stretching our names to four syllables, and we hid the lightning-bug jars and ran to the screen doors. The mothers brushed the cut grass from our legs and clothes and hair, oh just look at you young lady, and Sally the deaf girl knew it was time to go home. We had Rice Krispies and milk in the kitchen. I hated to pretend to cry when Sally wouldn't play right, but we had to, her aunt said, or Sally wouldn't learn. I wondered if Sally knew about the hot guilt flopping inside me when I rubbed my fists into my bent face, boo-hooing even though she couldn't hear. In the hot nights Judy and I slept in nothing but cotton panties. When I awoke sometime in the early morning, I sneaked out through the breezeway door and dumped the comatose lightning bugs out of the jars. I scared myself into seeing shapes beneath the willow tree and ran back across the wet grass. The screen door bumped against the frame with a muted beat like *ma-ma*, and I hurried back to bed and lay stiff with the image of the statues in the yard cast on the inside of my eyelids.

In dreams, Daniel would somehow wander among the children in their pajamas and I would be one of them, running in white cotton panties because it was so hot I was allowed to sleep almost bare. I could feel the sheet against my back and flung-out limbs, and the motionless Midwestern air crawling across the blue-painted sill into my room. I was never Daniel's child and as he hauled me into the air like a niece or a daughter, I grew and clasped my legs around his waist when he tried to let me down. At night our skins touched and blended into molecules.

4

It was late afternoon and the world outside looked like a child's scribble-drawing: erratic colors and a random brightness scratched into the black ashes and the black clouds.

Before I left the hotel room, I ran a little rusty water into the sink until the faucet began spitting foul-smelling air with the trickle of water, and I soaped and rinsed my body. My sweat smelled like garlic. I pulled clothes from the single suitcase in the room. The woman had been smaller than I was, but the man's brown trousers weren't too bad a fit. He'd bought a blue T-shirt that was embossed with a fuzzy orange sunset behind a palm tree, and I pulled the tag off and put the shirt on.

Most of the downstairs rooms at the Fujita were locked. Some of them were occupied, and the smells, which made me jerk away as if ammonia had been held to my nose, kept me from searching those rooms. "New brand of smelling salts," I proposed to the dog. "Essence of death. Guaranteed to wake even the dead." I found only rotten fruit and open packages of shrimp crackers in the unlocked rooms. In the laundry room at the far end, washers had overflowed and a dryer had exploded. Printing on the wall said: To our Costumer Pls. use U.S. Coin.

The second-floor rooms opened onto a balcony. As the dog and I ascended the open concrete stairway, I thought I heard something, a scrabbling in the cement rubble on the balcony. I opened door after door, calling *Konnichi wa* into the rooms. I left the doors to the dead closed. I did not even try to force the locked doors. In one room I found two silver cans of Sapporo beer upright in the shreds of a cardboard ice bucket and a cat food-size can of cuttlefish. I loaded the cans into the fishnet bag I'd picked up on the balcony.

The Kentucky Fried Chicken stand had been next to the Fujita. I thought sickly of extra-crispy chicken and of the red rice and hot finadene that every island restaurant and stall had served. The larger-than-life statue of the Colonel remained, tumbled in the sand, Southern visage down. I remembered laughing to see the Japanese tourists taking each other's picture beside the Colonel.

In the litter behind the statue, I kicked up a can of mushrooms. Product of the People's Republic of China. MaLing Choice Whole Mushrooms. Packed by China National Cereals, Oils and Foodstuffs. Across the pale button mushrooms pictured on the label were Chinese and Arabic characters, no doubt claiming nothing less important than that the contents were beautiful choice whole mushrooms.

I pulled Cimarron toward the Scout, with Snoopy's suppertime paean running stupidly in my head. *Suppertime, suppertime.* I could have stayed in one of the Fujita's open rooms but I drove home to the territory I'd claimed, carrying my cuttlefish and mushroom supper on the seat beside me. *Sup, sup, suppertime.*

The sign for Pedro's Wake was still there. I'd seen it many times, pointing into the boonies on a road that was really a path, until it had ceased to register.

I remembered that I'd been worried about diving last week with Malcolm, especially in the harbor where sharks were attracted to the tuna boats' processing discards. I'd never read anything about sharks' attraction to menstrual blood, and I'd been too embarrassed to ask at the dive shop, but it had seemed logical that the blood would pull them. I had been due for blood a week ago.

The sign for Pedro's Wake was a weathered board, with one end sawed to an arrow point, nailed to an old post. The words were hand-painted in uneven letters, with black drips beneath the *r* and the *W*. I'd seen other signs for other wakes, Danny's and Jesus' and Vincent's, but they'd been knocked down once the ceremony was done. Pedro must have been long dead even before the rest of us last week, but nobody had bothered his sign.

I didn't believe I could be pregnant. I'd made love with no one but Malcolm Yarrow since Daniel, and we'd been careful, Mal and I. Though I'd dreamed of babies for years, Daniel and I hadn't engendered them, and I'd been careful that no one else would. At least I'd been careful of that.

At first I'd meant to photograph the Pedro's Wake sign as local color. A funeral wake had seemed a sign of the past, a practice imposed by Catholic missionaries but made part of island tradition. At first, the sign had suggested something about the island's truth, and I'd thought I'd understood the subtlety of interwoven traditions, but still I'd been embarrassed to stop and photograph the old sign just like a tourist, and then I'd ceased to see it at all.

Now I stopped before the sign and looked furtively around. I reached to touch the crossbar and drove splinters of the wood beneath my fingernail. The dog scratched at the Scout's side window and whined, agitated at my dance of pain. When I tried to pull the splinters out, they broke beneath my fingernail.

If I had a baby, I thought, I'd name him Pedro. Then I thought I must be delirious with hunger and pain and fatigue and solitude and disorientation. I drove the Scout back to the dive shop, my hideout. The dog had crawled into the back of the vehicle. I wore my seat belt. I knew I was not pregnant but had merely ceased to function. Little Pedro did not exist and needed no wake. The sign, uneven painted letters on gray wood, pointed up an overgrown path into the jungle, unburned here, hot green and rampant here. My left index finger throbbed with the splinters.

I wanted to make a fire but I had no matches. Anyway, I was afraid. A fire would make me less afraid, a small, human-tended fire to keep the animals at bay, but also more afraid, for men were pulled to campfires and the clink of tin pans and blue-enameled coffeepots. Beyond a fire would be mountain cats, too far for their eyes to catch the firelight but glinting green nevertheless. Within the erratic light cast by a fire, men could pass a bottle, drink from tin cups, someone could sing a ballad, "Beat the drum slowly, play the fife lowly," like a sentimental movie scene, and in the strobe of the firelight, men could dance out the day's hunt or crouch over women.

I decided, as if I had a choice, to eat my supper cold. First I opened a can of liver-flavored Alpo for the dog and shook the soupy chunks onto the dive-shop floor. Cimarron gulped half of the food and then moved across the room and vomited the unchewed chunks. The gagging, saliva-filled retching didn't bother me; the familiar sound could have nothing to do with radiation sickness. Immediately she ate the regurgitated chunks and then finished the rest of the food. She licked the wooden floor.

Beneath the counter, where I slept, I laid out the can opener, the can of MaLing mushrooms, and the flat can of cuttlefish. There was a rush of saliva in my mouth. I didn't believe there was any other human in the world. I hoped I could make myself eat slowly and keep the food down. I pulled the tab on a can of San Miguel and drank slowly. The beer was warm and yellow. Slowly I ate the flesh of the cuttlefish and the mushrooms, washing down the briny taste with the beer, and then another beer.

With the dog beside me, I sat on my bedding beneath my counter and held one of the cans of Sapporo beer I'd found in the Fujita Hotel that afternoon. All day the sky had been dark and now the night was so black that I was blind. I felt the dog's thick gray hair. I held the Sapporo can in both hands as if it were an urn, and I could feel the flare and the soft ridges and the muted silver. It was an alien object, as if I were Cro-Magnon, and yet it was as familiar against my fingers as a pre-Columbian vase to an archaeologist.

The last human left, I remembered that ontogeny recapitulates phylogeny. I drank from the Sapporo can. Then which was I? the last of the race who had crawled, gilled, from the brine and stood upright and made fire and civilized itself to death? or the infant in the cave, preparing in the blinding dark to crawl out and find a mate of my species and learn again to use the fire drill and the particle accelerator? Or was I merely an individual with the race's life squeezed into a ball behind my ribs, a human remembering gilled breathing in amniotic water, falling on my vestigial tail as I learned to walk?

Suddenly I laughed aloud in the dark: falling on my vestigial tail indeed. The beer had made me drunk.

The dog thumped her tail uncertainly. Our noises spun out into the darkness and I lay down, drunkenly spinning and abruptly terrified. I put my hands out flat on the wooden floor, feeling that gravity could fail and the earth could spin me off. Vertigo swept through me, and I did not know if I was floating in the sea or lying on the coral earth or floating in space so bright it was black. And I held to the dog in despair, knowing the whole story, wherever I was in it, knowing the way we carried memory and consciousness of what we are—our veneer of humanity, the hidden worm-eaten heart.

In the dream, Daniel and I were in our old green Impala, except that the seats were dark green instead of white, and then he was sitting on the curb next to the passenger's side where I sat. A thin stream of muddy water ran along the curb. Then it was my mother sitting on the curb, and she kept dropping her dangly earrings into the stream and I kept reaching over the car door and plucking them out for her. We heard a sound and I thought it was a baby's crying from some nearby house, but the other person, my mother—or Daniel—was outside on the driver's side then, and I struggled to say, *Get in.* And the other person turned to see what was there and said, *It's the sea wolf,* and I glimpsed a shape like a bloody seal. I choked out the words, *Get in,* and woke myself with the words spoken into the stagnant gray air in the dive shop.

My own voice brought me abruptly to the world again, and my heart pounded as it used to when I'd awakened from my childhood daytime naps. My body must have lurched, seeing the bloody seal, or perhaps the dog had twitched in her sleep, for something had startled the gecko on the wall beneath the counter: it had dropped its tail. The stump of the tail looked cleanly cut and cauterized. I sat up slowly, but the gecko sped away, around the corner.

Beside my leg, the lost tail wriggled on the beach towel, and then was still. I shuddered and flipped it away.

"You do what you have to do," I told Cimarron pompously. "Jettison the tail to save the body. Lesson for the day." I lay back on my pile of mattresses, sticky with sweat and the dream.

When I was fourteen, my mother wouldn't allow me to shave my legs. "It doesn't show now, it's so fine," she said, "but as soon as you start shearing it, it'll come back black and stubbly."

But she gave me a miniature gold razor in a velvet bag. She showed me how to screw the little handle onto the blade. When I shaved under my arms the first time, she took the little razor from me and carried it downstairs.

"Oh, please don't," I said. "I'll just die."

But she proudly showed my father the hair-clotted gold razor. Often I went with her to the grocery store. Judy didn't have the compulsion. She'd never write another *I'm sorry, Mama* note. But I, who could take her moods no more than Judy, I, who dreaded the public embarrassment of our lives spread out like wares on a bargain table for the store clerks and the checkout boys and acquaintances she encountered, I was compelled to hang around her.

"Hop in," she'd say. "I might let you wheedle me into buying you a new record." She listened to our 45s with us.

But it wasn't the bribe I accepted. I was coming to know how to be a woman, and how not to be, but I didn't stumble along stoop-shouldered beside her grocery cart for those gleanings, either. "Straighten that back," she'd say. "You're slim, you're blond, you've got nothing to hide." I'd squirm under her hand, cringe beside her, knowing that everyone in the store had heard her, dying when we came to the records and she discussed the Belmonts and the Supremes, needing and denying her pep talks. I had a full spread of morbid secrets to hide, and she knew it.

My reward for giving my mother the contact we both required was Green Stamps. It was the only reward that Judy understood. I got to save all the Green Stamps from the grocery store. I let them collect in my underwear drawer, and then I'd paste them into the books and see how many more I needed for the record player.

"Oh, look at the sweet little kitty's tongue," said Judy when I licked my Green Stamps. "Does the kitty like its mucilage? Oh kitty-kitty, it likes its horsie hooves, yummy, yummy."

"You'll never touch my new record player," I said. "Never ever."

Though Judy was a year younger than I, she'd already started. My friends merely said "started," without specifying what. We couldn't use the health-class word, *menstruation*, or our mothers' word, *period*. Judy had started last summer, while I was at camp. Mother had told her friend next door that Judy had mentioned it matter-of-factly and they'd gone to the store and bought the supplies. "That was all there was to it," Mother said. She shook her head. "You never saw anyone so matter-of-fact."

When at last I had enough books of Green Stamps, Mother took me Saturday morning to the redemption center. She gave me the nickel to put in the parking meter and, as we walked down the Saturday sidewalk, she said, "I've got a bone to pick with you."

And I knew it wasn't something like not making my bed, I knew it was a secret lurching into her sight.

"I found a mess at the back of your underwear drawer," she said.

I knew there were nine pairs of bloody cotton underpants back there, stiff and brown, smelling like old blood.

"I don't know why you didn't tell me," she said.

We walked together among the Saturday-morning women, and I could only shrug.

"I'm curious," she said. "What did you use?"

We passed before the redemption center's window: toaster, plush animals, silverware, coffeepot, suitcase, radio, necklace, linens, everything displayed randomly.

"Toilet paper," I whispered.

I redeemed my blue-and-white record player. Every month my mother became erratic and angry as the wads wrapped in toilet paper piled up in the bathroom wastebasket, and every month Judy matter-of-factly bled. The record player was beautiful, gently grained, and it spun my 45s, with the center pieces pressed in and later my long-playing Sibelius records, immaculately. For years I irregularly gave up my secret pent-up blood.

I lay back on my pile of deflated air mattresses, hungry and nauseous. Would there ever be toothpaste again? Mothers would not bring their sick children trays of ginger ale and soda crackers. There would be no raisin-bread toast. Cats would no longer lie around in possession of houses when the owners weren't home. No husband would pat his wife's buttocks as he passed by for another cold one from the refrigerator. No neighbor would send her little boy over with a sack of zucchini from the garden. Beethoven was irrevocably dead.

The stump-tailed gecko waddled around the corner and stopped on the wall beside my head. I thought it was paler than before, now grayish-white against the whitewash. The dog dropped her head and blew out against her flews. Her black rubber nose and her black lips looked dry.

My body had a yeasty smell, and my hair, gummy with sea water and unwashed for over a week, was clotted and ropy. When I moved, the Japanese tourist's clothes gave off an odor that was a blend of old man's trousers, cheap new Korean clothing, and unwashed woman. My skin was sticky, with tiny balls of dirt in the sweaty creases.

The condition was nearly pleasurable, as coming home after a camping trip, smelling of sweat and wood smoke, used to be an affirmation of vitality. Now my dirt and my smell affirmed my regret.

After a short while on the island, I'd noticed that my hair and my fingernails grew more quickly than before. I could feel the ropes of hair down my back, and my nails were long and jagged. Regret, I thought. Nothing like a bit of understatement. Kitty regrets that she will be unable to attend your gala celebration. She is spending the season in the tropics, luxuriating in her own odor, picking at the scabs on her scalp with her ragged fingernails. She regrets.

Something would have to be done about this condition, I thought. Behind my regret wasn't vast grief but a tingle of anticipation, as if the phone might ring. I must grieve, I thought. I grieved for my lively dead mother, and I grieved at the death in Daniel's eyes, and what was the requisite amplitude of grief for the blue planet snapped into ashes?

"Come, dog," I said. "We find food." I believed she approved the gruffness.

I remembered my father's simple, loud way with foreigners, as if his words were lifted from the sentence diagrams of a sixth grader who could identify nothing but subject and verb. *I go. You stay.* In compensation, my mother and I spoke to foreigners elaborately, our vocabularies blooming like magnolias on intricate branchwork.

The morning sky was still gray but a lighter gray shimmer had been overlaid, as if I were seeing the thick sky through a new aluminum window screen. The wind had picked up during the night and the sea rose in large, smooth swells. A black band at the horizon separated the gray sea from the gray sky.

Cimarron nosed at something in the road. "Get away from that," I said. She did not move. It was a smashed crab. Pieces of shell were scattered around it, and within its substance—like butterscotch pudding—were two neatly curled claws, intact. Ants were working on it.

"What the hell, dog?" I said.

There were clues here. This crab was freshly dead. Something else had survived. And here were ants, as well, doing the old work. And something had killed the crab. I remembered the proof of God: Things change and must have a changer. The crab looked as if it had been run over by a car.

I had heard no vehicle in the night. I closed my eyes and could almost hear the rattle of a truck passing through a town at night, a touch on the air brakes as it slowed at the blinking yellow light, a rattle as it crossed the railroad tracks. And I sat down abruptly on the dive shop's front step, nearly falling, as the remembered world clattered around me. With my head between my knees, I waited for the clatter and the motion to pass, like dizziness. Men dollied loads of paper from trucks into offices where the paper would be fed into typewriters and printers and copy machines and then filled with words and numbers and graphs. Truckers passed through towns and then back onto the interstate. Men in red visored caps strode past the plastic banners snapping in the wind at Milty's Good Used Cars. Phones rang in offices, and secretaries chirped Kohlman, Biersbach, and Anderson and pushed hold buttons. Women rattled carts down grocery store aisles and loaded them up with macaroni and cheese, four for a dollar, yellow Angel Fluff toilet paper, Total cereal instead of Choco-Cookie Crunch, shoving the kid down again in the toddler seat. Machines stamped, people inspected, products rolled out.

And what did all that motion do to the planet? Had we put a wobble in the orbit? I felt the concrete step tilt and then slow beneath me. And what happened when the motion ceased all at once? The spinning top fell over on the table. The game was over.

Cimarron had eaten the smashed crab.

I could hear my students saying, "Oh gross, miss," and giggling. I missed the island rise-and-fall of their English. I missed *mees* and even *sāys*. I missed telling them of the world. When I was in high school, my own mother had returned to school and graduated with a degree in elementary education. She had, long before, forsaken art. In a classroom my mother knew how to handle kids—like yeast and warm water ready for flour, which she stirred in, a cup at a time, and then let rest but only for twenty minutes, and then she went to work, kneading. Sometimes the kids cried but they were moved, and they and their parents wrote her notes, which she saved. She was good, very good, at turning out doughboys eager for the oven.

Judy had been jealous of the kids. "I hate those brats over at Wiley School," she'd said.

But I came to understand the way my mother must herself have swollen, merely watching the active ingredients at work, and I did admit, I came to understand the tactile satisfaction in the shaping. I did so admit.

Rogelio Torres had sat in a front-row seat of my second-period reading class. He was a tentative, fat boy from the Philippines.

The class consisted mostly of boys, poor readers all, from two rival villages. They threatened and made gestures at each other, but they all made fun of Rogelio. The only other outsider was a boy from China, but he was quiet, whispering the correct answers when called on, and nearly motionless. Rogelio tried too hard to join one side of the room or the other. His fat, his small T-shirts, the fact that he was from the Philippines, and his funny pronunciations ensured that the local bad boys would mock him.

"Hey, Rogelio," one said. The bell hadn't rung yet.

"My name is Roger," he always insisted.

"Hey, Rogelio, what do you call a Filipino out walking a dog?" The fat boy grinned, ready to be the butt of the joke.

"You call him a vegetarian!"

I had the main bad boys back after school, and I gave them the tolerance-equality-brotherhood-America talk.

"Hey, sorry, miss," Joey Santos said sincerely. The students called all female teachers *miss*, pronounced *mees*. "We just hate Flips."

"Yes, and all of you on Tanô also hate the Trukese who hate the Yapese who also hate the Filipinos who hate the Japanese," I said wearily.

The kids looked at each other and shrugged as if to say, hey, dude, she's catching on.

"And the villages all hate each other, but they get together to hate the military and the rest of us haoles."

"Hey, sorry, miss," Joey said again. They looked puzzled.

"In my room," I pronounced, "you don't have to be friends. But you will fake it. Have you got that?"

At the beginning of every class, I pointed to the word I'd written on the blackboard. "This word is pronounced *sez*," I said. "*Sez*, not *sāys*." We pronounced it together several times.

I'd look out the doorway into the courtyard, turn the fan on medium if the weather was clear, or turn it off if it had rained, and allow the students a few moments to settle. "All right, troops," I'd say, "onward ho." We'd work on vocabulary or paragraph-writing.

I wished I could tell my mother about the lizards on the class-room walls and the black butterflies that flew in the open louvers, across the room and out into the courtyard.

In two months of teaching, I hadn't changed any student's conversational pronunciation of *says*. Rogelio Torres couldn't even say it correctly in the daily chant.

A few ants worked over the dark spot where the crab had been smashed on the road. Most of them were high-stepping it toward the dive shop. I wondered what the ants were going to do without us to smash crabs for them, and to leave crumbs under the toaster and Mazola on the stove top. Geckos deserted houses soon after humans did. People took away their residue, and so the insects had to find their crumbs elsewhere, and so the geckos, too, left to find something alive on the menu. That was the explanation. But I wondered if the geckos had simply liked us.

"Where there are ants, there's life," I told the dog. I was nearly hysterical with life.

The dog lay on the road, cutting off the ants' path, and panted mildly and smiled.

"But we mustn't find it in this condition," I said. "Must we?" I held my gummy hair away from both sides of my head. "See? Would you take such a smelly creature home? Would you intro-duce this to your friends? Would you?"

Your friends in the quarantine center are dead and your mother must have been obliterated with Daniel. I did not tell her this because I did not want to utter it. People talked to dogs and babies, I thought, to hear themselves—to hear their *sweet* selves. As a side benefit, infants learned language. I wondered what dogs gained.

At the island's center was a round freshwater pool. It was called Hidden Pond, though when Malcolm Yarrow had taken me there, a clan had set up a barbecue on the east slope and a dozen or so boys were lined up to swing on the Tarzan rope. Each boy, as we watched, had tried more complex acrobatics before hitting the water, and Malcolm had said, "We'd better leave before they kill themselves showing off for us."

I remembered that, and I thought in my hysteria that the people on the island had taken on our airstrips and our warheads, and they'd tried to walk our high wires of government jobs and BX supplies, and we hadn't left, and the results had been political corruption and welfare dependency and dynamiting of the reefs, and I wished, I wished I would cease making an analogy of every dead or alive thing.

With the dog in the passenger's seat, I drove the Scout inland, recalling Mal's path down an overgrown World War II landing strip. I remembered where to park. The switchback trail down to the pond had disappeared already, but I scrabbled straight down over the coral rock. Above, the land that had made me think of savannas had burned. Already, pale green shoots were showing in the black. I did not know how anything green could rise without sunlight. The slope to the pond was intact, unburned and dense. I followed the dog through the scrub.

The pond was dull black beneath the gray sky. Hidden Pond was nearly empty this time.

One dead boy leaned against a boulder and the Tarzan rope dangled at his ankles. I could not think how he had come to die alone at Hidden Pond.

He wore long red shorts patterned with purple and yellow flowers. *Hawaiian-flowerdy*, Malcolm had said. *I will not wear that Hawaiian-flowerdy shit*, he'd said. The boy's brown skin was bloated and cracked like clay earth in drought.

The dog had headed immediately for the water. Her head was propelled along the surface by the paddling engine of her legs. She lapped the water, gagged and hawked, and then lapped again.

With a heavy stick, I gouged a grave, much too shallow for the boy.

"I'm not up to this grave-digging stuff," I told the swimming dog. I wondered if I'd have the strength to climb the slope back to the Scout.

I pushed the boy away from his rock with my foot until he fell sideways. I jumped back as he fell and turned away, afraid that he would roll down the slope like a boy on a grassy hill, afraid that I would retch at the smell. I pushed him with my foot into the niche I'd dug, and he held together, and I covered him with handfuls of loose dirt, picnic debris, and leaves.

I took off my Japanese tourist's T-shirt and pants and climbed the dead boy's rock. I could not begin burying everybody I found. I launched myself from the rock. I yelled *aaeeyy* and hit the water. Below the surface, I scrubbed my hair. The water was cool, cooler than I remembered, and I thought it was black only in reflection, not in itself.

At fourteen, I'd been allowed to stay at a cousin's a few extra days after our family visit. Mom and Dad and Judy left me. The extra days didn't count. My cousin was older and big-sistered me—took me to the country club pool, taught me to jitterbug to thirty-seven thousand repetitions (my uncle said) of "Party Doll." I drank coffee, black, in the morning because she did. The desertion was what mattered. I could never leave *them*. But the relief of being left made it possible for me to jitterbug, to strut and dive in a yellow swimsuit.

What mattered was that on the bus trip home I sat beside a man in a military uniform and, asleep, allowed my head to settle onto his shoulder. I slept and now and then shifted against him, and he did not move. I woke with my eyes closed and held the position until the bus slowed as it approached town. And then I stirred and found myself startled and embarrassed at sleeping against him.

Now I did not remember him at all. I remembered the slow, smiling good-bye he gave me as he retrieved his duffel bag. My mother said, "And just what was that all about?"

My mother, Catherine Muriel Larson Falkenburg, daughter of Hulda Catherine Larson, lived immersed in time. She believed she lived in the present, day by day, flower by sketch, person by talk, now by now. But she couldn't step out of the body of the fat girl known as Sister. She couldn't grow beyond her mother's voice telling her: "Now Sister, you're going to nursing school, big girls should be nurses;" her mother's voice saying: "I wasn't coming to meet you, I was just walking the dog."

She was still her father's big girl, running to meet his ferry, waiting to be carried to Johanssen's Tavern where she'd sit on the bar and open the box with the new doll in it and decide on its name. Her father's friends pinched her baby fat and laughed at the names she came up with. Once it was a boy doll, and Sister could only say, "He be ... She be ... ," and all the men with their whiskey laughed. The boy doll became Heebie-Sheebie, and it was her favorite. She was still her father's big girl, sitting on the bar and drinking the chocolate sodas he sent someone down the street for. Most of the time she waited for him to come home.

My mother believed she lived in the present, but as much as she was still Sister, she was also a future Catherine who had done the things she now did and could tell about them. She was always waiting, anticipating the shopping expedition, the carnival birthday party she was creating for her girls, the summer trip to Lake Michigan. The pleasures were in the hoping and then in the telling, and so maybe it didn't matter if Judy and I weren't properly responsive or if a mood caused her to snap at the man with the rented pony or to jerk the car to the curb and turn on us.

Catherine Muriel was Hulda Catherine's daughter, and I— Kitty—was my mother's daughter as well, and so I'd spent my days waiting for something more to happen and jotting down reminders of whatever was happening so I could describe it in the Sunday letter to my mother.

Now there was no past and I lived moment by moment. Now there was no way to live but moment by moment, sky by cloud, sea by wave, jungle by banyan, now by now.

Every summer, we drove to northern Michigan to visit relatives: wide aunts living on sandy farms, Mom's cousin who had married again, a little man bent into a right angle, and most of all, Mom's father. He lived in the hotel he'd once managed and still commanded.

Dad would never stop at a motel; I used to think he was stubborn and only later thought he didn't have the money to squander on sleep. Judy slept on the backseat, knocked out by the Dramamine Mom gave her to prevent car sickness. At night, I slept on the front seat with my feet on Dad's lap and my head on my mother's lap. I was older and taller than Judy, but I was the one who slept up front.

During the day, we played travel bingo on cards Mom had drawn, and license plates, and count-the-cows. Judy and I bickered in the backseat. Mom promised, withheld, and dispensed little prizes and treats, according to our behavior and her mood.

She told us stories of Grandpa as a lumber-camp cook, Grandpa as a smuggler of whiskey from South America, Grandpa as a Great Lakes ferry steward, and she told stories of the presents, giant dolls and once a piglet, he brought her whenever he came home again. He'd spoiled her, her mother had said. He'd taken her for countless chocolate sodas and kept her a fat little girl. We drove past orchards and through pine forests, and again Mom told her stories of living in a hotel. Her own mother had died while she was in the hospital giving birth to me. I'd seen the dark green blanket in which my father had burned a hole while I was being born. My dead grandmother had been Hulda Catherine, and she named her disappointing daughter Catherine. And I was Catherine, called Kitty. My mother told me once that for years she'd slept with her mother's silk glove under her pillow. It smelled like her, she said.

At night, she sang. She began with "Itsy Bitsy Spider" and "Mairsy Doats" and "You Must Have Been a Beautiful Baby." Finally she always sang "Summertime." I didn't know if Judy ever heard her. I could smell the car seat and my mother's sachet and perspiration. I could see the headlights of passing cars through my closed eyelids.

Later, when I was a teenager, I noticed how often she burped. She didn't embarrass us in public, but at home she'd burp and then put her hand over her mouth and say, "Excuse me!" in a surprised way: Did *I* do that? That little sequence irritated me unspeakably. Now I wondered if those surprised little burps might have been guilt bubbling up. She was still the fat child whose mother had been dainty, whose father loved her up with chocolate sodas.

Her mother wanted her to go to nursing school. Big girls were supposed to be nurses. But she declared herself an art major. She slept with her mother's silk glove under her pillow. Finally she became a teacher. As did I, as did I. She needed her mother's glove under her pillow. And I, I needed men.

Judy was jealous when our mother went back to school. She fussed at the extra housework we were to do.

"I should think you'd be glad your mother's smart enough to do it," Mom said. When we were little, she used to say, "I should think you'd be proud to have such a young mother." She wasn't any younger to us than our friends' mothers or even than Sally the deaf girl's aunt. Mothers were not people but merely those who called us in at dusk.

But I was only glad when she took those classes, when she left me for "Elementary Language Arts" and "Mental Hygiene in the School."

"Where I grew up," my mother said, "the town was divided with an invisible line—Polish on one side, Scandinavian on the other. And there was no crossing that line."

"But how did you know which was which?" Judy asked.

The answer was words.

"The Poles all said *dis* and *dose*," Mom said. "If your name ended in *-son*, you didn't associate with someone whose name ended with *-ski*. And vice versa."

It was just noises, I'd thought. The way you made certain sounds, and the sounds that named you. Just noises.

So, years later, fat sixteen-year-old Rogelio Torres insisted his name was Roger.

Now I kept making the noises, talking to the dog, even singing in the Scout, just as if I'd flipped on the radio, mindlessly singing along to nothing. I had to have language in my mouth.

But when I was fifteen, it was meaningless noise. Though it was my punishment and my compulsion to be surrounded by the noise, I would not make my mother's cutting distinctions. I wished a *-ski* would ask me out and that she would make me turn him down. She wouldn't have, but at fifteen I was perverse.

To my mother, there was an invisible line between *dating* and *seeing*. "Kitty's dating the Walters boy, Chris, from the young people's group," she would say to Mrs. Reynolds across the street. *Dating* was clean and healthy. It made me think of Fig Newtons. But the older girl down the street was "seeing that Blackwood character"—as if they pulled down their pants in front of each other. *A little necking* was all right, but Judy and I were warned against *petting*. *Necking* translated to *making out*; I understood that. But *petting* sounded so friendly, so puppyish, that it was difficult to see the objection. But if I ever succumbed to petting, God forbid that it should be heavy. When Sally the deaf girl got in trouble, it was because she didn't know the words.

Once I'd said, "If you don't want Chris and me to do any

petting, you'd better let me shave my legs." She didn't laugh, but later I heard her tell it to Mrs. Reynolds on the phone.

I thought of my body and boys' bodies as pulsing with invisible lines. There was a line between the closed lips that must be held during kissing and when he touched his mouth to my neck, or the results would be French kisses and hickeys. There were horizontal lines across my shoulders and at both our waists—made visible before all by belts, buckled belts—and across our hips and halfway up my thighs.

I was netted by invisible lines and language.

I thought of Sally the deaf girl striking out with her solid breaststroke, as she did at the Lake of the Woods pool, until she got to the deep part where she'd float and roll in the bleached water beneath the corn-growing sun. No one at her special school, nor her aunt, had shown her the lines, and everything must have been mere hushed noise in her head, and she got herself in trouble. My mother and her neighbors didn't even say that some boy got her in trouble. She did it herself. Oh there was much head-shaking on Hawthorne Street.

I would lie on my sheets in my baby-doll pajamas and think that, when I was sixteen, I would be like Sally, deaf to the seine of words, unnetted, my body seamless as a dolphin's.

There were motions I must go through. Already I'd washed off the sweat and the salt. There were basic necessities, as they say, minimum basic necessities. There was no one to say it, but where there's life, I thought, there are minimum basic necessities. Words, cleanliness, mothers, and lovers were not among the necessities.

With the familiar smell of wet dog, I drove the narrow landing strip through the burned savanna. If the dog didn't sicken from the water of Hidden Pond, I might have a source, I thought.

Yellow-green shoots had sprouted already in the burn, and I

thought of devouring them like a dog eating grass. Abruptly my stomach lurched and I stopped the Scout, thinking I might vomit. I could not tell hunger from sickness.

On the cross-island road, I stopped again and backed up. Here was the old sign for Pedro's Wake, gray and ancient as a relic of the cross. Under the paint-dripping letters were faint words in red:

I AM ALIVE.
JESSE S.

The letters were nearly as uneven as the original ones. They had been written with a red felt-tip marker, I thought, but the ink had soaked into the old wood until it was more pink than red.

Surely the faded red words had not been on the sign yesterday. Under my fingernail I carried splinters from the sign. I would have seen Jesse S.'s words.

"Oh my dog, we aren't alone after all," I said. "We aren't alone." I held the sign as if it were the man, my hands gripping his shoulders.

I thought that I should leave him a sign in return. If I had a felt-tip marker, what would I write? *Call Kitty at the dive shop. For a good time. Kitty loves Jesse S.* With a piece of coral rock I tried to gouge a *K*, but it didn't show, and Jesse S. would never see it.

He was alive though. And I would have to find him.

"So what do you say, dog?" I asked. Already she was becoming *dog* instead of Cimarron. "I mean Cimmie. Will mademoiselle please pardon the lapse? And so," I went on, "we need food, clothing, and shelter. How come they always leave out water? And whoever *they* are, the ones who made up that list, they didn't live in the tropics or they'd have left off clothing. What's that you say? Oh, sure, they must've been missionaries."

What a clever conversationalist this dog is, I thought.

I couldn't get to the commissary on the air base, and I knew the Payless supermarket on Marine Drive was gone, but I wondered if any of the little shops were left. Once the island had borne a couple dozen Mom-and-Pop stores. I thought of pulling up to Chiu's. Inside, Mrs. Chiu behind the counter would smile and bob at me, and I would grin at the toddler penned behind the counter with her. Most of the shops were Chinese because, I'd been told, the Chamorros couldn't make a profit: the owners' relatives expected free food and their friends expected endless credit. Families took care of their own, and the weaving of families was intricate and extensive, and so the shops failed.

In the beginning, of course, no one needed shops. Tropical islanders merely waited for the bananas and the breadfruit to ripen, for the coconuts to fall. They spun a net in the lagoon at sunset. The palm thatching of the shelters held until the typhoon and was readily replaced after the bodies were buried. Everyone knew islanders didn't need clothes. Maybe grass skirts for festive occasions when musicians played the coconut-shell banjos and everyone drank the fermented banana flower and then made much love. Everyone knew that's what the island had been. In its day. That was before the conquerors and the missionaries and the military and civilization.

I drove past the dive shop, heading south this time. I knew the north was dead. Jesse S., whoever he was, would not be in the north.

I wanted to spot Jesse S. hiking down the middle of the road. I wanted Chiu's to be standing, and I wanted to walk right in and load up on cans of corn and peaches and Spam and SpaghettiOs.

"My dog," I said, "I am getting cynical in my old age."

She looked at me.

"Yes, the world's killed itself, and why shouldn't I get a trifle cynical? But anyway. Here's my point: Isn't it funny that life first mucked around in some tropics, but it took colder climes to invent civilization as we knew it, and now here we are, back in the tropics. Beginning, middle, end. The middle did us in."

So far, the south was nothing but blackened hills.

"Did you like that little lecture?" I asked the dog. "Are you enlightened?"

As I drove up the hills, the noon dusk gathered in eddies, catching in currents and swirling in black dust devils. I remembered the island's greens—the yellow-green of shiny new leaves, the sword grass, the rubber green banana leaves, crabbed greens, dying acid greens—greens that played in each other's shades to camouflage, violent greens that at the same time sweltered together until the island had seemed to vibrate. I'd said to Malcolm once that botany didn't exist on the island: the jungle was too wildly green for any science.

"Oh, that's just nonsense," he'd said.

"Right," I'd said, just playing at conversation. "Science is sense. This is all so raw. Maybe in a couple thousand years it'll calm down to vegetation."

"'My vegetable love should grow/Vaster than empires, and more slow,'" Malcolm had declaimed.

I should have loved him.

"Not bad for a military type," I'd said.

We'd been driving, and he'd suddenly pulled off the road into a tangle of uncut grass and weeds. "My vegetable love is growing," he said. "Except . . . except I don't think it's a vegetable, it's . . . yes, yes, poetry fans, it's a fruit . . . it's a banana!"

I should have loved him.

The island's greens hadn't been pretty—not bottle green, not emerald, not apple green. I started touching men long ago but I did not love. Now the burned hills between the road and the sea were viridescent. Malcolm had been fooled like the rest of them. Perhaps with him I would have dropped the camouflage. Probably not. When Daniel saw the flickering shades of the costume, he left. I did not blame him. I hadn't changed. My mother was what her mother had made, and I'd been sorry and still disgusted that she couldn't shake her childhood. I was what my mother had made. It was taking the end of the world to show me my own virulent green heart.

The dog whined beside me.

"Right," I said, "lighten up, Kitty. Who the hell cares what color your sins are. At least you didn't blow the world to hell. That wasn't your doing."

The dog was at my shoulder, whining toward the left. I looked toward the cliff and thought I caught motion. I drove slowly, watching the mossy black hills between the road and the cliff and saw nothing. Then I saw a sign—no, a cross—and I stopped and got out of the Scout.

The stubbled hill canted smoothly toward the sea and dropped off abruptly, I knew, though I couldn't see the rock cliff, only the burned hills and then the black ocean.

Beyond the eight-foot cross's nailed-together planks was raw earth, ground up as if giant earthworms had been at work. The death I smelled was gentled with the moist black smell of turned soil.

On the cross fluttered scraps of cloth, dozens of scraps nailed down and across the planks. The dog scrabbled at the window, and I looked around. Only the bits of cloth moved. Some of the scraps were blank but for the patterns of flowers or sailboats, but most of them held printed names. VINCENT FLORES. AUNTIE LUZ. LOURDES. MOTHER. BABY FRANK. JUAN BLAS. DEBORAH SANTOS, 16. One hand had printed all the names, it seemed, dozens and dozens of names in black ink that had bled into the cloth.

Someone had survived to bury the dead. Perhaps my Jesse S. had assumed burial duty.

The southern end of the island had been uncivilized. Un-spoiled, I supposed. I'd seen fishermen in the lagoon throwing their nets against a sunset. People ate the fish and crabs and fruit bats they caught. They ate bananas, coconut, breadfruit, and wild pumpkin, none of which they planted. Families were all related, it seemed, and took care of one another. Adolescent children were free to move from auntie to auntie when home didn't satisfy. Dwellings were thatched palm fronds. There was frequently an excuse for a fiesta or a fandango. The river provided fresh water, and the sea stepped, blue by blue, from the aquamarine shallows to the depths of the Mariana Trench. At sunset, the sky settled in unnameable oranges into the sea, and the clouds piled themselves on the horizon. Sometimes just after dusk, when the sky was smoky, the sea was blue-gray, lighter than the sky. The high full moon lit the clouds in a deep blue-white.

The trade winds blew in January and February. In early June, the Big Dipper made a question mark. Sometimes the sea and sky blurred the horizon. Sometimes dark blue banded the horizon. Always the horizon rose far above where the eye believed it should be.

I got back into the Scout and drove on, past the mass grave, knowing that paradise hadn't really existed. Something— civilization perhaps, as much as the island might have resisted— had spoiled it. It was easier to dynamite a reef than to fish. The fruit bats had become an endangered species. The jungle couldn't provide enough, and people bought Spam, ship's biscuits, octopus from Japan, and frozen fish from the Philippines. Intermarriage and incest were rampant. Unlimited generosity made small businesses impossible. Shelters were more often corrugated tin and packing crates than palm thatchings—and everything blew away in typhoon season anyway. With no sanitation system, the river was polluted, and diseases like lytico and shigellosis killed off the babies and the old people. At most fandangos the bride was pregnant. Just barely beneath the greens and blues of the jungle and the sea was the debris of civilization—aluminum cans, Pampers, Coke bottles, 1967 Ford Mavericks.

I had come to the island for the myth, I supposed—for pure humanity. That was the way to escape the human self, I'd supposed. I drove on in the scorched orange Scout.

I couldn't have an argument with civilization. Not while I was driving, anyway. I'd never really wanted the imagined simplicity of primitive culture. No human was one with nature. No human was purely animal. The kids from the southern village dyed their hair punk green and learned to break-dance better than any Chicago kid and lip-synced Madonna between classes. What made us human, after all? Not our ability to cut open coconuts. Not our cleverness in devising nets for the lagoon. Not our need for the fandango with the coupling. We were human because we'd processed the pork parts and canned them as Spam. We were human because we had to leave the village and the cousin who had been chosen for us. We were human because we saw the band at the horizon, we saw the Big Dipper in June as a question mark.

The sign read PUNTAN DOS AMANTES and I took the turn. When I had been here with Malcolm, three tour buses waited while the Japanese tourists—honeymooners, most of them—followed the sidewalk up to the cliff's edge and, grasping the rail, looked down to the waves beating the rocks a hundred and fifty feet below. Here, the sign told them in English and Japanese, was where the lovers tied their long black hair together and jumped from the cliff rather than be separated.

The men held the rail and stared down intently, and the women immediately swooned back from the drop. The new wives in their pink plastic sandals and their baggy pastel shorts and yellow blouses waited while the men somehow assessed the quality of love, and then, holding hands, they wandered to the vendors' awnings and bought island T-shirts and island wood carvings made in the Philippines. The bus drivers lounged on the grass with tropical patience and the knowledge of kickbacks. They gestured to the tourists: Go ahead, you try local drink, you buy. Drinking from straws stuck in green coconuts, the couples wandered to the new statue of the two lovers.

This time only one tour bus waited at Two Lovers' Point. There were no people, only the twenty-foot bronze statue of the lovers.

Her right arm lightly held his back, his right hand was mildly cupped just above her buttocks, and their left hands met to bind their hair, his arm reaching over his head. Their legs were too long, like any young animal's. Before, the pair had seemed a graceful, golden ideal of youth. Now the huge statue was blackened with a green tinge like a fly's body. His unpursed lips were on her hair still. They might as well have died for love, I thought, but here they stood, poised for the ecstatic leap, blackened in the black afternoon above the sludgy black sea.

I remembered that it had been a Buick Skylark with a narrow backseat. It was winter, old winter, with grainy yellow-and-gray snow heaped on curbs, and steam grew like mold on the windows as soon as we parked. The penetration was painless, the act without sensation. I could not believe that being touched with a penis did not send me swooning away from some edge, or prepared to leap; it could have been anything—plastic, wooden, rubber—but surely not flesh.

Our mother had warned me and Judy to wait, wait. "Once you start, you won't be able to stop," she'd said.

Judy did wait, and she married Mitch a virgin, she told me later. "For a while at first I thought Mom was right," she'd said. "It was sort of addictive. But then later it didn't really seem to matter much. To Mitch, either, I think. At least we got the kids out of it."

She's a cold one, Mom used to say.

Coldness was survival against your flashes of heat: what did you expect? I thought to my mother.

I didn't wait, but not because of Mom's tantalizing warnings, nor because of the hours in backseats and basement rec rooms. The boys seemed to be ravaged with need as with disease, and perhaps that was part of it. And when they touched their inanimate bodies to me, I became real.

That first night, Mom walked into my bedroom as I was pulling my nightgown over my head. She picked up the blood-spotted underpants I'd dropped on the floor and held them up as something precious. "I see it's that time of the month," she said. "I think you're getting more regular." So for a week I had to fold up clean Kotex and leave toilet-paper-wrapped bundles in the bathroom wastebasket.

In the abstract, she feared for my innocence, but in practice she had faith. She always waited up for me, as mothers did, not out of worry that I was lying in a ditch somewhere, as she said, but for the vicarious life my details gave her. She, of course, had been too fat to be popular. So I offered her the movie we'd seen, the tasteless outfit that Suzie Sellers, with whom we'd double-dated, was wearing, the crowd at Shorty's and the pizza we'd eaten, scraps of conversation. The little truths glazed the lie of the last hour, after Suzie Sellers and her boyfriend had been dropped off. She swelled with my teenage details. As I shed them, I faded, until I pleaded fatigue and left her—until I could once again grow real under some boy's need.

Legendary tragic lovers usually suffered because their families, their cultures were different. On the island, there had been no Montagues and Capulets. In the island tale, the girl's father planned to marry her off to the foreigner, and her tragedy was to love another islander. I wondered what this meant. What had the story meant, later, to the villagers at the south end, knowing the northern end had been taken by the foreigners? What had it meant to the honeymooners, all the Japanese men wed to Japanese women, looking over the railing at the surf a hundred and fifty feet below as if bodies rolled in the foam?

The bronzed girl and boy of the statue had touched each other lightly, innocently. Now, blackened, they'd aged. They still looked alike, brother and sister, but now his lips touched her hair knowingly, and her light touch was postcoital bitterness. Their yin and yang were graceful still, but I thought of the black sky pulling around them like an eggshell holding some calcifying mutant.

Like a tourist, I followed the sidewalk to the railed cliff edge. I looked out, not down, but there was no horizon. The black clouds rolled into the sea and pulled the coagulated water around them, like rolling wet snowballs, and rolled, dripping and globoid, into the sky. The motion seemed to hold the island at the center of a whirlpool. I pulled for breath and held the railing.

Below me, past the singed scrub protruding from the cliff face, bodies bobbed and ducked like inflated beach toys. The waves pulled back, rose and curled, paused, and then rushed to the cliff. They flew against the cliff, fell to the gray foam, and pulled back again. The bodies plunged and splashed like serpents at their aquatics.

During the Second World War, the Japanese conquered another of the islands and settled in whole families along with the officials who were to oversee the natives. When the U.S. finally took that island, the Japanese wives believed the propaganda about the raping and murdering American Marines. The women took their children to the highest cliff, and one by one, with babies strapped on their backs and children held by the hand, they jumped. Three hundred died on impact, thirty-three drowned, and seven were retrieved by the Marines.

I could not know if the tourists, the honeymooning pairs, had witnessed the flash, understood it as only the Japanese could, and silently leapt, their hands twined like hair. Perhaps, though, having taken on the McDonald's franchise, rock and roll, some Western individuality, and Adidas tennis shoes, they'd dropped the fanatic and holy racial face like absolutely righteous teenagers evolving into relativistic adults. Perhaps they'd died—or been killed—on Two Lovers' Point and then been dragged or rolled to the edge. I wondered how long they could pitch in the foam before they fell apart. I wondered if it mattered if they'd jumped or been pushed.

64

5

"**G**as station," I told Cimarron. "Watch for a gas station." I remembered seeing a single gas pump in front of a store in the southern bay village, Siti. Perhaps it wouldn't matter if I couldn't work the pump. Perhaps the ones who had made the mass grave, with its festooned cross, would be there to help.

Marine Drive, which circumnavigated the island, was a two-lane paved road, furrowed and buckled, spotted with potholes that were ringed with tar from repairs that hadn't taken. In the south, the road climbed, dipped, then climbed. Before us the sword-grass hills rolled to the cliff and the sky lifted from the slaty sea. As the island began to round itself into the southern end, the road dropped to the black-sand beach where once Magellan had landed.

With the headlights on in the afternoon dusk, I drove up the hills slowly to avoid potholes and to watch for motion on the burned hills.

The truck was beside me so abruptly that it could have risen from the road bank.

The truck careened toward me and I headed for the dirt shoulder. The truck swerved back to the left lane, and I maneuvered onto the tarmac, and abruptly it was beside me again, forcing me once more onto the shoulder.

In panic I speeded up, and the truck dropped behind. It was an old red pickup, and I thought there were two men in the front seat.

My hands and body were shivering. The dog had been thrown

65

to the floor. She did not try to climb back onto the passenger's seat, and I was afraid she was hurt. The red pickup stayed behind, but I held my speed at seventy, bouncing on the fractured tarmac. Then the truck speeded up. Keep at least a car-length separation for every ten miles per hour, I thought stupidly. The truck rammed the rear of the Scout.

I slewed onto the shoulder, shivering in panic, and jerked back onto the road. "Stupid, stupid, stupid," I said: how stupid to die in a stupid car wreck when the world had killed itself.

The old red pickup was beside me again. I looked and saw two brown men. I lifted my right hand from the wheel and made a pleading shrug. I knew my mouth was open and my lips were widened in fear, and abruptly I closed my mouth to erase the distorted smile. In the shivering dark I could not really see but I knew they were laughing, and then I could see the passenger's arm in an orange sleeve reach out the window. Something shot against my windshield. The glass was starred. The pickup slid behind me, and as I tried to hold to the road at eighty shivering miles per hour, the star sent rays across the windshield. The road lurched as if it were sentient, and collaborating with the old pickup.

Again the truck was beside me but this time it passed and pulled back into the right lane. Just ahead, it braked suddenly, and I saw the flare of the brake lights and swerved into the left lane to avoid hitting it.

Again the men pulled up beside me and again the orange-sleeved arm aimed out the window at me. I heard a crack.

They were *shoot*ing at me. *Oh my dear Cimarron dog, they are shooting at me.*

I slid down in the seat so that I could barely see over the dashboard. I could not see the road's pits and broken tarmac but I held my speed, presenting as small a target as possible, shaking and crying.

People: men were after me, but would there be people in the village? I began honking the horn.

The pickup was beside me and I kept low, the Scout bouncing out of potholes, and I increased my speed, still honking. The men in the old red pickup must be howling, I thought, at this terrified woman beeping at a dead world.

At last I felt rather than saw the road descend. As I slowed to take the curve at the bay, in the sudden windless silence I heard my dry sobs, a droning *uh-uh-uh*. The dog climbed onto the seat and pecked her nose toward my cheek, unsure about licking. I sat up enough to see that the pickup was still following but at a distance. In the rearview mirror I saw the truck's headlights shut off. The black sand around the bay was invisible.

The village of Siti was on the other side of the road, across from the beach. I was sure it was. There had been a Mom-and-Pop grocery with one gas pump in front and, inside, a trough of iced beer and fresh snapper, mahimahi, and crabs. There had been a tombstone-shaped marker explaining in English and Japanese that in 1521 Magellan had landed here, killed several Chamorros for their natural curiosity, and written on his map *Island of Thieves*.

There was no village.

The afternoon deepened, and I slowed. I couldn't see beyond my headlights. The invisible truck might be behind me. Again I began honking. *Oh please be here, people be here.*

The pickup's lights blared into the Scout then.

I sobbed through my nose, twice, and shoved the dog away.

The men must have known the village was gone. I breathed through bared teeth, furious at the men who might be the only other people. I didn't crouch in the driver's seat: let them try to shoot me. But I speeded up as I made the straightaway up the western coast. The road climbed, more gently than in the hills of the eastern side. The pickup followed circumspectly, now with its headlights on, now in darkness.

In a few miles I would reach my dive shop, just before the harbor. I didn't dare turn on the overhead light to check the fuel gauge. The men might guess I was nearly out of gas. What a lovely phrase, I thought: *out of gas*. I heard echoes: *Sorry I'm late, but I ran out of gas. Oh, I'm so pissed, I ran out of gas and I had to lug that leaky gas can two blocks.* If I ran out of gas now, the man with the orange sleeve would shoot the door locks open and then shoot Cimarron, and they would both jerk me from the Scout into the boonies as so many other women had been taken. Weekly the newspaper had told on them: TWO JOGGERS RAPED, MANGILAO WOMAN ATTACKED IN YARD, AIR FORCE WIFE ATTACKED, BEHEADED. I drove fast, northward, with no plan beyond letting the dog escape and running myself if they were far enough behind.

As I neared my dive shop, I turned off the Scout's headlights and tried to follow the black road in the black afternoon. Now the truck's lights were on, and after I'd passed the dive shop, I saw the men turn at my hideout. I didn't know if they believed I'd turned there, but they must have known it was my place. I drove north past the harbor's breakwater road, toward the hotels.

The Scout died then, and the wheel stiffened under my hands. I wrestled it counterclockwise so the Scout coasted onto the left shoulder and down a gentle bank. The right side of the road was naked but on the left were at least a half dozen black palm trunks. Cimarron whined and pawed at the door. "Cross your legs, animal," I said. "Let's make sure this heap really is out of gas."

I stopped grinding the ignition and opened the door. The dog bungled over my lap and was out. She charged twice around the palm trunks and abruptly squatted.

One of the palms carried a ragged tuft of fronds. Its base seemed a cloven hoof. With the toe of my shoe, I dug between the spatulate toes of the hoof, dropped the Scout's keys in, and smoothed the sandy dirt over them. At least I wouldn't simply give away the vehicle to anyone with a can of gas.

I stepped into the jungle, hidden but hardly knowing where to go. I tried to follow the dog, stooping and crawling even. She made her way aimlessly, and when she led me back to a brain-coral rock that we'd passed before, I sat down.

Well, and now?

I was far enough away, deep enough into the jungle, that the men wouldn't be able to find me. But I had nowhere to go. I supposed that we could only wander now.

Before, we civilized people did not merely wander. We pretended to roam only on weekends. Daily we drove to the factory, we carpooled the kids to Roosevelt School, we took the bus to the office downtown. On the weekends, we went to Safeway, to the laundromat, to K Mart for some cheap new tennis shoes. We went. We moved. Saturday night we drove to the Cinema-Plus if we could stand the rowdy kids who were always sitting behind us. On Sunday we loaded the van with a cooler and drove fifty miles to the beach, where we spread our Budweiser towels, lay on them, jumped up and threw Frisbees and swam in the cold water and set up the grill and lit the charcoal and drafted the kids to hunt green sticks and drank beer and checked the beach bodies and roasted the wieners and dismantled the beach chairs and drove home and unloaded everything sandy, sodden, and blackened, and sprayed the kids' sunburned backs with Solarcaine and turned on "60 Minutes," half over, and burped beer and onions, and shook up a martini and school-nighted the kids to baths and beds and— remembering the drive in the morning to the factory in the car that needed three hundred dollars' worth of carburetor work—did not love anything.

We never simply roamed; we always went someplace.

When we went hiking, we found the trails and followed them, making the circuit back to the parking lot where the cold beer would reward our vigor. If there had been rails on both sides of the paths, we would have been angry, but we stuck to the marked routes, stepping politely aside for other hikers to pass, urging our dogs on when they began sniffing each other: *Come on now, Red, that isn't very polite.*

And we went to the same places. We sat in the same row at every theater. We staked out the same stretch of beach. We hiked the same set of trails. We even went to the same places in our heads: kept the car's FM buttons set, read the same book with a different title on the spine.

We were not nomads. Not vagrants, not strays, not tramps.

We knew what we were. Knew where we belonged.

Sometimes we woke at two A.M. and imagined sliding the flaking wooden window frame up and stepping into the moonlit backyard. We would be vagabonds, gypsies. We would live on deserted islands, we would be hermits, we would live off the land. Then we would take a pee, check the kids, and get back in bed. "Honey?" we would whisper. "You awake?"

Now I wandered. I supposed that soon I would head for the hotel ruins. We always needed some *place*, some covering even in the tropics, some base. I called the dog and wandered through the burned jungle toward the beach, thinking to wander toward the hotels. If there had been someone at the Fujita before, at least he hadn't pursued me.

The jungle thickened toward the beach. Here the palms and the banyans were woven together by vines. I polished the end of a banana frond: under the gummy soot the leaf felt like thin plastic. It would be shiny gray-green, I thought, if I could see colors.

I heard the dog charging through the matted vines. "Hey, dog of mine," I said, too softly for her to hear, "slow down. Lead me through this mess." I held my hands before my face to catch the spider webs and soon my arms were strung with gummy webbing. Tripping on roots and coral rocks, I stumbled after the dog, no longer wandering, ready to return to the burned jungle with its sparse black pipe stalks. Let me out of this life stuff, I thought, trying impossibly to wipe webs from my mouth and eyes. I was blind in the woven jungle. The woven, canopied jungle, I thought: it should be lovely. Then I caught my foot and I was down. My thigh scraped on coral rock; the pants ripped and I felt blood.

I remained down. I could hear the dog digging. Then behind

70

me, somehow insinuating through the vines, the organic sound of a car grew, grew, and then withdrew. I didn't know if the car had passed or stopped, perhaps by the Scout. I didn't know if the old red pickup had stopped and if the two men were able to read my track in the dusk.

Suddenly something scuttled over my hand and I leapt up, knocking my head against a branch. "Oh damn it," I moaned, "damn it." Cold nails had run over my hand, and I shuddered. It must have been a crab, and as soon as I pictured a hermit crab or a blue rock crab running over my skin, my stomach growled with hunger.

A horn honked twice, a friendly heavy and light beep, and I could hear the wheels fighting for traction. I thought I could hear gravel spin against the Scout. I must have been too far across the burn and into the jungle—but I thought I could hear the red truck bouncing down on the road and squealing away toward hotel row. I'd have guessed that the thick sky would have absorbed sound, but perhaps the black wind carried sound across the new silence as over water.

Finally I parted the wall of vines and stepped out of the jungle into scattered ironwood trees and then scrub and beach grass. The dog crashed through behind me. I squatted to pet her and smelled her breath—fishy. She must have eaten a crab, maybe a coconut crab. Her dog breath was foul, and I wondered if the crab had been rotten.

"All right, maggot breath, let's see what's along this beach."

I unzipped my trousers and they fell to my ankles. Just yesterday I'd had to hitch them down. I stepped out of the pants and left my shoes on, knowing better than to risk stepping barefooted on sea urchins. The water was dark and carried a freight of dead fish, splintered boards, and broken brown coconuts, but I had to wash off the spider webs before they shrouded me alive.

As I stepped into the water, orange light cracked the clouds, and I jumped back as if the ocean were electrified.

The sun was still out somewhere, still striking the lurching earth when its clouds split.

Near the invisible horizon, the clouds let through a thin band of sunset. I waded into the water and crouched to scrub my face and hair. Orange vibrated into an aurora of green and purple, and the lights spread across the water like a sheen of oil. Abruptly the aurora drew into a ball and bounced across the swelling sea. I fled to the beach. The phosphorous ball rode a wave, flared incandescent green, and sizzled out.

By the narrow orange light of the horizon, I pulled on the trousers, called the dog, and headed across the stretch of sand back to the ironwood trees. There would be no twilight, and I had no flashlight with me.

The wide beach was strewn with water marks of seaweed, lines that seemed reflections of the moving horizon. Automatically I stepped over them. Step on a crack, break your mother's back. The highest line was thick with debris, and trying to step over it, I slipped on the slick seaweed and pinwheeled my arms to stay upright.

What a fool, I thought. My mother was dead, even before the rest of us had died.

I returned to the ironwood trees. I wanted some shelter, some hiding place, but I couldn't crawl back into the jungle. Beneath the long dripping needles, I thought the trees might be alive still.

In the dark I made out a shape too symmetrical to be natural — a car seat. I dragged it into the stand of ironwood. Behind it, I could lie hidden from the open beach. I heaped dry ironwood needles for a bed and lay down with Cimarron against my back.

I stared into the springs of the car seat. I ran my hand over the back's ripped vinyl. It was brittle. I couldn't tell what color it was.

I felt queasy.

I remembered an adolescent case of stomach flu. All night I'd thrown up. The first time, Mom had cleaned up after me, scrubbing the carpet and changing my sheets. She put a purple bucket and towels by the bed. I hit the bucket every time and emptied it into the toilet, and every time, all through the night, I woke her. I must have been fifteen, no child, but she filled a glass with water and had me rinse and spit, and she led me back to bed.

Now I thought I might throw up, and I stood. This must be radiation sickness.

Pacing on the soft needles between the trees, I kicked something that rolled like a partly deflated football. Cimarron chased it into the beach grass and tried to carry it back to me. I could hear it drop and then hear her teeth on it.

"What is it, girl? Whatcha got?" I said. "This really isn't the time to play, you know."

This dog had never been to the ocean, having been carried in her airline kennel directly to the quarantine center, but Daniel and I had taken her and her mother to the lake. Daniel's dog wouldn't get wet, but Cimarron had walked straight into the water and swum so far out that we thought we'd lose her. When she climbed out at last, she shook ice water on us and charged back into the water. We threw sticks, and she bucked the water to retrieve them, though she lost interest once she had the stick in her mouth and let it go.

Now she brought me a coconut. Again, the saliva leapt in my mouth, and I couldn't tell sickness from hunger. Suddenly my tongue felt dry and large, and I realized I'd had nothing to drink since the can of Sprite that morning, before I'd driven south.

I had been determined not to eat anything but canned food. Surely, I thought, everything else would be contaminated. The coconut felt smooth and plump—green—though I couldn't tell in the dark. I shook it and heard liquid. My tongue thickened and my stomach lurched, and I hardly cared if I'd die tomorrow: I had to have the coconut.

Before I'd come to the island, I'd occasionally bought coconuts in the grocery store, but they were small and brown—hairy taters,

Daniel called them. I'd never opened a coconut, not even those dry inner balls from Safeway.

I threw this one on the ground, and of course it did not split. I jumped on it and only drove it into the sand. I groped until I found a rock and tried beating the coconut. I aimed it at a tree trunk and heaved. You throw like a girl, Daniel would have said.

I was sick. I needed the slick watery milk and the white flesh of the coconut.

Finally I lay down on my ironwood needles, with the coconut in my arms. "Oh please, oh please," I heard myself saying. Cimarron licked my face and lay beside me.

Sally the deaf girl got herself in trouble and her aunt sent her away. By the time we started junior high, we weren't really friends anymore. Sally went to a special school and returned to her aunt's for vacations and summers. Her aunt called and invited me over, and dutifully I walked down the block. I waved at Sally, as if she were across the street, when she opened the door. I grinned and showed too much gum. Her aunt fed us pizza and Cokes. Pizza was slumber-party food, with a half dozen girls in striped flannel jester's pajamas following Chef BoyarDee's directions. Even Sally must have known that her aunt was trying too hard. She made Sally speak to me, as she was learning to do at her school, but I couldn't really understand her utterances. I grinned and nodded and drank my Coke and said I had to leave.

Through junior high everyone thought I was normal. I went to dances in the darkened cafeteria: a strobe light dotting and dizzy-ing us, a local d.j. spinning the 45s from the stage, the short crew-cut boys on the left, on the right the tall girls with grosgrain bows clipped in their hair, a girl crying alone in the fluorescent-lit girls' bathroom, another girl crying with two comforting girlfriends by the dark row of lockers. In junior high I rode the bus with my friends downtown on Saturday, and we spent our allowances on

Bobby Vee's records and mohair sweaters, and then we met some boys in the balcony of the movie theater. In junior high, I was my mother's daughter: oh I was popular.

Dancing with little Mike Millhausen—who called me up and sang "Kitty Lee, Kitty Lee, oh how my heart yearns for thee" to the tune of "Peggy Sue"—I knew I was not normal. Spreading the pizza dough with greased fingers, I knew I was not normal. Trying to teach poor Judy the twist, I knew I was an adult dumped into a teenager's body. I knew it was all ridiculous, silly—the phone calls, Mike M.'s clutchings, the giggling in the kitchen, the music. It was as if my mother were the teenager, trying to hide her avidity for the details, wishing she could try the twist. I was at once the popular girl condescending to be nice to the queer one and the adult knowing how trivial were the friends and the fads.

Some boy kissed me at a playground at night. We were caged inside a jungle gym. Later some other boy put his hands on my undeveloped breasts and my thigh. But it was as if it had all happened before, as if I were remembering and repeating what no longer mattered since it wasn't the real first time.

Judy had her girlfriend or two and later her yearly date, but she never was what all kids yearned to be—popular.

"Listen to me," I overheard Mom telling Judy, "it's the unpopular ones who go somewhere in life. Of course, I don't mean your sister. But it's the outsiders who end up as the scientists and the artists and the leaders."

But neither of them was comforted. Every ninth grader believes that only the popular ones were corporeal.

And I knew I was an imposter, a grown person in red-striped pajamas. I drifted above the strobe light and watched my body do the twist and for the next dance be held by some boy singing "I'm Mr. Blue" in my ear.

I read *Green Mansions* and moved on. I wrote secret poetry denouncing God and conformity, and I discovered Beethoven—

and I was popular enough to get away with these queer things. But these were not quite enough to jiggle my body into its shadow.

My mother had been blurred in others' vision because she was fat, she believed, and Sally the deaf girl's dumbness made her nearly invisible too. When Sally's aunt cried in our kitchen, Mom hurried Judy and me away, but of course we listened through the register.

"I just don't know what else I could have done for that girl," she wept. "How could she do this to me? I even loved that girl."

For a month, though Sally was sent away, she grew more solid than she'd ever been, as the mothers' Wednesday morning sewing circle stitched into her, as the fathers, watering adjacent lawns in the evening, shook their heads and wanted to get the son of a bitch that'd do it to a deaf girl. The aunt put her house up for sale, and soon Sally disappeared more quickly than a corpse.

I believed I understood how it must have been for Sally, how kissing and touching were silent anyway, but the weight of a body on hers even in the dark defined her shape.

Once I'd climbed into the backseat of the Buick Skylark, a dozen boys in the next two years petted me in backseats, on a blanket in a cornfield, in rec rooms when the parents were out for the evening, in a basement bomb shelter, petted me until I allowed submission. I gave little but my quiet body.

I should have had a reputation, but Kitty Falkenburg was such a nice girl, who satisfied her mother, who always had her nose in a book and earned her *A*'s and loved that long-hair music. A rumor didn't have an inch of fertile ground to drop seed in. Guys will talk in the locker room, Mom warned. I did not know why the boys held their secrets about me.

One night Larry Benson and I were parked in the country, off a back road where there was no night traffic. Larry turned off the headlights, but I continued to see the dry corn shocks spread across the windshield. We kissed for the requisite twenty minutes, and then we pulled down my stretch pants and his white Levi's,

76

and all the time I believed that through the muffling windshield I heard the corn husks snarling together.

Suddenly the car was full of light and Larry scrambled into the driver's seat and pushed me down. He reversed onto the gravel road and took off. The car that had pulled up beside us followed with its red light spinning. As soon as I had my stretch pants pulled up, I said, "Stop, stop. We're just a couple of kids parking. What can they do to us?" Even my mother wouldn't be upset by a little necking beside the snarling corn. But Larry accelerated, sliding and recovering on the gravel, and then hitting a paved road. He careened into turns, gaining distance, and in my fright I laughed, thinking of the adventure I might relate to my mother once it was over. As we neared town, Larry pulled suddenly into a driveway and killed the headlights.

"Get down, get down," he said, and we both crouched.

In the silence, I heard Larry's panting and the corn husks rubbing together like insects' legs.

The police car pulled in behind us.

"Stay down," Larry whispered.

And so the two policemen found us on the front seat, pulled into fetuses with our heads together.

From the station they let us call our parents, and soon my mother and father and Larry's mother were there. My mother righted the bow clipped in my hair and cried. Larry's mother insisted that her son was just a boy sowing his wild oats and that boys would be boys. My father said nothing but led Mom and me to the parking lot and drove us home while Larry was ticketed and fined, and his mother defended her boy, and his father watched a late show in the den back at their house.

In our station wagon, the silences simmered while my mother tried to decide if she was mad and worried about her wild teenage daughter or indulgent and almost proud of the harmless adventure, while my father suppressed whatever he wondered, while I heard Mrs. Benson's phrase: *Sowing his wild oats.* I almost laughed, wanting to correct her: corn, not oats. But I pulled out of my shaking body in the station wagon's backseat, sat beside it and patted its shoulder: right, right, keep up that shuddering, do not think of poor Larry Benson, his corn unpopped, do not laugh hysterically or calmly.

Tucked into bed as if I were sick, I remembered how oats were sowed and I heard the muted snarling corn.

Monday morning between English and U.S. History, I—who said I was Mrs. Donald Reynolds—made an appointment with a gynecologist. On Wednesday after school I rode the bus downtown by myself and checked in with Dr. Wan's receptionist and in the little room put my heels in the stirrups and spread my knees. None of us believed I was Mrs. Donald Reynolds from out of town.

"You healthy?" Dr. Wan said. "You eat right?"

He peeled off his glove and spread it out on the edge of the metal wastebasket.

"Here," he said, "you take this."

He set a sample packet of pills and a prescription on the counter in front of the jar of cotton balls, and hurried out.

Before, I hadn't thought that Sally applied to me. Yes, we took our shapes from boys lying on us. But Sally had been the one in trouble: I had drifted so far out of my body that nothing could engage it. Mrs. Benson had plunked me back into my body. In the police station, she put her arm around her son and stared at me malevolently. She knew my stretch pants had been yanked back up during the chase. Boys needed fields for their oats, but she didn't have to admire the wildflowers sprouting at the furrowed edges.

I hid the pills in a beaded clutch purse I'd had for a prom, and I swallowed one every day, never forgetting—and sometimes, especially in the summertime, I heard through the screened window that brown dry corn.

At the beginning of my senior year, I was chosen editor of the literary magazine. I'd been with no boy for the past few weeks of the summer, and now with this sacred job, I decided that I would quit the sex. For the rest of the year I'd be the unspoiled Kitty they thought I was.

Peter Murphy joined the magazine's staff of six, and after the others left our Thursday after-school meetings, Peter and I continued to argue and defend the merits of the submitted stories and poems.

Peter was a poet himself, he said.

"I thought about not joining the staff," he said. "Even though Aunt Edie said I ought to." Aunt Edie was what we all called Mrs. Eisenfeld, the English teacher for college-bound seniors, having discovered that her first name was Edith.

"How come you weren't going to?" I said.

"Well, I'd like to give you some of my poems," he said, "but if I'm on the staff, it'd be like a conflict of interest."

"That's all right," I told him. "Hand them in. Nobody'd think anything."

"You don't get it," he said. "Whatever of mine is ever published, it'll be because it's damn good. I don't even want them to know who I am."

I looked across the table at him. We'd stacked the poetry entries into piles that Peter had labeled Absolutely, Could Be, Forget It, and Rotten. He was a very lean boy, nice looking, really, and he had a mild accent of some sophisticated sort, though he'd told me he'd been raised in the Midwest "among farmers and the small-town bourgeoisie." I'd never really seen an instance of integrity before, though of course we talked about it in humanities class. We knew many who had no integrity, especially politicians, though I'd never applied it to myself.

I looked down at the piles of poems. I couldn't tell Peter that I admired his integrity, after all. And he might see the contamination in me.

Soon enough, Peter was showing me his poems, which I thought were excellent though not beautiful.

"Good! Good!" Peter said. "I don't *want* beauty. I want truth. I don't care what Aunt Edie says Keats says: they *aren't* the same. She just doesn't get the poem. She ought to ask herself just who the hell is *saying* those last lines."

My girlfriends wanted to know how come I was going out with that creep Peterhead Murphy.

My sister had acne that year. Mom took her to a dermatologist once a week for sunlamp treatments. Judy sat at the Tuesday supper table with a sunburnt face, white rings around her eyes, and blood-clotted pimples, each with a white crust ringing it.

"If I were you," she said, "I'd go out with the popular guys. You're popular, so you can get the popular guys."

"All the popular guys care about is football and making out," I said. "Peter cares about stuff like poetry and music and ideas."

Mom passed the casserole, and I saw her exchange looks with Dad. I couldn't tell if she was relieved—I wouldn't get in trouble with cerebral Peter—or disappointed that I might relinquish my chance at football homecoming queen. I thought I saw a quirk of amusement in Dad.

I stood up. "I don't care what you all think," I said. "All you care about is what the neighbors think and your little suburban house."

I turned on Judy. "And your problem is that you *care* about being popular. Being popular is stupid. Besides, if you didn't care so much, you just might *be* popular."

I strode to Judy's and my room and slammed the door.

Peter took me to concerts and the university's free lectures. Homecoming passed. We didn't go to the dance. Instead we drove to the state park and walked in the dusk woods, imagining the pairs dancing with the pins of their corsages and boutonnieres sticking their chests. Peter held my hand. We walked on the dead leaves, and the yellow and red leaves still on the trees seemed to retain the light of the set Midwestern sun.

"'Gather ye rose-buds while ye may,'" Peter recited, "'Old Time is still a flying.'"

We'd studied Robert Herrick's poem in Aunt Edie's class.

Peter moved my hand to the front of his pants.

Now it was right, I thought. Now it was new. It was my self, my virginity, I was giving him, despite all those others.

Still, the sharp dry elm leaves stabbed my bare skin and Peter panted, holding himself above me with straight arms, closed his eyes, held his breath, and then sobbed it out. Quickly he pulled away.

"Oh God," he said.

I pulled on my underpants and sat on my slacks beside him. My bare thighs were very white.

"You weren't a virgin," he said.

I put my head on my knees.

"I should have known," he said. "Jesus. I thought you were so pure. That big act."

I stood. "Listen, Peterhead—that's what they call you, you know that? You're the one who's a phony. All this business about living life to its fullest without all those stupid bourgeois values— and then when you find out someone's actually done it, you act like some maiden aunt or something."

I picked up my pants and strode bare-legged back to Peter's father's car. He'd locked it. I pulled my pants up my scratched legs. For the first time I was crying for some boy, in my own skin, my spoiled skin.

In ten minutes he followed me. He actually knelt and held my hand to his cheek. "Oh God, you're right," he said.

For a month he was righteously proud of his fallen woman, and we were friends as we hadn't been before. He told me about his awful hardware-store stepfather and about growing up shy until he quit caring what anybody else thought and about his poor mother who loved her husband but didn't like him. "You've got to have more than the bedroom," he said.

Finally he asked who had done it to me, and I considered making up some stupid story about a cousin attacking me or something, but then I told him about the dozen boys and my need not for sex but for *some*thing, I didn't know what, but that was the closest.

"Before I knew you," I told him, "I felt so dirty. I felt tainted or something."

Peter was silent. He shifted away on the car seat.

"Taint," he said. "I know what that is. I heard some guys saying. Taint is that little spot on a girl—'taint pussy and 'taint ass."

Peter quit the literary magazine, though I finished my job of final selections, of showing the production staff how to arrange the pieces. Peter submitted an anonymous late poem about Vincent van Gogh and a prostitute model. I knew it was Peter's, and anyway it was too late to include anything else, and the magazine, *Idylls*, didn't need our taint.

As soon as the magazine was done, I got sick. For three days I slumped into classes, exhausted by the trip from my locker. I didn't care that Peter Murphy watched from two rows over and must have thought he was the cause of the depression.

I couldn't talk to Mom anymore. I had no more stories to feed her. She fussed after me, and I turned on her.

"I just can't wait to get out of here," I said.

I supposed she cried. I supposed I was sorry.

After Christmas, I tried to return to popularity. But my friends had seen *Where the Boys Are* and discovered the Beatles and gone out for cheerleading and passed around Suzie Sellers's brother's dirty book while I'd been absent from my body. They'd wrapped angora around their boyfriends' class rings to make them fit and they'd learned to do the jerk. I was like a big sister come back from college, and though they tried to take me back and fixed me up with their boyfriends' friends, it was too late.

For spring break I went with my friend Janice and her parents to their Lake Michigan cottage. Her father taught sociology at the high school and knew enough to leave us alone. In hooded sweaters and old pants, we walked the cold beach. The water was cold and rough. Past the breakers, gray-white veins rose and broke on the gray surface.

We gathered driftwood and dug a fire pit in the wet sand. At last we got the twigs and dried grass to light beneath our driftwood tepee. We sat in the windy gray afternoon by our blowing fire, trying to read and keep the sand from our eyes. I knew my hair would be sandy.

"Don't you love coming home from the beach and scratching sand out of your scalp?" I said, and we started giggling.

We were both reading Jack London's *Martin Eden*, though I was nearly finished. Janice was my only friend who read as I did.

When we quit giggling, we watched the veined water. "Sometimes I think I could just walk straight out there," I said.

"Oh no," Janice said. "I could never do that." She flung her hand toward the fire. "Oh there's never going to be enough of life."

"Well, just you wait until—" I began.

She looked at me and we both knew I'd given away *Martin Eden*'s end.

"You rat," she said and threw sand across the fire at me.

She finished the book anyway, of course, and we memorized Swinburne and traded lines like passwords. *From too much love of living*, I'd say. *From hope and fear set free*, she'd say. *We thank with brief thanksgiving*, I'd say. *Whatever gods may be*, she'd say. *That no life lives forever*, we'd say together. *That even the weariest river winds somewhere safe to sea.*

I still remembered that moment Janice and I knew each other's mind. I still remembered the passion of wearing a seventeen-year-old body when I was alive and even the somehow satisfying lethargy when I withdrew from the contamination. Nobody lived in such a stark world, such an unshadowed world, as a teenager.

By graduation, I was spending my weekday evenings at the library and my weekend nights with one boy or another, Judy had changed her name to Judith and then to Judi, and I could barely speak to my parents for fear of the invertebrate sounds or the tears that would emerge. Mom kept trying but there was nothing to tell her—no more half-truths about parties and friends, and certainly not the truth about my sickness—and so I ignored her.

I went to the senior prom in an expensive white-and-pink dress. Dad took pictures of me and Kevin Apple. Later Kevin and I left the all-night party at three A.M. to park by yet another cornfield. This corn was young and yellow-green. And afterwards Kevin and I made it back to the party and the breakfast that Sharon Hopper's mother was serving.

At graduation, I stood with my robed friends and discussed tassel placement. To "Pomp and Circumstance" we rolled and halted up the auditorium aisle. Along with my friend Janice and Peter Murphy, I took my awards and my scholarship. Afterwards we flipped our tassels to the other side of our caps. The girls unhooked their black gowns to show their graduation dresses and began crying.

I must have slept on my ironwood-needle bed, because I awoke abruptly when the dog moved. She growled deeply. I peered around the car seat but I could see or hear nothing on the beach.

What had my childhood to do with the island? I was merely here. I had never been innocent. Guilty, I'd hidden my bleeding. I'd never been deflowered but only acted out my shame.

Cimarron whined and licked my face, as she used to when she wanted out in the night.

"Look, fool dog, you're already outside. You can just do your duty any old where," I said.

She headed toward the beach. I lost her in the blackness. In a moment she was back, licking my face and whining. She must have tried to drink from the ocean: I could smell the salty water on her tongue as she licked my cheek.

Perhaps the island had once been clean and flowering, but it had long since been despoiled. But what had I to do with that? Every living thing had always carried its own seed. If darkness had again fallen upon the face of the deep, it hadn't been my doing.

I still felt sick. I did not know why I was still alive. In the black and gray of the island, the sea, and the sky, I was as insubstantial as the ironwood trees, as the horizon, and I could not tell hunger from sickness.

6

A brittle clap woke me, and I jumped blindly at the sound. Immediately I saw that Cimarron was gone.

A horizontal shaft of light hit the car seat I'd slept behind. The clouds were parted like a grim mouth. After days of darkness, I thought the thunder that had awakened me must have been the crack of the sunrise against the car seat's vinyl.

So this is the famous crack of dawn, I thought. I tried to laugh.

I'd been dreaming of food. I was no longer hungry, but I remembered the pleasures of cooking. I remembered packaged bloodless meat. I remembered chopping onions, despite stinging eyes, because the food processor made mushy pieces and juice. I remembered the texture of fresh mushrooms between my thumb and forefinger and the feel of the sharp knife slicing through them to the chopping board. I thought I could smell the variety of spices and seasonings when I'd opened the cupboard—dill, paprika, coriander, sage, tarragon, cinnamon and cloves, thyme, pepper. I remembered stirring in shredded cheddar and sour cream.

So this is the crack of doom, I thought. Everything is lost.

"Cimarron," I called softly. "Where are you, pups?"

There had been those who'd eaten dog.

The daily world was gone. No more cucumber and tomato chopped for the salad, no more buttered popcorn late in winter evenings, no more mozzarella spread on the pizza. The details were gone. No more crab dip recipes. No more curlers and clipped toenails. No more soap powder measured into washing machines. No more squirting window cleaner onto bathroom mirrors. No more linoleum. The dailiness was gone. No more "Six O'clock News," no more cold water poured into the Mr. Coffee in the morning, no more eggs over easy, no more cut grass in the summer.

Long ago I'd lost my childhood. Once I'd been able to catch lightning bugs in damp summer evenings, but I'd soon recognized that I was as deficient of something as Sally the deaf girl.

And now the world had lost its innocent daily details.

The dog rushed out of the jungle as if she were being chased. There was blood on her muzzle. Cimarron opened her mouth and gagged, heaved twice, and then dropped her head to vomit. She must have gulped the chicken. Before I pulled her away, I saw clumps of brown feathers, the beak, and a yellow foot.

I didn't know if she'd eaten so fast that she couldn't hold the inedible parts or if she was sick or if the bird was contaminated.

"Come along, you disgusting creature," I said. "Let's go home."

I decided to hike back to the dive shop where at least there were hidden cans of Sprite and dog food. I thought the two chasing me must have stayed at the hotel ruins last night, and if they were in a room in a double bed each, they might have slept through the crack of thunder.

First I stepped bare-legged into the ocean and, squatting when I reached waist-deep water, ducked my head under. My hair would dry gummy with dirt, oil, and salt, but in the meanwhile it felt cleaner to have wet hair on my shoulders.

As we walked along the black water's edge, Cimarron brought me sticks and decaying zori to throw. When she retrieved something, she'd toss her head and flip it away instead of fetching it to me. Soon she'd drop something else at my side: a child's deflated water wing, a glass fishing buoy.

"A little chicken for breakfast and you're ready to take on the world," I said. "Even if there's no world to take on."

About halfway to the harbor, I saw a wrecked shape at the water's edge. With her tail in the water, and her torso and head face-up on the beach, lay a larger-than-life plaster mermaid. I was sure I recognized her as the Sirena statue that had been perched on the rocks of a grotto downtown — four miles straight across the island. She was intact, her pale green-scaled tail slicing the water, her right arm across her waist, large brown-nippled breasts and transfigured face directed straight up, her white eyes rolled back. Sirena had been, according to local legend, a young girl who neglected her chores so often to play in the water that she was turned into a mermaid. This Sirena seemed to have lived with the fishes for a long time, judging from the quality of her bosom and her ecstasy. I could not imagine how she'd been transported intact four miles across the island.

Near Sirena's downtown grotto had been a perpetually revolving statue of the Pope. In the Chinese Park, Confucius had stood by a pair of picnic tables. I wondered what had become of them.

Much of the beach had disappeared, as if the water had risen. All along, the sand was littered with debris. Once, a beachcomber would have called it flotsam and jetsam. But there was nothing so cheerful about dead fish that the dog tried to roll on, mangled ropes of seaweed, burst aluminum cans, jagged hunks of corrugated tin, or a hugely bloated water buffalo with one horn stuck in the sand and its head twisted to its spine.

The wind grew, tossing up breakers far out, seeming to bloat like the dead. The gray sky gathered and ran like mercury.

At the northern part of the harbor, just before the breakwater, was a floating graveyard. Dozens of bodies were sucked out with the water and then heaved back against the rocks. The currents must have gathered them and now they were trapped, eddying where the beach met the jutting breakwater. The bodies, like small whales, were thrown against the rocks, and when the sleek skin was ripped by the coral, the bodies deflated, emitted a yellow-green gas, and sank. I held the putrescence in my nostrils for a moment, fighting the gag until it turned into gasping sobs, as if it were my duty to witness. Oh we humans had been so enraptured by the ineffable loveliness of sand, of blue rock crabs, of deciduous trees, of cornfields, of coral, of field rocks, that we thought we were exempt from decay.

I sent Cimarron into the dive shop first. Creeping from the beach to the shop, I'd heard nothing but the wind on the water and among the dark pearly clouds. If the men were hiding in the shop, she'd bark and warn me. I hoped they wouldn't shoot her.

The men weren't there, but they had been. The air mattresses had been stabbed dozens of times. My beach towel had been ripped in thirds. My books on diving and coral-reef fishes had been torn apart. The hose to my regulator had been severed. Someone had defecated on the stabbed air mattress.

But they hadn't found my food cache beneath the floorboards. Immediately I opened a can of hot Sprite, drank, choked on the bubbles, and drank. Outside I dipped a wash basin into the barrel of rinse water for dive gear. Cimarron emptied the basin and I refilled it.

The only food left in my cache was dog food—three cans of chunk-style Alpo and a bag of dry Purina. The second bag was still in the Scout. I opened a can of Alpo and dumped it on the dive shop floor for Cimmie, and she gulped it in spite of her dawn chicken hunt. The Alpo smelled like beef tips in gravy, like beef Stroganoff just before the sour cream is added, like beef stew—I almost expected the dog to spit out the bay leaf.

I opened a second can. I had no spoon or fork. I picked a hunk of meat out of the Alpo gravy with my fingers. I'd never tasted anything so perfectly prepared. The meat—probably horse, I thought—was tender, and the gravy was thick and brown and rich. When the can was half empty, I tipped it up and drank the rest of the gravy and then shook the meat, chunk by chunk, into my mouth.

89

"Oh pups," I said, "I never knew what I was missing. Now if only we had a nice dry red wine."

In college I met Daniel at the first mixer. Our dorm big sisters had warned my roommate and me that the sophomore and junior guys would be there looking over the new girls; we shouldn't hope for seniors, who already were paired. We were asked to dance again and again to the Lettermen and the Byrds. Near the end, Daniel stepped up to Valerie and me.

"I'm Daniel Manning," he said. "I don't dance. But I'd like to walk you back to your dorm."

He looked at both of us. Valerie said that some sophomore named Dave was going to take her to the snack bar. So Daniel walked me back to Towsley Hall, and I never knew if I was really the one he'd wanted.

Daniel Manning was lean, almost scrawny, with dingy blond hair that he wore longer than most students. He dressed neatly enough, but he wore white socks and his pants were always belt-less. He was talkative but aloof, hiding an intensity, I thought, more passionate than my high-school boyfriend Peter's.

He didn't call for a month after the mixer, and when at last he did, I canceled another date to accept his offer to attend the college production of *Our Town*. We went out irregularly for two years. We liked each other's company, and in the shadows of Towsley Hall, he sometimes kissed me, but we had no grand passion. He seemed almost ascetic, I thought, but I accepted his every invitation for the relief of his company and friendship after all the others' open-mouthed kisses and parked cars and walks to the cemetery at night. Daniel Manning would never take me to a Purple Passion Party where everyone dipped from a bucket of vodka and grape juice until the bathroom was full of vomiting girls and the back lawn littered with sick and passed-out guys. Daniel never even tried to unsnap my bra or unzip my pants.

I changed majors from philosophy to psychology to English. Daniel knew from the beginning that his major was history. Sometimes with him I felt like a patchwork body—Daniel was so seamless.

At the end of my junior year, Daniel graduated and moved into his own tiny apartment and immediately began graduate school. My roommate, Valerie, was scared to go home and tell her parents she thought she was pregnant. I took her home with me, and we told my mother, who was unshocked and kind. One of her fellow elementary school teachers knew someone, and among them they got Valerie her abortion. I never told Valerie about my years on birth-control pills. I didn't tell her that she was stupid to get caught: I didn't believe that. Her catching pregnancy was innocent compared to my cautious licentiousness.

Valerie went home to New Jersey for the rest of the summer, and I found that I could talk to my mother again. I told her about Daniel, smiling a bit at his morality and at my relief. My mother and I could talk because I did not have to dissemble. In relief, I decided that I would marry Daniel.

By August I was spent by the flat Midwestern heat and by my mother. I slept until noon and woke open-mouthed and sweating in the bright bed, sapped by the thought of the afternoon and the family supper and evening remaining before I could go to bed again. When my mother wasn't tight-lipped because I'd slept so late, she was reciting her good deeds and the compliments she'd received.

"—and Helen Williams said she'd met me years ago and had been charmed by me, and I say to myself, now what had I said?"

"Something witty, I'm sure," I said.

"I ran into Harvey Jervis's mother in Carson's, I had him in sixth grade years ago, and she said I was the best teacher Harvey ever had, he still talks about me."

"I wonder what Harvey Jervis is doing now," I said.

"Sometimes I don't know why I go to those women's fellowship meetings, most times I just sit there, but sometimes I get into a crazy mood and everybody thinks I'm so witty and clever."

"I can imagine," I said.

Every time she delivered leftover altar flowers from church to the nursing home, every time she returned the extra change when a clerk gave her too much back, she recited it.

Judy was no help. She was a math major, and she spent hours at the kitchen table filling pages with equations. We couldn't understand her. "We don't use numbers," she said. "Just letters." She and Mitch were engaged, though they were going to wait until they graduated before they married.

"What are you going to *do* with your math?" Mom wanted to know.

Judy shrugged. "I don't have any interest in applied mathematics," she said.

"I don't think I like applied anything," I said.

Mom looked tolerant. "Well, you could always teach," she said.

"Oh God," Judy moaned.

"I guess it's good enough for some of us," Mom said.

"Now don't get offended," Judy said. "You're a great teacher. But I just know I wouldn't have the patience with all those dumbheads." And she picked up her pencil.

Late afternoons, Mom and I lost the irritations of the sweltering days, and we worked on supper together, chopping vegetables for salads, unmolding Jell-Os, making a cold chicken salad, mixing brownies to go with the ice cream. I knew precisely the right sizes to chop onions, green peppers, cucumbers, hard-boiled eggs, cooked chicken. I knew the right amount of celery salt to add to the potato salad.

Dad would come home, and the four of us would eat on the breezeway, praising the cool food and talking gently of neighbors and the mill levy and the size of the willow tree in the side yard. After supper, Judy would leave for her volunteer job at the nursing home, Dad would change into Bermudas and join the other shirtless men watering their lawns up and down the still-curbless blocks, and Mom and I would clear the table, spoon leftovers into Tupperware, and do the dishes together.

"Let's see if those Tupperware pitches are really true," she said one night. She burped the lid down on the bowl of spaghetti, just as the home demonstrators said, and threw the bowl to the ceiling. It splatted to the floor and sent cold spaghetti and sauce all over the kitchen.

We laughed until we had to go to the bathroom or wet our pants.

After the dishes, we'd check on Dad watering the yard. I wondered what suburban men did without yard work. I sneered to myself at the narrowness, and then Dad would turn the hose on me and I'd run away, laughing at the coolness and the comfort of it all.

In the dark, Judy and I talked. The night diffused through our screen windows and over our uncovered bodies. As little girls, we'd slept in our cotton underpants in the summer. Now we slept in baby-doll pajamas.

"Mom drives me crazy," I said. "All that stuff about her school. All that bragging. How can you just sit there and play with your numbers—excuse me, letters—and just ignore it? Doesn't it bug you?"

"Not really," she said. "Don't you get it? Sure, she protests too much. When you get down to it, she's not really sure she's so darned good. And you know, it's not that she's a bad person—she's not, she's one of the good guys. But the thing is that she doesn't know it for sure herself."

"Well, hot damn," I said. "Maybe you're the one who should have tried majoring in psych. I guess you're probably right, too. But she still drives me crazy."

Outside, in the summer night, sheet lightning slammed quietly on the horizon.

That summer, my roommate married her high-school boyfriend and so, when I returned to school, I had our little room to myself. Valerie wrote that she just couldn't return to school after what had happened but she couldn't stay at home, either, and so she'd agreed to marry Gregory Hulett, who was a narc—I shouldn't tell anyone—and packed a piece. She wasn't crazy about any of it but what could she do? By the time she got my forwarded letter begging her to come back to school—she could still register late—she and Gregory Hulett were on their honeymoon in Miami. I wondered if she'd told him about the abortion. I wondered if he wore his piece to the beach.

By myself in our little room, I was lonely. Valerie and I had been true friends, even if I had worn my good-girl body all the time. Finally I might have told her.

She called me from Miami. "I don't know why I did it," she said. "He calls that gun his baby. Now I'll never have any true love." She cried, and when Gregory returned to their motel room, she hung up.

Alone in our room, I played our favorite records—Tchaikovsky's Violin Concerto and *Swan Lake*—and read Dostoyevski and Updike and Edith Wharton and Ralph Ellison, depressed as if I'd lost a love. The housemother of Towsley Hall tried to give Valerie's bed to a stray freshman, but I wouldn't have her.

Daniel took me to the college's production of *R.U.R.* and held my hand all the way through. Afterwards we walked to his tiny apartment. "I have some wine I want you to try," he said.

"I don't like Ripple," I said.

Yellow leaves were falling on us, and the streetlights exuded the dry brown smell and waxy light that were the essence of fall. I felt as if we were walking on a set, holding hands as directed.

"Oh my dear," he said, mock-disappointed. "I have something truly exquisite."

"I don't like Boone's Farm, either," I said.

"Oh ye of little faith," he said. "What awaits has an actual cork that ye may sniff."

Daniel's apartment was one room with a single bed on one side

94

of the divider and a refrigerator, hot plate, and small round table on the other. The bathroom, down the hall, was shared by all the roomers.

He plied his corkscrew and sat us down on the bed to drink from jelly glasses.

"I think it's time we made love," he said.

Abruptly the tears rose. I lifted my glass, caught a tear I couldn't restrain, and drank.

"Hey now," Daniel said. "You're not supposed to cry until afterwards."

He set our glasses on the floor beside the bed.

"Do you mind the light?" he said. I shook my head. The yellow bedside lamp gave off the same waxy light as the streetlights.

He touched me carefully, and after the wine, I felt as if his hands were washing me with pliant yellow light.

"Oh my beautiful love," he said.

"Yes," I said.

I'd read Molly Bloom's yeses, and I almost giggled, but then I forgot and said, "Yes, yes."

He lay on me long after.

"What color would you say this yellow is?" I said.

"I don't know," he said. I felt the effort of his words against my chest. "Maybe cadmium. I'm not sure what that is, really, but it feels right."

I'd never had an orgasm before. Valerie and I used to laugh about not wanting to say "organism" in biology class for fear of mispronouncing it.

"I know this may not be the first time for either of us," Daniel said. "But I don't want to know about anybody else. And I'll never ask."

I wouldn't let him walk me back to the dorm. "You stay," I said, and kissed him, and left him, lean and cadmium, on the narrow bed.

All the way back, I wept. It was the wine, the joy, the indelible past, and the guttering fall. I arrived at Towsley Hall past curfew and pounded on the door. The housemother opened the door in her green housecoat.

"All right, young lady, you'd better tell me what this is all about," she said.

"Oh leave me alone, I'm a senior," I said, and went to my two-bed room to continue weeping.

The gecko on the dive-shop wall wasn't the one I'd seen two mornings ago. This one had a mismatched tail. The body had a fancy pattern, like worn intaglio, but the tail was plain gray. The line between was clear, as if the tail had been soldered on.

Suddenly the gecko spurted across the wall, and I saw that it was chasing another gecko, this one small and pale. I wondered if geckos changed shades to match surroundings. I'd seen chame-leons outside my apartment—a green one on a banana leaf; one, lying on a beach shoe, with its head and its thin tail bright blue. The geckos seemed able to change only along a continuum of weak tans and grays.

"You know what, Cimarron?" I said. "I think Judy was a gecko and I was a chameleon. Whatever sense that makes."

Abruptly the mismatched gecko gulped down the pale one.

"Did you see that? A cannibal gecko," I said. I wondered if mutations could be appearing already. I'd never seen a gecko nab another before, but perhaps they had. Perhaps what remained would be biologically skewed.

I thought for an instant about trying to kill the cannibal gecko. But what would be the point?

Then the perfectly familiar sound of an engine interposed. I closed my eyes in the pain of memory. This could be the Reynolds family pulling up to their shingled house across the street, home from the drive-in, and Carol and Donnie would run around the yard in their pajamas before Mrs. Reynolds would call, "All right, you two, you'll step on a rusty nail out there barefooted in the dark." This could be Daniel coming home from work; soon I'd hear the wheels on the gravel driveway, and Daniel would pick up the evening newspaper, and we would eat an early supper. But engines weren't friendly anymore. I thought of friendly fire and looked out the dive-shop window. I couldn't see anything—and then a red pickup rose up a slope in the road. The dusk shuddered around it like heat.

If I ran out the front, they'd surely see me. Perhaps they wouldn't even stop, but I couldn't risk being caught and punctured like the air mattress. I grabbed the empty Alpo cans, called the dog, and left by the rear door. Behind the dive shop was a foothill of rocks and unburned, ashy trees, and then a rock cliff. We couldn't run, but I thought we could hide. I set the cans behind a boulder and pulled a fallen branch over them. Cimarron stopped to sniff and circle the ground we'd been using as our bathroom. "For God's sake, not now," I said, but she assumed the posture as the red pickup stopped. I couldn't see it, but I heard the tires shriek on the pavement and then scatter gravel, and I scrambled up the rocks. The dog overtook me. I grabbed at her to pull her down behind a boulder with me. I got her tail, and she yipped, but the truck's doors slammed, and I didn't think the men could have heard.

The wooden door of the dive shop slammed. I hoped the floor where Cimarron had licked up Alpo gravy was dry. I could hear voices, one young and high, but I couldn't make out words. The dog was panting rapidly, and I stroked her hard to keep her quiet.

The back door's hinges squealed.

"All right, boy," one man said, "go get 'em. You Flips eats enough dogs that you're probably part-dog your own self."

"Oh, shi-it," the other said after a moment. His voice broke. "It's all over my own Nikes."

"Shit is right," the older voice said. "Fresh shit, too. I bet even a dumb Flip can figure out what that means."

I heard something slammed wetly and repeatedly against rock.

"At least it's dog shit," the older voice said. He laughed. "But maybe you'd rather step in a pile of *hers*."

In the silence from below, Cimmie's quick panting seemed loud.

"Due to the fact of the smell," the older voice said patiently.

I heard the hollow rattle of empty cans thrown onto rock.

"Everybody outta the pool," the older man hollered. "Come on, come on. The dog eat, the dog shit, we know you haven't departed the area."

I recognized the governmentese that had pervaded Chamorro English.

"We're getting so tired of the sceneries," he called.

They began throwing stones and coral rocks up into the boulders. When I was hit, I immediately pitched the rock toward the cliff above me so they'd hear a report. I hardly cared whether they found me. I almost laughed. I was too clever to be captured. A rock hit Cimarron's flank and she pulled away and headed down the boulders, losing her balance and then gracefully leaping until she was down. She charged the men and pulled up short before them, growling, and then breaking into a deep territorial bark. Even as a puppy, she'd had a funny, low-down voice that Daniel and I had laughed at. The men ran into the dive shop, and I started down the side of the boulder heap.

The door hinges squealed, and I heard Cimmie utter a long, low *whoo-who-whooo*.

"Don't you talk to me that way," the older man said.

What he had in his hand had to be a gun.

"Don't you dare," I said and climbed the rest of the way down. Long ago, my mother had taught me the schoolteacher's voice. It couldn't be used often, but when needed it could stop a playground fight, a dog about to attack, anyone before he spoke forever irretrievable words. I'd used it to stop an impending food fight in the cafeteria and once to stop four boys preparing to heave a kitten into the air. The man held the gun on Cimarron and then slowly moved it to aim at me.

"No, don't," the other man said in anguish.

"Rogelio thinks I will shoot you," the older man said. "And he gots no use for dead meat."

"Miss," Rogelio said, pronouncing it *mees.*

I remembered the fat Filipino boy in my reading class. He was still fat, but before he'd had the larded look of little boys with obese parents. Now he looked grayish, as if his brown skin were dusted with ash, and bloated. He wore a tight orange T-shirt that read CHAMORRO DUDE in cracked fluorescent letters. He looked like the dead washed onto the beaches.

"Hey, Roger," I said. "I'm glad to see you made it." I reached out to pat his shoulder, and he jerked back.

The older man was short and dark brown, perhaps fifty. He wore plaid Bermudas and no shirt, and his belly rested loosely on the shorts' waistband.

I remembered how the village boys had mocked Rogelio Torres in class, and I recalled my puerile lectures on brotherhood.

"Roger," I said, "have you seen anybody else? How'd you find him?"

"The man says go with him—"

"Shut your face up," the older man said. He aimed the gun at Cimarron again. "My name is Anthony Joseph Taitano. Maybe he gots one reason for being with me." The gun followed the dog as she nosed the ground.

We three, perhaps the last people, stood speechless behind a wooden shop, before a rock pile and a cliff. Rogelio Torres, ashen and bloated, stared down as if he were trying to make out the upside-down pattern of the letters on his T-shirt. Anthony Joseph Taitano probably hadn't even had to rape him. Kit Manning couldn't even control her dog.

"Do you want to come with me, Roger?" I said.

"The man says—" Rogelio started, pronouncing it *sāys* again. There was no correcting anything.

"No, *mees*, that's not how it is," Taitano said. "You come with us." He laughed lewdly. "She come with us," he said to Rogelio, who stared at his Chamorro Dude shirt. "Stupid fucking Flip. Look at me, stupid. Come on, look up, and we might make you have a turn with this scummy white bitch."

Rogelio looked at Taitano and then at me.

I recalled the common use of *make* for *let*. What did language have to do with volition, I'd wondered to Malcolm Yarrow. It's just the way they talk, he'd said.

"First we gots to waste this fucking dog," Taitano said. "Then we honeymoon at the Hilton. If we can find one room without dead gooks in it."

As he pointed the gun at Cimarron, I slammed into his shoulder, and while he was off balance I ran around the side of the dive shop with the dog running beside me.

"White bitch!" Taitano yelled. "You gots nowhere to go. This is an island! And I have stayed here forever. If we don't get you, the typhoon will."

I started across the road toward the breakwater. Perhaps I'd be able to find my cache of dive gear and swim away from them. But what about Cimarron? And, despite the gun and the threats, they were just a scared kid and a blustering fat man. I'd never feared any of my students; though they'd hidden a bomb in another teacher's car, I was sure none of them would ever hurt me. This was only poor derided Rogelio Torres, not very bright but desperate to be accepted among the Tanô boys. He probably didn't even realize how I'd tried to protect him.

I ran north on the road, with Cimarron charging ahead. I couldn't see anyone following me. I sprinted along, light and safe. Taitano and Rogelio were too heavy to catch us. They'd tried to run me off the road, but I didn't think Taitano would shoot me. He had nothing to fear from me, except that I might lure Rogelio away. I might well be the only woman left.

Looking back, I saw bright bobbing lights, and then I heard one of the men yelling something, a wild ululating cry. I ran past the breakwater. Here partly burned jungle separated the road and the beach. I could hear the men behind me, and I was suddenly winded, with a pain in my side. I ran into the jungle. I wasn't sure if they had seen me. Cimarron was far ahead of me, and I let her go. The islanders had been afraid of large dogs, and Rogelio and Taitano had run into the dive shop to get away from Cimarron, but I didn't think she would attack them. They might not kill me, but even a Chamorro might be hungry enough for dog meat.

The jungle was patchy, with dense oases circled by burn. The burned ground had shrunk down, and blackened coral rocks protruded. I ducked in a patch of thick growth.

"I . . . gots . . . to stop," Rogelio panted.

"Pussy," Taitano yelled. ". . . lets her get . . . gonna kill me . . . move your ass."

Ashes and soot stuck to my sweaty skin. With the men heading up the road, I turned south, plodding from oasis to oasis. Now I might be able to reach my dive gear and make a sea escape.

Near the harbor the cover disappeared, and rather than run in sand, I returned to the road. I had lost my dog. I was panting and my side ached. I heard a distorted chirping of birds, as if from a warped synthesizer. No birds were left on the island, I knew, and I limped on in the dusk.

Then behind me a wild cry sounded, like a movie Apache's, and I saw my own shadow, thrown onto the road by the flare. I hadn't heard them following me. I thought wildly that Taitano was in good shape for a fat man.

I ran for the rocks and tangantangan brush of the breakwater. I carried the image of my misshapen shadow. I ran out the breakwater's dirt road, energized again with panic. In the roar and suck of the ocean against the breakwater, I heard monstrous, wet bells. I knew I must be hallucinating, but the bells still clanged in the viscous waves. A light flashed behind me, and in the nictitating flare, my shadow drew into my body, and I turned. Rogelio had disappeared. Before Taitano could reach me, I raised my fists and flipped my middle fingers, and with the hallucinations abruptly gone, I jumped onto the low concrete wall on the ocean side of the road, and dropped to the heaped boulders above the water.

Taitano yelled above the crash of the waves, and I saw him, limned by torchlight, standing on the concrete wall.

"You gots nowhere to go," he yelled.

Below, the waves crashed on the rocks, but I climbed down onto the next boulder, thinking that if I leapt far enough out, I could swim out of the current before it swept me back against the rocks. Before, I hadn't truly been afraid of Taitano. Even after a nuclear holocaust, I'd still been inviolable Kitty. Tears rose sharply.

"I can make you live," Taitano yelled, "or I can kill you."

I couldn't make it down the rocks to the ocean before he shot, and I couldn't have survived the crushing waves against the rocks anyway.

"You gots to be up here," he yelled. Rogelio was beside him on the cement wall. Taitano raised the gun. I heard nothing. A sliver of rock hit my calf, ripping the trousers and nicking my skin. This man would kill me. Shaking, I climbed back up. The jagged rocks and the delicate tangantangan were sharply clear in the dusky afternoon.

Taitano grabbed my arm and put the gun to my head.

"No . . . man," Roger panted. "He says . . . just get her . . ."

Taitano walked me down the breakwater.

"Who says, Roger?" I said.

"The *man* says—"

"Shut your face," Taitano said. "I'm the man here."

He yanked me along.

"Let go," I said. "I'll go with you. You're hurting my arm."
He shoved me ahead and the two of them followed.

"Okay, *mees.* Home again, home again," he said when we reached
the dive shop. "In you goes." Even a savage wanted some *place,* I
thought. Savagery now needed walls, not a beach.

"Secure the area," Taitano said, and Rogelio closed the doors
and shoved over the bolt at the back door. The front door locked
from the outside only, and none of us knew where that key was. I
wondered what other man Taitano might be hiding from.

I thought I saw a face at the window. But the window was dark,
and I knew there was only tangantangan brush against it.

"I'll make you go first," he said. Holding the gun on me, he
reached behind him to touch Rogelio. He found the zipper. He
kneaded the crotch. "Down, boy, you takes them down. I gets to
watch you fuck the teacher."

"You're sick," I said. "Rogelio, you don't have to do what he
says."

"Roger," the boy said. He shoved his dirty tan trousers down.
He wore no underwear. "You calls me Roger."

Taitano looked over his shoulder at Rogelio's crotch, and I
thought for an instant about trying to grab the gun. It was shiny,
like a toy. He held it so close that I could see the grid of the black
grip.

He reached forward and knocked the gun barrel against my
head. I lurched back, feeling nothing, and then the numbness
broke into pain.

"You're bleeding, miss," Rogelio said. I put my hand against my
dirty hair and looked at my bloody palm.

"Look at the Flip's tiny sausage," Taitano said, disgusted.
"*Lanya.* Nothing but one little ounce of chorizo."

I wanted to sit on the floor and hold my head. Rogelio's
shrunken penis was ringed with gray folds. He pulled up his

trousers. I stayed on my feet. Head wounds bled a lot: I thought I remembered that. All this blood didn't mean anything. The pain clanging in my head didn't mean anything. Blood soaked the shoulder of my T-shirt.

"I can do it my own self," Taitano said. "This stiffs up your chorizo. Watch this."

He swaggered toward me. Satyr, I thought. His left hand searched under his overhanging belly for the opening to his Bermudas. Dizzy, I thought I could see the hairy fetlocks and the hooves as he minced toward me.

I heard the sound of the hammer pulled back, *rat-chet*. He held the barrel against my bloody head and with his other hand gently unzipped my pants. Watching my face, pointing the cocked gun at my head, he slowly bent and worked my underpants down to my ankles.

"No, no," I said. "Roger, you stop him. Don't let him do this."

My head throbbed. I could feel blood and tears forced out with each pulse.

"Down," Taitano said, gesturing with the gun. He extracted his fattened penis from the Bermudas. With that belly, this isn't going to work, I thought and almost snickered. I imagined a fat fish swimming in circles, lopsided, and suddenly I remembered the pictures in some Sunday supplement—the fish circling instead of spawning, turtles leaving their eggs, unprotected on the sand, to cook in the sun. The animals had been exposed to radiation, the article said. Birds attacked instead of dancing. Irradiated, they forgot how to mate.

"Down," Taitano said, and he swung the gun back.

This time I ducked before he could hit my head, but with the pants around my ankles, I staggered.

"Haole bitch," he said. He held the gun at arm's length and pulled the trigger. The gunshot was deafening, and stupidly I looked down at my body to see where the blood would well up.

The bullet had made a small hole, just its own size, in the back wall. Taitano pushed and I fell to the floor. He kicked aside my pants and stood over me.

"Hey, chorizo dude," he said, "come here."

He cocked the gun again. How many times had he shot? Would there be six bullets? In the movies, the hero kept track. He'd be able to bluff. The shiny gun was huge, and I thought Taitano had shot only twice.

Using his left hand to aim, he urinated on me, aiming the stream back and forth, wetting my thighs and my stomach and my chest. I turned my head when he reached my face. He urinated on and on. "You are liking golden showers, *mees?*" he said. At the end, Rogelio unzipped and squeezed out a few drops on my shoes.

They weren't going to rape me. The urine stank, and it was nauseatingly bitter when it splashed my mouth. But it was only urine. I might be the last woman alive, and all this pair wanted to do was urinate on me. Perhaps that was the effect of radiation. Perhaps the skewing of the old pattern had been encoded: no more propagation. Every ride had an end.

Taitano spread my legs and knelt between them.

He put the barrel of the cocked gun between my legs.

"Oh God oh God oh God," I cried.

"No problem, *mees*," he said. "I am keeping my own finger on the trigger guard."

I squirmed back on the floor.

"I am putting my own finger on the trigger," he said.

I stopped, and he walked forward on his knees. He tried to push the gun barrel into me. "Pussy so tight," he said.

The metal was hot. He shoved the barrel into me. The gun's sight tore my dry flesh. I held myself still and silent. My body cramped but I did not move. Taitano pushed the barrel farther in me and switched hands. I made myself a statue, unmoving, mute, deadened. Taitano's right hand worked on himself. Rogelio was rubbing himself erratically as if he didn't know how. Nothing could enter stone. The gun jerked with the rhythm. Stone. Stone. Stone.

Taitano panted. He closed his eyes.

Suddenly and smoothly, I slid backwards and rolled to the side. Taitano's eyes opened and he groaned. "*Lanya*," he groaned. He pulled hard at himself. I jerked my pants up and was out the front door.

Cimarron was on the front step, and she ran with me across the road toward the breakwater. I didn't turn to see if Taitano was following yet. He'd finish his labor first, I thought. On the beach, I chased Cimarron away from the harbor. "Go! Go away!" I yelled at her. The dog slunk to me, wagging her tail low. The wind chopped at the water.

In panic I found my cache of dive gear wrapped in a beach towel and half-buried under coral rocks. I pushed the dog away and got the regulator attached to the tank, and then I saw the flare and the two fat men lumbering across the sand. I heard a shot.

"Good-bye, my sweet sweet dog," I said, shooing her away, and shrugged on the b.c. and the tank.

The water was a swamp of bodies. I had forgotten that drowned, bloated graveyard.

Behind me Taitano shot one of the floating bodies. It burst. A piece of flesh, like a tongue, hit my cheek.

I lurched into the water to my waist and sank among the bodies. Even when I got the mask on and cleared, I couldn't see in the black water. The bodies filled the water from sand to surface like giant molecules. Sobbing into the mouthpiece, nudging the thin rubber skin of the bodies, I crawled into the harbor.

Without a weight belt, I floated toward the surface. The bodies bumping me were a horror, like being buried alive with executed prisoners as they fell into a mass grave. I shuddered constantly, alive still and fastidious among the dead. But there was nothing to hold to, and I floated to the surface. I was not far from shore, but my vision was blurred by burning salt water in my eyes. I saw a blurred crowd of men on the beach.

"There!" one man said clearly, and I saw a long arm reach out.

I dove, feeling my rear break the surface, expecting the bullet, anticipating the numb moment and then the pain, shuddering and laughing as my hands touched the sand, but no one would laugh at the indignity of being shot in the butt, and then beginning to rise again. I floundered back down, feeling the bottom for rocks that I might stuff in my clothes. Abruptly I felt something sharp in the sand and remembered the sea urchins. If a diver touched them, their barbed spines broke off under the skin and caused excruciating pain. I floated up among the bodies. I could not stay down and drown, even if that was the lesson of horror.

I rose beneath a body, and suddenly beyond despair, I held on to its clothing. Slowly I kicked to propel us away from shore. I was weary. I was a ruined inanimate body. I was simply one of the dead. I reached under the shirt. The body was face down. I touched cool smooth skin and tiny tight nipples. I turned face up beneath him thinking, Oh my dear my cold dear hold me, sculling him out toward the sea, both of us satiated, taut from too much love of living, thinking sea burial.

Then he deflated and settled on me, and alive still, I pushed myself away. I thought that Taitano must have shot the body. I did not know what had happened to Cimarron. I was alive, and I swam hard out into the harbor.

The harbor deepened and I left the slough of bodies. If I tried to make it across the harbor in deep water, I'd run out of air. And I'd never have the strength to swim steadily enough to stay down. Risking sea urchins, I groped along the bottom until I found a pyramid of rocks that the shock waves must have arranged. With a small rock in each trouser pocket, I still began to float up, and so I added rocks to the pockets of the b.c. and fastened them with the Velcro strips and put a baseball-size chunk under my shirt, tucking it in my trousers and underwear.

A few feet below the surface, I kicked slowly. I couldn't read the pressure gauge in the dim water, and I had no way of knowing if I was headed across the harbor or in circles or back toward the shore, but the bottom dropped into invisibility and the surface chop grew rougher and I felt almost as if I were being towed in the right direction.

While the swimming was easy, I thought of Cimarron. I didn't think she'd tried to swim after me. If she'd stayed on the beach, Taitano had probably shot her. I pictured her firm black dog's body floating among the bloated gray humans. I pictured Taitano butchering her on the sand. Surely she'd run away when I'd disappeared. Surely she had. The rock under my shirt scraped my skin. On her own, Cimarron might be killed by a pack of boonie dogs or she might starve. I took out the rock and held it to my chest with both hands. Abraded bloody flesh might draw sharks. I hoped my head had stopped bleeding. Perhaps Cimmie would find more chickens. Perhaps she'd locate fresh water. My legs ached. If I'd died a year ago, Daniel and my parents and Judy and some men would have grieved. I felt my right calf cramp, more a tightening than a pain, and I hunched over to rub it. Now. Now nobody would find my abandoned body. We were all nobody now. I held my rock to my chest with both hands and resumed kicking my way through the livid water.

I couldn't get enough air. I sucked at the mouthpiece and kicked harder. Oh my dear, I thought to no one, oh my love, this is burial. There is no sweet blue air. Then I remembered that I'd been breathing from the tank on my back. There was no more air. I dropped my rock and kicked and broke the surface. A white-capped wave hit my face and I choked, trying to keep my head above water while I coughed the salt water from my windpipe.

Finally I recalled the rocks in my pockets and shed them. I was three-quarters of the way across the harbor, and I could not see the shore where the bodies eddied and where I'd escaped Taitano and left Cimarron. Holding my breath with every wave that hit my face, I unfastened the b.c., shrugged out of it, and pulled underwater by the weight, managed to detach the tank. I put the vest back on and blew into the little mouthpiece attached to it until it inflated enough to hold me high in the water.

I swam toward a narrow strip of beach below the cliff at the other side of the harbor. I swam. I swam dead until another wave hit my face and the pain of water in the lungs brought me to life.

Finally I crawled through the breakers and lay on the beach like any castaway. I lay on the sand in the inflated red vest like a jellyfish. Finally I did not die, and the tentacles calcified into bones, and I did not die but stood and stamped on the sand and made a dance of footprints along the narrow wet stretch of sand below the cliff.

7

"**I** think we ought to just have a civil ceremony," Daniel had said the night before my graduation. We'd heated two cans of chili for supper at his apartment. "A justice-of-the-peace operation all right with you?"

"Jesus, Daniel," I said.

"No, I don't picture him there," he said. "Just our folks."

"What can I say? This is so sudden. So romantic. I mean, it may be the candlelight dinner, the champagne, and the diamond ring—but I guess the answer is yes."

"Of course," he said. "Now let's get naked."

I hadn't cared about the graduation ceremony, but Dad said he figured they ought to get at least a few pictures of me in cap and gown out of the deal, and so he and Mom and Judy came up for graduation.

"Oh you're looking so *good*," Mom said. I hadn't been home since Christmas. "Filled out just enough." She beamed and reached for me, and I returned the hug stiffly. Suddenly she held me away. "You aren't pregnant, are you?"

"Jesus, Mother," I said.

"Okay, okay," she said. "I know you're my good girl."

After graduation beneath the June sun, Dad took his pictures—me and Mom; me, Mom, and Judy; me and Daniel.

"Hurry up, I'm about to die in this getup," I said. "Could you believe those speakers? I thought they'd never quit. And trite?"

"There's a service," Daniel said. "Anyone who speaks at a graduation is required to subscribe."

Mom and Dad looked blank.

"Sure," Judy said. "It's like a phrase book. New beginnings. The world's future. Passing the torch."

"You got it," Daniel said and punched Judy's shoulder. "The nation's hope. The university's pride. Fulfill your dreams."

"Don't be snooty," Mom said. "An education is a great achievement."

"A crowning glory," I said. "New horizons."

"The hope of the future," Judy said.

Daniel knew when to shut up.

At his apartment, Daniel had champagne iced down, plastic glasses in the freezer, crackers in a plastic bowl, and a cheese ball, rolled in nuts, that he'd made himself. I could have wept with embarrassment and pride, thinking of Daniel Manning working in his tiny kitchen at the cheese ball.

"Come look at this new shirt I got him for his birthday," I said to Mom. The blue shirt had embroidered eagles on it, and leading her to Daniel's closet, I thought she would appreciate the taste she'd taught me, and perhaps, too, I understood the intimacy I was suggesting.

When I opened the closet door, we both saw my pink underpants on the floor. I kicked them into the corner with Daniel's dirty clothes. We admired the blue shirt with the embroidered brown eagles. I was sick with the champagne and with the image of my pink underpants wadded on the closet floor. I was sure I had not remembered them, sure I had not wanted her to see them.

"An announcement," Daniel proclaimed, holding his plastic wine glass above his head. "Your daughter and I plan to be married." It wasn't in Daniel Manning to ask anybody.

"And not a moment too soon," my mother said.

Nobody said anything, my mother hiccupped, and nobody said anything.

Finally Dad said, "We are deeply in love with our daughter."

They were in love with me? I had not known that. What did that mean? My father loved me and Judy, as fathers were required—but in love? Did the "we" mean Mother shared the passion? Were they in love with Judy also? What passions and secrets did my father and Catherine Larson know? I could not stand the silence and the shimmer of emotion like heat.

"Does that mean all right?" Daniel said finally.

"New horizons," Judy said.

Two years later, Judy married Mitch in the big Congregational Church with me as matron of honor in a peach gown, Mitch's brother as best man, bridesmaids, flower girl and ring bearer, the works, rehearsal dinner, reception, dance band, flowers, photographer, Mom in her cream mother-of-the-bride outfit, presents of silver bowls and blenders, Mitch's brother dancing with me, too close, champagne toasts, depletion of Dad's savings, rice poured into Judy's suitcase full of bridal negligees, Daniel sitting outside on the steps, drunk uncles.

But Daniel and I made it a minor ceremony. Mom, sure I was pregnant, didn't urge anything grand. Relatives gave us some money, a set of towels with large black-and-green angelfish stenciled on, a toaster. We stayed in Daniel's room for the summer. For his research fellowship, he dug up material for a history department professor's book on acculturation of the English immigrant in New Haven. During the day, I went over to Jefferson High School and arranged the desks in my room and did up the bulletin boards and studied the *Adventures in Literature* text. I typed up little lectures on the authors. Late afternoon, I carried our dirty clothes to the laundromat on the other side of the block and grinned at the other new wives who also must have been loving the smell of the stained sheets they placed in the washer and the feel of his long-tailed shirts and his underwear clean and hot from the dryer. Every night I tried something from the new cookbook or the food section of the *Press* or the label of a mushroom soup can. At night we talked in the single bed, we whispered what we wanted, we sported us while the love sheened on us.

The clouds were irradiated, as if they contained dense nebulae. The bright foam of the breakers seemed lit from beneath the water. The afternoon was dusky, and I thought I could almost see the clouds and the breakers hurling and catching photons.

Anthony Joseph Taitano might have believed I was at the bottom of the harbor with graveyards of broken staghorn coral and mess trays and mangled cable. Or he and Rogelio might have driven around to the other side of the harbor and be pacing the cliff top until they spotted me on the beach below.

My jaw ached from gripping the mouthpiece for so long, and my mouth tasted like rubber and brine. I'd never been so thirsty. I thought of the iced cans of beer that Malcolm Yarrow always had waiting after a dive. Mostly I thought of faucets.

Staying close to the cliff, I started along the beach toward the sea. Taitano would probably expect me to head inland. When the water was sucked back, I thought I could see silver coins and bars in the shallows. Then the breakers smashed them. The beach narrowed further, perhaps because the waves were higher. I bent to a receding wave and drank. My mother used to make me gargle with warm salt water when I had a sore throat, and I'd gag on the trickles down my throat. The seawater tasted hot and my stomach burned. I retched. You weren't supposed to drink seawater. I knew that. I didn't know how long dehydration took to kill.

For some reason, it seemed, I wasn't going to be killed, and so I took the dive mask off my forehead and stripped off the trousers and underpants and, close to the rock cliff, squatted over the mask. At first I couldn't make myself pee, but at last I relaxed the muscles enough to half fill the mask. And still squatting, I held my nose and put my lips to the black rubber and drank. I gagged, sloshing urine onto the sand, and then finished it off.

At the end of the harbor, the surf blasted against the rocks strewn along the coast. There was no beach here. I climbed to a higher rock, where only spray hit me, and sat to watch the water sucked seaward where it paused to madden in the turbulence of deep-veined water and sand. As people used to watch fires, I watched hypnotically as the waves ran on the water and detonated against the rocks.

Abruptly I remembered the spoken word *typhoon.*

Taitano had said: *If we don't get you, the typhoon will.*

I wondered if the islanders' famed communion with weather still applied.

Staying high on the rocks, I climbed along the coast until a gap between boulders forced me down toward the waves, and then I saw the reason for the gap: it was the entrance to a cave.

I imagined I heard a single violin playing within the cave. The white limestone in the cave and the white breakers below bounced the available late afternoon light between them. I climbed from the flooded sea-level floor to the second story. The violin seemed to be playing the second movement of Beethoven's Violin Concerto. I couldn't tell how far into the cliff the cave went. A drip of cold water hit my cheek, and I jerked back into the rock wall. The cave was dark and I couldn't see the white sea. When another drop of cold water hit my head, I reached up and touched slick limestone udders. If I'd been tall enough I'd have licked the fat, polished stalactites. I couldn't hear the violin. I put my hands to the rocks' lubricity and sucked my fingers. Finally, I held the dive mask out until a single drop ticked onto the inside of the faceplate, and then I lowered the mask below the slow ticks until it sat on the floor. No stalagmites in the works here, I thought. I couldn't drink enough to calcify into a white stone statue. The cave muffled the surf, and I believed I could hear the violin again, though I knew there could be no violin there.

Every Stradivarius had a name, Daniel had told me.

You mean like Fred? I'd asked.

The left corner of his mouth pulled to the side as it did when Daniel couldn't bear me.

A year ago you'd have laughed, I'd said.

A chitinous arpeggio joined the imaginary Beethoven. My body recognized the crab scuttle with a painful rush of saliva, and I jerked my hand to it. Then the crab had the web between my thumb and forefinger, and I felt the pincers meet. I shook my hand but the crab held on, and finally I bent over and, with my hand on the floor, awkwardly stomped on the shell. I thought of the coagulated pudding of the smashed crab on the road in front of the dive shop. The web of my right hand beat like a severed artery. I was sick. I thought of a plate of crab legs and a little pot of melted butter with a thin blue flame beneath it. By feel I pulled the legs off the crab and pulled out strands of meat. Many people of the world used to eat raw fish, I thought. I cracked the shell of the legs and dug out the remains with my teeth. I imagined the violin's rosined bow jumping on the strings. In the dark I could not see what I was scooping up. I isolated bits of shell with my tongue and worked them out of my mouth.

What would Daniel have done? I wondered for the first time. Would he have scooped up smashed crab with his fingers? Would he have heard a Stradivarius at the back of the cave?

There must be violins safe in the world.

The people must be dead, though. Daniel must be dead. Fred Stradivarius may be intact, but the namers must be dead.

When Daniel finished his dissertation on Thomas J. Morgan and the Chicago socialist movement in the late 1800s, we drove the old green Impala to Florida. For two years I'd taught ninth-grade English at Jefferson High School. We didn't know what we'd do next, and we discussed possibilities off and on from Oklahoma to Georgia and down the coast to the Keys.

"I'll teach if I have to," Daniel said, "but I have no tolerance for the worm brains who take required history courses. Even less for department dickheads."

"Heil, Herr Dok-tor Manning," I said.

He pushed his hair back and gave me a look. He thought he was losing his hair and he had a habit of pushing it back with both hands, leaving his high forehead bare and his hair parted in the middle.

"Just kidding," I said.

He was impatient with my school anecdotes, exasperated at my involvement with the kids, unwillingly cajoled into helping me chaperone the Speech Club's dance and joining the faculty's spring picnic. Unasked, he offered irritable solutions for whatever class problem I mentioned.

"Look, I'm just telling you," I'd said once. "Maybe I just need you to listen. And maybe try to understand."

"You want answers, tell me," he'd said. "You want understanding, go tell your mother."

"Sometimes you're about as moody as she is," I'd said.

But we had taken to talking almost daily, my mother and I. She borrowed my unit on mythology. We discovered that the same activities could work with sixth graders and ninth graders. We had a common language. Once we were in a shopping center restroom, Mom in a booth and I at the mirror, discussing something other than school, and another woman said, "I bet you two are schoolteachers. There's just something about the voice, I guess." She laughed. "I'm a teacher, too."

Daniel and I erected our orange two-man tent, a K Mart special, and zipped together our green Montgomery Ward sleeping bags. At the Key Largo campground, the Winnebagos—loaded with bicycles, television, and gas grills and towing small cars—and the family tents with breezeways and lawn chairs all loomed over us, crouching by our single pot on the fire. We were jobless, spending most of our savings on the Florida trip, and we were certain that we were superior to the blue-hairs and the old farts in the trailers and to the families outfitted with collapsible canvas stools and kerosene lanterns and a guitar.

The campground had a mangrove swamp rather than a beach, but we swam in the pool. I had a glowing red bikini held together with plastic rings at the hips and between the breasts. One evening Daniel stopped his laps and I, at the other end of the pool, dove and swam underwater toward him. Eyes closed, I reached his feet and tickled their bottoms. I ran my hands up his calves and thighs, caressed his penis, and when it grew, put my mouth against his trunks. Out of air then, I surfaced. Daniel was three yards away. The man I'd caressed was hairless and red. He grinned sheepishly.

"Oh geez," I said, "that'll teach me to swim with my eyes closed. I thought you were my husband."

"No, you just stay blind," he said.

In the tent, I told Daniel about it, and we laughed. We turned off the flashlight and made love inside the single green sleeping bag, with the Winnebago laughter and the campfire guitars looming over us.

The next day we went on a boat past the mangroves to Pennekamp, the underwater park. On the way, I was seasick but faked attention to the guide's little lectures. Daniel never knew how close I was to vomiting over the edge and swimming back. At last we anchored and donned our dive gear, spit in our masks, and somersaulted off the boat. Twenty feet down, holding hands with Daniel, I'd never been healthier. We swam down to the Christ of the Abyss with his green arms supplicating the parrot fish, his green head back, facing the thin lead skin of the surface.

Then a little fish attached itself to my belly. Panicked, I knocked it away. I tried to gesture to Daniel, but in my dive class I'd learned only signals for *okay* and *out of air*, nothing for *little fish suctioned onto belly*. It came after me, and swatting at it, I swam to the boat as if a shark were after me and climbed aboard, leaving Daniel to finish the dive with strangers.

117

Later he scolded me for leaving my dive buddy, and then he laughed.

"That little sucker was a remora," he said. "And that makes you a shark."

"No, but it means maybe there *were* sharks around there," I said.

"A female shark," Daniel said, laughing.

We went to the cypress gardens, and Daniel took a picture of me with parrots perched on my outstretched arms. I was sunburned. My wild salty hair was tied into doggie-ears. I wore short shorts and a blue-striped top. In the photo, I am laughing, scared, at the birds on my arms.

Along the river bank were a few scattered alligators, sunned into immobility. Daniel and I held hands and walked among the tourists.

"No, no, Mommy," a little boy shrieked.

His mother had him by the hand. She laughed. "Don't be scared, Petey."

"No, no," he yelled. "I'm ascared of them."

"But they're not real," she explained patiently. She crouched down beside him. "The park people just put them there so we can see what they look like. Don't be scared, Petey. They're just plastic."

Daniel and I stood holding hands and watching the mother and the shrieking kid.

"Oh for God's sake," she said in exasperation, "you are over-reacting. Look: the goddamn alligators are *plastic.* I'll prove it to you."

She strode over to the nearest alligator and kicked it firmly in the side.

The alligator slid abruptly into the river. The mother jumped as if she wore jets. The little boy screamed and screamed.

Daniel and I laughed until we had to sit on the grass.

All the way home we stopped at caves and basket factories. We saw the world's largest prairie dog, the world's largest clam, and a bear in a six-foot cage. We didn't talk of jobs or Daniel's dissertation committee or Jefferson High School or my mother or money.

Almost home, Daniel stopped the green Impala on the shoulder and put on the hazard lights. "Come here," he said, and he kissed me. "God, I love you in that red bikini," he said. "God, I love you, Kit."

And I kept that glowing red bikini for all our years, even after it lost its elastic and was swept off if I dove into a pool.

In August Daniel accepted a position as staff writer for *PetroWorld*, a slick-paper, full-color monthly magazine put out by an oil company. Daniel would write on assignment but also initiate in-depth historical and social pieces. He'd travel, mostly to the Middle East. He would have editorial freedom, he would write investigative pieces, no matter that the sponsor was an oil company.

We moved to Chicago. Daniel collected a decent salary. We rented a brick house and acquired furniture and eventually Daniel brought home a dog. It was too late to find a teaching job but I thought I might substitute and try for something the next fall. We made some friends and went to some parties in chrome-and-glass and white-walled apartments or in lofts with Chinese screens to make rooms and with mattresses on the floor. I was embarrassed at our wood furniture and hide-a-bed couch.

In December, Daniel went to Libya.

Substituting for a civics teacher at Westside Junior High, I met another sub after school, also turning in a key and lesson-plan book. He was a solid man in a blue crewneck sweater, and we walked to the parking lot together. It was Friday, and the slush was littered with crayoned Christmas tree pictures that must have blown from the adjacent elementary school.

"This is wild," he said, "but let me ask you something. I have this problem."

"Here," I said, "this is my car."

"I'm Smitty," he said. "Oh, it's Ron Smith, but what am I gonna be but Smitty? Could we sit in your car for a minute? You must be freezing."

And I was shivering.

"Anyway, I have this new job, P.E. at Lincoln, starting in January, but see, they're having their Christmas party tonight and I'm supposed to come and meet everyone and bring a date which I don't have and so I know you don't even know me yet, but we probably yelled at some of the same kids today, and I'm wondering if you'd go to that party with me."

"I'm an English teacher," I said. "Let me tell you about run-on sentences."

"Oh," Smitty said. "Well, jocks . . . Anyway, I saw your name's Catherine Manning."

"Kit," I said. "And I'm married."

"Fuck," he said, closing his eyes. "Oh, I'm sorry. Pardon my French. It's just I'm going to look like such a jerk. I just wanted to show off some pretty lady like you."

So I told him Daniel was in Libya and I didn't play around and where to pick me up for this one night only.

Smitty was embarrassingly grateful when I answered the door in my yellow sweater dress. I didn't know if he noticed that I'd taken off my ring. He drove slowly: the afternoon's slush had frozen.

"I'm a little nervous about all this," he said. "I must admit."

I didn't know if he meant the icy streets, the party, the new job, or me.

"It'll be all right," I said. "Just take it easy." That covered everything. And I would just take it easy, too.

The party was in the back room of a barbecue restaurant, with piped-in Christmas music and a pile of name-exchange presents on the back table.

"This is my friend, Kit," Smitty said. "This is Mr. Richards. He's the fool that hired me. Oh, that didn't come out right."

I took Smitty's arm. I laughed up at him. I did what I could for him.

After ribs and beer, Mr. Richards put on a beard and red hat and handed out the presents. "You can tell who drew their friends' names," I whispered to Smitty. They opened a perfume atomizer, a daily calendar book, a little olive book of poems, a pair of red-and-green shorts with JINGLE MY BALLS across the front.

"Some of these guys are going on to this bar in Old Town," Smitty said. "But you might not want to drag this out, I guess."

"I guess the night is young," I said.

At Trudy's Tarbox, Smitty bought a round of drinks and we danced to jukebox music chosen by other customers, trading partners with a math teacher and his wife, a reading teacher and her husband, and a basketball coach and his girlfriend. The coach bought the next round.

"God, this is fun," I nearly shouted to Smitty above the Four Seasons singing "Big Girls Don't Cry." "I haven't danced in about three years, unless you count twisting in the kitchen by myself. Daniel doesn't dance."

Two of the couples left and we had another drink with coach and girlfriend and danced a slow one. Smitty held me circum-spectly but whispered, "I really want to hold you. But I'm not too far gone to forget the rules." I thought I could feel his palms throbbing through my sweater dress.

Outside a light snow was coming down and the air was almost warm. On the way to the cars, we passed a bar with a live band.

"One more round?" Smitty said.

"Not us, bud," the coach said. "We got to get home and to bed. Though not necessarily in that order."

Smitty and I ambulated from bar to bar, testing the house wines. I'd see Smitty's blue oxford-cloth shirt swaying to the music and then I'd fix on his face floating above the shirt. We'd sit across from each other in booths and test the wine, and Smitty'd confess another segment of his college love—meet-the-siblings (her parents dead), abortion, engagement, arguments.

"Not necessarily in that order," Smitty said.

At the final bar we sat on the same side of the table. When we danced, Smitty backed up to the bar to stay upright. We may have been the only customers left. Smitty sat on the bar and pulled me between his legs, and this was how we danced. The waitress watched a tiny TV behind the bar.

I found a bathroom with a complicated lock. Finally I sat and tried to hold the door closed while I peed. As I pulled my dress down, Smitty pushed open the door.

"Please," he said. "Please. Just let me look. Just for a minute. I won't touch."

"No," I said and closed the door.

When I returned to our booth, Smitty was there with two full glasses of wine before him, his head leaning back, his eyes closed.

I slid in next to him. "Don't you worry about it," I said.

He said nothing. I saw a trickle of saliva at the corner of his mouth.

"Hey," I said. "Smitty—hey, anybody home?"

He didn't move, and abruptly I was afraid to touch him. I'm sitting in a booth with a dead man, I thought.

The bar was dark and the waitress watched the tiny television.

Finally I nudged him, ready to jump if he toppled. He gurgled. I shook his warm blue shoulder. He gave a long indrawn snore.

I looked at the dollar bills he'd left on the table. I slid the strap of my purse onto my shoulder. Holding the table, I stood and held on until the dizziness passed. I picked up my coat from the other side of the booth and walked out the door of the bar into the Chicago snow. I worked my way down two barren blocks, from windowsill to windowsill, carrying my long coat. Daniel had given me the coat. It had fake fur lining. I was hot. I crossed the street, holding a post until the light changed, though there was no traffic. WALK, the letters spelled. I thought of Smitty in the booth, drooling onto the button-down collar of his blue shirt. I hurried down the next block, staggering as my heels slipped on the snow-beaten sidewalk.

At the end of the next block a taxi waited for such as I, and the driver took me silently home through the dead city.

When Daniel returned a day later, I still had my flu. I knew that I would never drink wine again. Daniel brought me ginger ale and soda crackers when I asked. I held him and cried onto his shoulder though he did not know it.

"Hey, don't give me that nasty bug," he said. But he held me.

I read the newspapers thoroughly for the next few days, but nowhere did the *Trib* note a fresh Old Town murder, and no teacher named Smith made it to the hospitalization list or the obits. Once I thought I saw Smitty's gray car drive by, but there was a multitude of new silvery cars in Chicago. After Christmas, I called Lincoln Junior High and was told he was in class. Would I want to leave a message?

The message was, Thank you Smitty for somehow making it from a booth in an abandoned Old Town bar to Lincoln Junior High School. The message was, Thank you for allowing me to discover my own fidelity.

Daniel's moods were worse than my mother's because they lasted for two days instead of two hours. There was no placating Daniel. He'd have taken no notes: *I am sorry, I'll be a good girl from now on.* My mother's moods always meant that she was feeling neglected, and the words, accompanied by tears, would resurrect her. She demanded the words. I never learned that Daniel wanted silence, nothing but furred winter blackness surrounding him.

"What's wrong?" I'd say.

Daniel would wince, as if words were penlights shined sharp into his eyes.

"Nothing's wrong," he'd say.

"Then why are you shutting me out? I know you, Daniel. Something's wrong. I feel so lost when you go away like this."

123

I was an alien, walking among the people in a rubber human-suit. With Daniel I was alive, I used to think, the way a human master's dog would grin, would know the cupboard where the Milk-Bones were kept, would talk in nearly human voice and be answered in English. When Daniel disappeared, I grew feral.

Two days later, he'd emerge and talk. "They're fucking with me," he said. "They promised all kinds of freedom to pursue anything, write whatever I found, go after the shit. Every time I find out about some secret cartel or some lobbyist slipping it to some senator or some sleazy raghead oilman with fifty-seven wives, it's a slap. 'No, no, you misunderstood. We just want the scenic wonders of another hump of sand, forget the thuggees on the other side of the hump. Just shoot some shy young eyes looking out of purdah and forget the pregnant belly. Forget the Butcher of Baghdad, who dropped chemical bombs on the Kurds.' It's *National Geographic* time, kiddies. God, I hate this pimp work."

I'd suggest looking for something else, but Daniel didn't want help.

"And it's going to get even nastier over there," he said. "I don't want to be around when they get their hands on real weapons."

I didn't ask who *they* were or what might get nasty. It was all far away from Daniel and me.

"Look, I know you don't want to teach," I said, "though it's not that unpleasant a job. But what about another magazine?"

"I'm not a political fucking scientist," he said. "Besides, it's all pimp work."

I stayed a true wife, and we'd walk along the winter lakeshore, holding bare hands so we could tickle each other's palms suggestively. Chunks of raw gray ice rode the swells until they were caught in a breaker and pounded to the shore.

I never saw Smitty again, and I stayed a true wife. Much of the time Daniel was of sound mind, of sane heart. I should have learned to leave him alone when he turned murky. "What's wrong?" I'd say. "This is the one who loves you. Remember? Talk to me."

I complained to my mother once, and she was pleased at the confidence, though it couldn't make up for my failure to consult about the marriage in the first place, my failure to discuss, wonder, plan, plot, dissect, fear. She and I would have wrapped the wedding and Daniel in yards of web, then unwrapped the undeveloped chrysalis and poked at it, then rewrapped the body. When I did complain about Daniel and his moods, she said, "Sounds kind of like a maniac-depressive to me." I'd always known when to keep silent with my mother. Besides, we all took what we didn't know and fixed it to fit our tongues and jaws. Maybe there were maniacs among us anyway.

My mother dieted most of her life, until finally she lost her appetite and lost all the extra weight. Her mother had tried to slim down the ten-year-old Sister, the sixteen-year-old Sister. She'd served spinach and fish. "When you're hungry between meals," she'd said, "chew ice." Finally she did chew ice, a sign we didn't read: Anemia. I remembered the women's magazines' promises: "5 Pounds Off in a Week," "Thinner Thighs in 30 days," "The No-Pain No-Gain Diet," "Eat Chocolate and Lose Weight!" She kept charts. She bought a tiny scale for weighing food. She ate yogurt. She drank Sego. She despaired. Once one of my high-school friends said, "How come you didn't tell me your mom was pregnant?" "It's just the way she was standing," I said, but I wondered for two weeks until the moodiness clocked in. For years she lost pounds and then drew them back. She knew how to dress—the right lines, navy blue, the overhanging jackets—and for a while I thought my dad must love her solidity. Then I would vow never to grow the flabby upper arms, the dimpled thighs. I would tell her, "You look fine. Quit worrying about it. Why kill yourself to be a size fourteen? Don't let your mother rule the whole rest of your life. You know how to dress. You know how to hide it."

Once she tried to get Judy and me to participate: We were to stop her whenever she wanted to eat anything between meals. I declined but Judy tried. She followed Mom around in the evening and caught her with a box of crackers. "I don't care what I said," Mom said. She was weeping. "I don't need your spying and your snide remarks if I want a few crackers while I read." She carried the box of Cheez-its to her room. I never told my mother that my friend thought she was pregnant. Judy and I were never fat.

And though she promised, before we were born, to love us no matter how fat we grew, she loved us anyway, no matter how slim.

After two days of any diet, Mom felt righteous. Whatever she ate then didn't really count. She'd made herself a promise and stuck to it. She deserved a reward for that if nothing else. Having abstained for forty-eight hours, she could eat a quart of chocolate-mint ice cream and go on with life.

And so, after Smitty, after getting myself home intact, the others didn't count. I was Daniel's, whether he was in Chicago or Saudi Arabia, whether he was loving me or sinking in a mood. I was always Daniel's.

Months after Smitty, having proven my virtue, I allowed George Waxman to suggest a Friday night pizza. George was the assistant principal of Mark Twain High School, where I was subbing for two weeks after an English teacher had a miscarriage. He was an older man, maybe forty-five, and he looked foolish with strings of mozzarella cheese stretched from his hand to his mouth, and he did not count. He touched my elbow when we walked outside. His face was middle-age handsome and kind.

"You look too nice to be an assistant principal," I said.

"I am nice," he said. "Would you come over for a glass of wine?" he said.

And because I'd resisted Smitty, I knew nothing mattered, and I followed his green Vega to his apartment and parked at number forty-four, his relinquished spot, and drank two glasses, only two glasses of white zinfandel, and nothing counted. He touched my elbow and I turned to him, and he put his nice face to mine.

"Oh dear Kitty," he said. "Oh dear Kit. Oh dear."

He took me by the arm, as if he were escorting me into his office for an interview. In the bedroom we undressed separately in the dark and then lay together on top of the rib-cord bedspread.

"Oh Kit," he said. "Oh dear Kit." The nice man arched his neck and howled and then settled back down on top of me.

"That's the trouble with men. That was too fast for you," he said. "But I've been waiting for someone like you. I'm sorry."

"It's all right," I said. "It's all right. You're a nice man."

When Daniel was away, I visited George Waxman. I always wanted to know if he'd howl again. He was always sorry, but it wasn't his fault. The satisfaction didn't really matter. I wanted him in an abstract way. None of it counted.

Soon George Waxman believed that he loved me. "I know the ground rules," he said. "You made it clear from the start that you're married. I can't help it if I want more, can I?"

He instructed the school secretary to try me first when any of Mark Twain's teachers called in sick. At noon we'd drive to a city park and eat the lunch he'd packed: tuna salad sandwiches and a can of cling peaches or fruit cocktail. We'd discuss school and then his love for me, looking at the snow loafed on the picnic tables until the Vega's windows steamed.

Soon I could hardly bear George Waxman. I couldn't stand the way he smacked his lips when he ate. I wanted to hear the details of his passion for me but I couldn't stand them either. I hated the crumbs on his trousers and the tuna on his breath.

He called our house late one evening, ostensibly to check on a missing attendance report.

After the call, Daniel said, "Bit late for school business, isn't it?"

"That's what I thought," I said. My voice smothered guilt with wryness, I hoped.

127

George Waxman pulled into the driveway one morning before Daniel had left for *PetroWorld*'s office.

"Christ, George," I said at the door. Daniel was still shaving.

"We need you at school," he said formally.

"What's this 'we'?" I said. "You got a frog in your pocket?" It was one of Daniel's expressions.

Daniel said, "What's going on?" I loved the lean man in the blue towel wrap. I loved his clean lathered face.

"I guess you know they're desperate at a school," I said, "when they send the assistant principal."

"We tried your phone," George Waxman said. "Wasn't working. You'd better call the phone company."

"Well, give me forty-five minutes," I said. "I'll be there by second hour."

And I did go to school, though of course no teachers were out and no sub was needed. I could have done it by phone. But I dressed in the burnt orange skirt and vest that George liked. At school, I waited like a tardy student in the main office while the assistant principal finished designating punishment for a boy who'd stolen a soldering iron from shop.

"Come in, Mrs. Manning," he said. He closed the door.

"This is it, George," I said. I touched his hand on the desk. "I'm sorry. But it's going to screw up my marriage." I didn't have to touch him, but I did.

He swiveled in his executive chair to face the wall. He put his hands over his face.

"I'm sorry," I said. "You knew all along. But I'm sorry." I wondered if he was crying. "You're a nice man. You know I care about you."

Twitching in irritation at the man, I could hardly wait to leave his mouth noises, the way he'd try to kiss me with fruit cocktail still in his mouth, his fishy breath, his pleas for my time. I went to him and touched his shoulders. "I do care about you, you know," I said.

128

He looked up then. "Please stay, my dear Kitty," he said. I could not tell, through his fingers, if he was crying.

I turned one more time to look at him before I left his office. He was watching me in my burnt orange skirt and vest outfit. I closed the door after myself. George Waxman never called again. I turned down all subbing jobs at Mark Twain High School. I never saw the nice man who howled, who loved me, ever again.

Always my mother needed recognition. She needed praise. She needed someone to sight her through a lens and sharpen the focus on her blurred body. And she needed us—to hear the anecdotes, to read the parents' notes about their children's new love for school, to view the defined body.

Her third toe hooked under the second, and so did mine. She'd noticed that when I was a day old and still Catherine, not yet Kitty. She had a single whisker on her right cheek, and when I was sixteen, I grew one too, just above the jawline. I shaved it with the miniature gold razor she gave me. Later Daniel noticed when I forgot to shave it, and he told me once that it bugged him, a stupid petty thing like a quarter-inch whisker.

Always I needed men. Daniel was a man, my own true love, and our loving was ravening, was comforting. We were wedded. My need was not lust. I needed a man, another man, to see the slim body I knew how to dress and to move, to pursue it until I granted the touch, to proclaim love and to turn away with his hands over his contorted face when I ended it, to watch me move to the exit, to remember sweet little Kitty beneath his hands. I needed men to fix me in their sights and hold the cross hairs steady and never shoot the plastic rifle and never know the game.

After George Waxman I lured dozens and allowed a half dozen to take the scent.

I'd catch some man's look at a party, at one of my schools, in some little restaurant where I was having lunch alone, book in hand. And I'd know that I could change his life, hold him in my thrall. It was the power—and I could not help but exercise it—to be part of someone's life from then on, if only in memory or thwarted desire or masturbatory fantasy. *Kitty was here* in this scenic spot, in this public world.

Ascending from a two-day mood, which I told myself justified the current affair, Daniel was gentle as a Thorazined inmate. We would talk about leaving Chicago and *PetroWorld*. We would make sweet love. One *commits* adultery, I thought, but *makes* love. Daniel would talk about the Chicago socialists in the late 1800s, his grad-school focus, which wasn't his true subject. Every historian has his personal and his public passionate subject, Daniel believed, and they should be the same. He wrote stories about oil refineries in the Middle East, but it was a job and he didn't really care about their politics now or even about the history. I got out my old Revised Standard Bible with the maps in the back, but the route of the exodus from Egypt, the lands of Canaan, and the location of Babylon were abstract to both of us. Daniel probably never knew what his true subject was, and I thought his black descents were a catatonic search for something to dwell on, to dwell his life in.

Finally I said, "Daniel, my love, let's have ourselves a baby."

"Hey, I changed your sister's kid's didie once," he said, "and once was plenty."

"Notice how those kids always climb all over you."

"Notice how I try to shake them off," he said.

I stopped taking the daily pills. I shed all men. I was Daniel's and the baby would certainly be Daniel's. Pregnancy and a baby would be enough intensity.

Daniel despised company parties, but I'd thought we ought to go. "I don't want you to stay on with that bunch of greedy Texas cowards," I told him. "I really don't. I just think you ought to play their game until you find something better." I was scared he'd quit before he found another job. I knew I was a coward, too. I was scared he'd stay with *PetroWorld* until he could never extricate himself.

At the party, we dipped our glasses into the champagne fountain and ate a supper's worth from the hors d'oeuvres buffet. We took turns going for refills of stuffed mushrooms, caviar and crackers, steak tartare, and cold shrimp. We giggled in the corner. Occasionally a Texan would come over to shake hands with the real historian. We all dipped into the champagne fountain.

"You're historical," I told Daniel, "and I'm hysterical."

A large man clamped his hand onto Daniel's shoulder. "Frederick Jenkins," he said. "Field services. They all call me Shorty."

I could see the stenciled roadside signs: VOTE FOR FRED "SHORTY" JENKINS, HE KNOWS WHAT YOU'RE THINKIN'.

"Field services," I said. "Does that make you a scarecrow?"

We all dipped our glasses into the fountain.

"No ma'am," Frederick Jenkins said. "That means I try to stay as far away from rigs as possible. But there's other fields."

We grinned at each other: we both knew the game.

"You got yourself a pretty little lady, Danny," Jenkins told Daniel. He held up his glass. "Here's to the pretty little ladies."

Jenkins and I touched glasses, but Daniel held his glass low.

"Yeah well, you ought to see this pretty little lady trying to get herself knocked up," Daniel said.

"Hey now," I said.

"She's always taking her temperature," Daniel confided. "I'm afraid if I slip her some tongue I'll get mercury burn. She's got enough charts to keep accounting busy for a month."

"I guess there's nothing wrong with wanting to have my husband's baby," I told Frederick Jenkins.

"You know why they call me Shorty?" he asked us both. "Because of this tattoo I've got on my dick. Says *Shorty*."

Daniel laughed.

"Oh yeah?" I said.

"Yeah," he said. "Until I get me a boner. Then it says *Shorty's Bar and Grill, Albuquerque, New Mexico, September, 1956.*"

I knew I must not laugh. I put my hand over my mouth and coughed.

"You should see her," Daniel said. "After I fill her full, she sticks her ass in the air and does the bicycle. Doesn't want to lose a precious drop."

I'd only done that once. I hadn't known he'd seen me, though.

"Maybe because there isn't a drop to spare," I said. I turned to Frederick Jenkins. "*His* tattoo says *Dan's*. And when he's got a hard-on it says *Dan's Pub*."

"You can't have third parties in a marriage," Jenkins said. "I guess I sort of encouraged this, and I'm sorry. She really is a pretty little lady. I hope you folks quit keeping score."

In the morning, we drank tomato juice and nursed our hangovers. We took aspirin and tried to laugh.

"God, that was awful," I said. "I don't remember a thing."

"Dan's Pub," he said. "I remember that." He tried to laugh.

"My ass in the air," I said. "I guess I remember that."

We slept again and finally sat up at noon.

"Oh God," I said.

"There's this Irishman at the office, a photographer," Daniel said. "He says there's only one sure cure for a hangover: eat a big breakfast, take a big shit, and then fuck."

"You're getting crude," I said, "hanging around those Irish photographers."

"Go fry the eggs, woman," he said.

"Let's just skip the first two."

"You think old shorty's up to it?" he said.

Every month, for years, it seemed, I'd feel a little sick in the morning, I'd feel a fullness that was only the blood ready to drop. In bed I'd surreptitiously stick my hands under my buttocks to elevate them slightly. At least six times I was sure I'd felt the sperm enter the egg. But we never had any babies.

On the island, I used to find gecko eggs on the windowsill in my apartment. I'd put the eggs in a jar on the kitchen table, trying to witness a hatching, but with every egg, one day I'd come home from school and find nothing but a tiny white shell with its doors unhinged. I'd see pregnant geckos on my kitchen window, a pair of eggs visible through the breathing skin, one on each side of the spine. And when the eggs were expelled, I'd wait weeks and then one day after school I'd find only the white shell and the newborn fled, having climbed the four-inch glass wall.

Later the men turned impotent on me. They had their minds on meetings in New York or on ex-wives or on college sons' dope debts. It wasn't me: I was the sexiest woman they'd known. Yes? I'd say. Tell me. The words helped. And I could not bear to hear wives' or analysts' reviews.

They weren't all impotent, and none was impotent all the time. But I began to despise each one more quickly. They had smoker's breath or affected accents after six months, years ago, in London or drug problems or brilliant daughters or sandals in December or clam sauce on their beards or potbellies or newly discovered roots, now that the folks were dead.

Warren was the last.

"So has what's-his-face left for Outer Mongolia yet?" Warren asked me after school.

"Daniel is his face," I said. "He's in Kuwait. Somewhere in Kuwait. Even as we speak."

Kathy Williams, who taught French, looked into my room. "Listen to this translation," she said. "'I have bought my dog a toy. I have bought my dog a food. I have bought my dog a cathouse.'"

"My little guys'd probably like that," Warren said, "horny little devils." He had a pair of Chihuahuas.

After Kathy had retreated, he said, "So, tomorrow night? We'll do dinner . . . and whatever."

"Let's just eat it, if you don't mind," I said.

"Oh will we ever," Warren said. "Sixish."

"How about just plain six?"

Friday after school I loaded my briefcase, the leather one that my parents had given me for Christmas, with the papers to be graded for Monday. By six I was at the door to Warren's apartment, starving.

He answered the door in a black velour bathrobe.

"I'm early, I see. Well, hurry up. I'm starving," I said.

"Come keep me company," he said and took my hand to pull me into the darkened bedroom. He leaned a half dozen pillows against the headboard. "Sit," he said. "I just want to finish watching this movie first. Okay?" He poured wine.

"I think you're a bit ahead of me on this," I said. Warren smelled sticky. He slid bonelessly to the bed and pointed the TV's remote control. So in my black slacks and white ruffled blouse I leaned against the pillows beside him.

"What movie is this?" I asked. I drank my wine.

"*Penny Poppers*, it's called."

On the eight-inch screen, a woman was on her hands and knees. "That's our Penny," Warren said. "Good old Penny." Three men were at her various orifices, silent because Warren had the volume off. They all lurched and twitched like amoebae under a microscope.

"You ever watch this stuff?" Warren asked. He began working on the tiny white buttons on my blouse.

"What all have you had to drink?" I said.

He bit at a button and tried to take it off with his teeth. "Just some gin," he said. "Tee many martoonies. Just some of this wine."

He rewound Penny and the three men and watched them bulge and flow against each other again. I took another drink. I could see the cilia waving on the shapes of their bodies.

Daniel and I had never used paraphernalia, never rented the videos. About once a year, Daniel would buy a *Playboy*, and we'd tease about it. Daniel and I just touched bodies.

Warren filled my glass again, and I drank. "I need to catch up with you," I said. I didn't want to sit up primly in my ruffled blouse. All this, maybe, was the last I had to try. I stood and kicked off my black shoes and wriggled out of my pants like my mother getting out of her girdle and began working on the buttons.

"Don't be so shy," Warren said as I pulled up the sheet. It was black satin. "Here: drink." He'd taken off his robe, and his skin was very white against the sheets. He looked slightly puffy. I drank and he refilled the wine glass. He rewound the tape and watched Penny take on a very hairy man and a blond woman. "Touch me," he said, and I held him until he put his hand over mine and moved it. I reached over for my glass. I drank and followed Penny, a few seconds behind.

Sometime later he brought out the raspberry love oil. "What're you supposed to do with this?" I whispered.

"You rub it on and you lick it off," he whispered. "How do you like Clyde?"

"Clyde?" I hardly knew what we were doing.

He extracted something from me. "Clyde for the clit," he said. It was a wet plastic finger, a little spined penis.

"I *hate* that," I said. "Get that away from me."

I was drunk, and my lips were sticky with raspberry love oil. Something hummed.

"Lay back," Warren said. "Just relax. You'll like this gizmo."

I floated, fuzzled, in the vibrations. The television screen snowed: poor Penny in the Chicago snow. I thought I heard the flapping of film at the end of a big reel, and in a moment I'd have to direct a student to get the light and I'd feed the end of the film onto the sprockets and rewind while the kids jabbered and pushed at each other. "Take it easy, troops," I said.

When I opened my eyes, Warren was holding the vibrator on

me with one hand and pulling at himself with the other. The two Chihuahuas were on the bed trying to lick the raspberry love oil.

"Get them *off*," I said. "There are *limits* to all this."

He pushed at the dogs but they held to the bed. We were weightless in zero gravity and the stupid dogs had Velcro on their feet.

"I *hate* them," I said.

Warren disappeared with his tiny obscene dogs. Later I woke and hung over the toilet bowl for a while, but I couldn't get rid of any of it. Warren lay face up on the black-satin sheets with one hand holding his limp penis. Sicker even than the time Daniel and I'd eaten tainted pork at Poor Alfie's Bar-B-Q, I dressed and drove myself home.

I thought the tires were slipping, losing traction on something: clean new snow that no one had driven over before, or petals shaken on the road, or smooth summertime rain. This was the end of what someone had begun. Not sweet Smitty, who'd had nothing for it all and hadn't even landed in his own bed. Certainly not Daniel: none of this had anything to do with Daniel. Not Peter Murphy or any of the high-school boys. But someone. I remembered summer trips to Michigan and my mother singing "Summertime" in the dark. The road was clean and dry, pure and dry, but I felt the tires slide. I wanted only to have my father driving, with my feet on his lap and my head on my mother's lap. Her mother had said: No, I wasn't coming to meet you. I was just walking the dog. Now go pick up that suitcase, Sister. But my mother had said: You are blond and slim, and you have everything going for you. Yet I lived with her need. I could smell her sachet. I could feel the silk of her mother's glove under her pillow. In my sickness, I knew this was the end of need. My father's love and Judy's and my love couldn't teach our mother that the deficiency dwelled in a pocket, a bladder dense with blood and vessels and consciousness, and that it needed only a need—and itself—to live on in the host. And I am needless now, I thought. I am sorry,

Mama, I am sorry sorry. I made it home on the thick-scented road, wet with two A.M. air. So hush, I heard her sing, hush.

In the morning, I was purely sick and grateful. Now there would be no more sick mornings. I remembered faking tears when Sally the deaf girl wasn't playing fair. Her aunt said we had to. No one used any real sign language. I would put my hands to my face and hunch my shoulders, hot and sick at faking it. I would feel my face scrunch up, guilty, close to real tears. Sally would pat my shoulder and play the game right. There would be no more men, no more of the game, the come-on, the palpating of hearts, the handling of bodies, the sham regrets.

I didn't believe I'd been unfaithful to Daniel, though I couldn't have explained it to him, and though the appearance was the same. Only a couple of the men had understood that, and I'd shucked them along with the rest. I was unfaithful only to myself.

Now I would devote myself to teaching: and I believed I was a good teacher. Now perhaps Daniel and I could adopt a baby. Daniel and I might learn to sign our proper language. Though I could not cure my mother, I might resurrect myself.

Warren rattled the door at noon. He wore clean tight jeans and a blue shirt. His puffy face was yellow and his breath was sour, but Warren always looked sharp. The girls in his math classes loved him and plane geometry.

"You look like you've been dragged through a knothole backwards," he said.

"You have such a way with words," I said. I would dismiss him when we were well.

"I need tomato juice and beer," he said. "You got any tomato juice and beer?"

"I thought you might have expired after I left." I sat down on the living room floor. "I know I did."

"I really am sorry," he said. "I came over to tell you. I got you drunk, never gave you any dinner, and brought out all my toys. I really am sorry." He sat on the floor beside me.

"I asked for it all," I said.

"There's more," Warren said. "I didn't tell you, but there's no way you could have caught up with me. I'd done some coke before you came over. I'm not proud of that. But I'm telling you now. I wanted to be up for you. I wanted staying power. So I did a little coke. And you maybe don't know it but you don't do just a little coke."

We lay on the two-toned orange shag carpet, sick and honest, and slept. When I awoke, still sick in the angled light, Daniel was standing over us.

"Oh God," I said. I moved Warren's hand off my hip. "This isn't what you think," I said. "This isn't real."

"Shall we kick it and see?" Daniel said.

I scrambled away, so he wouldn't kick me, or maybe to offer Daniel a target, and he drew his foot back and kicked Warren's groin, and then he left.

The cave was absolutely dark. Waves detonated higher and higher on the cliff below. There were no moonlit breakers, no phosphorescent creatures; there was only black water giving tongue. The pants and T-shirt I wore had dried stiffly on me but now were wet with spray. I pulled for breath as if I were still underwater. My head throbbed. My forearms and knuckles felt raw and swollen from coral scrapes. My body ached from the rape with the gun. I was exhausted enough to die.

I crawled slowly toward the dive mask catching the drips from a stalactite. Surely the ocean hadn't risen enough to take it, but I couldn't find it in the blackness. The cave, the ocean, the world were not merely lightless, not simply achromatic. *I dwelleth in the black of night*, I thought, knowing such words were foolish. *Lead me to the pure water rising in the dive mask, lead me high into the earth's cave and sleep, leadeth me into some dawn.*

My skin must have been red as steamed flesh, but there would never be colors in the world again. I pulled at the loose skin as if I could flay myself.

Through the water beating on the rocks I could hear seals: baneful, terrestrial. These were no sweet seals but misshapen, flayed creatures slouching toward me. I could not see them in the absolute black, but they came on.

I put my hands to the rock, but in the blackness it had grown smooth and slick. There would be no more dawns. There would be no earth but the slick and clumsy shadows on unlit walls. In the black surf the seals howled.

Surely there was another earth, a lighted ground where Kitty had lived, a coexistent place where Kitty had not moved aside so Warren could take Daniel's kick to the groin, or where Kitty had not fallen simply asleep next to Warren on the shag carpet, or where Kitty had never allowed Warren and his toys to touch her, or where Kitty had grown intact in her mother's light.

The world was gone, gone, and the monstrous seals barked in the dark. Some god who had watched the sparrows fall had killed off everything so he could watch one sparrow flutter against wet cave walls, against her depravity, and fall, and know the complete depravity and the slick blackness. The unlit shadow gesticulated and understood the egotism: that any god might kill the world so that she would come to know that she'd deflowered herself, that mothers were mothers' daughters, that the sins were omissions against mother and Daniel, were commissions against the mirrored self, that all iniquity inhabited islands, that guilt was ingested with the papaya and the star apple, was rightly swallowed with the thin coconut milk.

Daniel knew me. He'd learned. I'd worn a red bikini to the ocean with Daniel, and for years no one knew that I couldn't really wear a bikini: I'd kept the fat so well hidden. But Daniel had found me on the floor, and he'd learned. He had never asked about anyone who had touched me before we'd first made love in the yellow light of his room, and we'd continued to lie down together as if we were folding wings around each other. Now Daniel must be dead with the world. I thought of Anthony Joseph Taitano sodomizing fat Rogelio Torres. Why was it the sybarites survived?

I remembered a joke: Southern sheriff, on finding the bullet-ridden body of a black man, says: "Worst case of suicide I've ever seen."

Once the world had seen Hiroshima, it had to see Nagasaki. The child had touched himself. The fear pulled us back then, but no one forgot the forbidden intensity. There were years of adolescent titillation—basement bomb shelters stocked with flashlights, Campbell's soups, and Scrabble; elementary school drills with instructions to hide beneath the desks; the radio's voluntary cooperation: *This is a test, only a test, if this had been an actual emergency, you.* . . . College students listened to lectures on the detonation of less than half the world's nuclear warheads—750 million dead immediately, 340 million dying, heat and fire, mutual preemptive strikes, nuclear winter—and they grew rapt at the power. The foreplay intensified, and the written and the spoken and the shouted words grew rapturous, and the vision of the white explosion grew, all building to the fever: *Do it, do it*, until the only end was release.

Old joke: kid, being told that masturbation caused blindness, decided he'd do it only until he needed glasses.

And now we were blind. Worst case of suicide the world had failed to see.

With another of his own kind, Daniel would have engendered babies. But I had contracted my mother's deficiency—which was self-consciousness, which was the knowledge that beneath the pink rubber skin was indelible taint.

Once I'd been a child in a dark bedroom and I'd kick off my covers and call, "Mama Daddy, Mama Daddy, cover me up." And always my mother would replace Judy's stuffed rabbit, Apricot, and then pull up my blankets and pat my back, but not kiss me because she knew I would pull back. She wore a satin nightcap to hold her hairdo, and she smelled of Vicks. She should have said: "You're a big girl now, you can pull up your own covers." She died before the rest did.

I crawled as deeply into the cave as I could, scraping my arms against coral rocks I could not see. Outside the skinless, muscled seals barked. Even now I wanted to hear her singing in the dark. *Cover me up.*

8

The sky was the yellow-brown of fading bruises, and the swollen sea turned its foam downward before it could break. I felt as still as the airless morning.

In the bruised light I found that the dive mask, beneath the stalactite still, had collected two inches of water. I put the black rubber to my mouth and drank. I had to tip my head back to swallow. My tongue was swollen, and I could feel sores on my fat lips. The water tasted slightly salty and heavy, and I imagined the elements from the periodic table being milked from the stalactite.

I found no pieces of crab shell inside the cave and I wondered if I'd dreamed I'd eaten raw crab. I remembered a sentence from a letter I'd been composing in my sleep: "We run 'round and 'round in the dog-moist morn." Now what in the world did that mean? I couldn't remember to whom I'd been writing. It was time to give up interpreting dreams anyway.

The web between my thumb and forefinger throbbed where the crab's pincers had closed.

On the rock just inside the cave opening were white spray-painted words: JOEY BLAS FUCKS GOATS.

The water was high on the rock face below. I didn't know if the high water and the heavy swells were the tides or the weather. But there was no purpose in staying. I could continue to catch stalactite drips but there wouldn't be enough water that way, and how many rock crabs could I catch bare-handed? The islanders had said *stay* for *live*, I remembered. Where do you stay? I had stayed all night in the cave, but I probably couldn't live there, even if no typhoon manifested itself.

Someone had dug the mass grave I'd seen in the south; someone had erected the cross and printed the names of the dead. Others were staying on the island still. They might understand the weather—the deep swells, the airlessness, the bruised sky— unless the bombs had skewed interpretation of such signs, too.

I knew I should leave before the water rose to the cave or before Taitano found me, but I sat, weak and limp, watching the water from the cave's portal.

In the stillness, I remembered weather—all that motion, crashing, flashing within our dome like a paperweight globe, bounded by ozone instead of glass, periodically shaken. I remembered lightning—the repetitive flickering kind like a window shade flapping in the next county, loosing yellow kitchen light; and the cracking visible kind like a child's drawing of the bolts. I remembered wind and dust devils and tree limbs ready to snap in a fall evening and leaves flying down city streets. I remembered rain splatting onto dusty windows and the black earthen smell of rain on leaves.

Remember after-storm mornings, I thought: the gutters running, the litter of branches, a huge maple branch crashed onto the neighbors' roof, the antenna broken, the neighborhood wonder of it all, the kids swimming in the flood and later getting earaches; remember the sheet of water running from the top of the car down the windshield when you pull out of the driveway in the bright gray morning.

Remember all our blue air, all our scattered shoals of clouds, the heaps of cumulus—all our amniotic air.

This morning, days after the war, I had not died. I'd had a hand in the world's death but I was too weary to kill myself. Besides, the rest of them hadn't died weary—Judy and Mitch with their happy children; Daniel with a new job and a new country; my father accidentally dyeing his underwear pink but writing letters beyond grief; all the world getting up before the alarm went off, going to work, eating suppers; even my mother, teaching sixth grade, taking chemotherapy after school, shopping for the grandchildren's birthdays, sick and weariless until her early death.

My mother used to wake Judy and me on school mornings by calling down the hall: Up and at 'em! Or she'd call: Daylight in the swamp! Or she'd sing: Oh what a beau-ti-ful morn-ing! From our blanketed beds, we wanted to kill her.

All right, I said. Up and at 'em.

I performed twenty-five toe-touches in the cave's entrance, facing the sea. Then I turned and began climbing up the rocks.

I worked my way slantwise up the rough cliff, moving one foot until it discovered a hold, then the other, not looking down. You weren't supposed to look down. The torn material of the trousers caught and ripped from thigh to calf as I pulled myself up, and I nearly lost balance. For a moment I lay against the rock, my cheek on the rock, my chest feeling the jagged rock through the T-shirt, my hips squirming to feel the rock like sand against my belly, my feet splayed to hold me to the cliff. I thought that I would look like a gecko on a wall, were there anyone out in the harbor.

The gecko squirmed up a wall by moving the legs on one side of the body together, inward, and then the other pair. I wondered about the toes' suction on the whitewashed plaster, and the wall's delicate seduction of the belly. I could almost sleep against the jagged rock, and I yawned, my face stretched, without covering my mouth. Of course, asleep, I would lose suction and slide down the cliff, shredding my skin, and drop to the shelf of the cave's entrance and rebound into the sea.

So I found another toehold and lifted my body up the rock again. I'd had a hand in it all, I knew, the burned island and the mass graves—the tourists' bodies beneath Two Lovers' Point, the swamp of bloated bodies at the harbor's entrance, the bodies buried and named beneath the cross. It didn't matter who had started it. So what must the hand do now? Slap itself with the other hand? I took hold of a knob of rock and climbed. Chew itself off at the wrist to escape? Above the cliff's layers were heaps of boulders, and though I still climbed upward, I could step from rock to rock, and then I was upright against the air.

Poets used to kill themselves. And it wasn't from too much love of living. It was from watching the hand commit what the hand could commit, and it was from watching the hand then take the pencil. Oh, they didn't really kill themselves: they took their own lives.

My foot caught and I went down on one knee. The rock tore the intact pant leg. My knee bled shallowly. It hurt and, like a child, I stood up and climbed with the blood running proudly down my shin. No one would print the proud phrase: *She took her own life.*

Near the top, the rocks were rougher, more sharply jagged, as if the lower rocks and cliff had once been underwater for a few short, abrading years. As the rocks rounded inland, I could see gray sand between them and blackened vines netted over them, and then there was a swath of burned scrub before the remains of a jungle. I stepped among the thin burned trunks. So what was the hand to do but reach before the face and protect it from the leafless branches and from the spiderwebs that already mapped the jungle again? What else but acknowledge the blood and protect what was left?

In the fall before he left, months before he found me on the floor with Warren, Daniel called in the late afternoon.

"Hey, listen, I'm going to bring a guest home for dinner," he said, with pleasure rounding his voice.

"Oh geez," I said. "I've got a zillion papers to grade tonight."

"To hell with the kiddies. They can wait another day. This is an important *guest.*"

"Well, could you at least stop and get something for dinner? Chinese or something?"

"Just see what you can find in the freezer," he said. "This guest won't be too picky." The pleasure broke his voice like slow bubbles breaking on the surface of a thick white sauce.

So I took dinner rolls out of the freezer, shook off the ice crystals, wrapped them in foil, and put them in the oven. I put a clean cloth on the table and set it for three with the good dishes. There was a box of Swanson's fried chicken in the freezer, and I hoped Daniel's guest would believe I'd fried it myself. I shucked three ears of corn, pulling off the strands of silk impatiently.

"Honey, I'm home," Daniel said, laughing.

Honey I'm home?

"I'd like you to make the acquaintance of my new friend here," he said.

A dog looked furtively from behind Daniel's legs.

"I can't believe I've just fixed a chicken dinner for a dog," I said. "Jesus."

Daniel unsnapped the leash from the collar, but the dog stayed, slightly crouched, beside him.

"Have you ever seen a more beautiful dog?" he said. "Siberian husky."

"How much did you spend for that coyote?" I said.

"More like a wolf," Daniel said. "What's the matter with you? I thought you'd love her."

Her face was cream, with a white stripe on the mask above her eyes. Her coat was a black, gray, and cream that made silver. The insides of her upright ears were cream edged with black. I crouched in front of her, but she wouldn't look at me with her Oriental eyes.

"You know Felicia? Boone's secretary? Her kids found her in the alley behind their house and finally caught her. She didn't want to be caught. But she must have been damned hungry. So Felicia brings her to the office. 'We've already got one parrot,

three cats, one mutt, three goldfish, and two kids in a neighborhood zoned residential,' she says."

"So of course the generous Dr. Manning has to feed the home-
less," I said.

"What are you being so pissy about?" he said, squatting beside
the dog. "I thought you'd like her."

"Oh I do," I said, hearing my own complaining voice. "I don't
know: I set the table and fixed dinner for a *dog*, and I've got all
those papers to do tonight, and maybe you should have asked me,
not just done it. But I'm sorry. Really. She's a beautiful animal."

We ate the meal, and Daniel ate two ears of corn out of obliga-
tion. The dog crouched beside him. We wondered how she'd
been lost. She wore a tag from Kankakee, but the owner's phone
had been disconnected. It took months for Daniel to win her.
She was a compliant dog but always a bit aloof, like a divorced
woman.

"She'll protect you when I'm gone," Daniel said. "I worry
about you, even in this neighborhood. This city's getting more
dangerous by the day."

"I don't think she's much of an attack dog," I said. "Anyway,
that's not why you brought her home."

"I confess," he said. "I wanted her, that's all. But she might be a
deterrent, who knows?"

As soon as Daniel left for Texas and some billionaire story, I
took the dog to a vet to determine if she'd been spayed. I was sure
Daniel would agree to have the job done, but I didn't want any
discussion of the female business, of heat, of pregnancy.

"Well, your lady here hasn't seen the knife," the vet said. "We
can do it now—but we'll be aborting her."

The dog crouched and shook on the stainless steel table.

"You mean she's *preg*nant?" I said. No wonder she was such a
wary animal. I hadn't even considered the possibility.

"Two weeks gone," the vet said. "Mom's always the last to know
about the wandering daughter." He grinned.

"We only just got her," I said, angry, taking no responsibility for the animal's condition.

He held up both hands. "Hey, just a little joke."

I made an appointment to bring her back Monday morning, unfed, for the procedure. We were calling it a "procedure."

At home I leashed her and walked her around the cold Saturday neighborhood. The bare ground was frozen. Two boys in snow-suits sat in a sandbox, grimly clanking dump trucks together. The dog's breath smoked more than mine. You can see your breath, Judy and I used to say, as if our living could condense into vis-ibility. A group of young teenagers climbed into a station wagon, laughing bleakly. None of them sat beside the mother who was behind the wheel. We all needed the warmth of snow, I thought.

When I returned to the house the phone was ringing, but I couldn't get my gloves off and the key turned in time to answer it. I thought that it must have been Daniel, calling from the hot cattled plains. I had never been to Texas, but I imagined African grasslands and the steamy visible breath of longhorns.

Somehow I had released my vague resentment of Daniel's dog as she walked lightly beside me, gracefully yet a bit uncertainly, like a thirteen-year-old ballerina, like a wolf learning domestica-tion. I sat with her on the kitchen floor. I offered her a Milk-Bone, which she took daintily and laid on the linoleum.

"What do you think? Want to be a mama?" I asked her.

When Daniel called in the evening, I didn't tell him about the dog. "She's fine," I merely said. "I think she's beginning to like me a little bit." I said: "What's Texas like?"

"I'm just in Dallas," he said. "Lots of city. Lots of glass. Down-town closes down at six o'clock. I went to see the Kennedy Memo-rial. Saw the grassy knoll."

I coaxed the dog up on the bed with me, though sometime after I fell asleep she left to sleep on the floor beside me, and Monday morning I called the vet's office to cancel the spaying and the abortion.

Daniel had named her Chinook, but I thought of her as Lucy. She reminded me of one of my students, Lucy Taylor, a girl whose tan skin and hair nearly matched—a serious, integral girl.

"Hey, what is this?" Daniel said a month after I'd learned that Chinook was pregnant. He had his hands on her side. "Either this dog's got one hell of a case of worms or she's got a bellyful of pups." He shook his head. "And I thought she was filling out thanks to the Skippy and my tender loving care."

I smiled.

"You already knew, didn't you?" Daniel said.

We held our palms to Chinook's side. One of the puppies had hiccups. I was relieved that Daniel had finally noticed.

"I wonder why you didn't tell me," he said.

I didn't know why. I hadn't been able to tell my mother when I'd begun menstruating, either. I wondered if I'd have told Daniel if I myself were pregnant. The body was stealthy.

"We wanted to surprise you," I said. "Didn't we, girl?"

We prepared a low box with old towels in it and kept it beside our bed, and Chinook began sleeping in it. I checked out library books on whelping. I gave her breakfasts of oatmeal and egg yolks. I walked her every day after school. I learned that I must be prepared to remove the membranes covering each puppy's head if the mother failed to do it or the puppy could smother. I bought a little pair of blunt scissors to cut the cords if Chinook didn't do the job.

Daniel was in Oklahoma when the pups were born. I woke at two A.M. when Chinook's panting shook the bed.

"Oh no," I said. "You can't have them here. What do you think we fixed this nice box for?"

She whimpered, and suddenly a puppy was expelled.

"Oh my God," I said. "Oh my God."

Chinook looked at me anxiously and then started licking the puppy. I watched her bite the cord and then eat the afterbirth attached to the cord. "Oh my God," I said. The book said to hold each puppy to a breast right away and then move it to the box out of the mother's way while she was still whelping. I reached for the washed puppy and Chinook snarled.

"All right," I said. "You know what you're doing, I guess. You don't need my help."

I put my bathrobe on and sat beside her on the bed.

The puppy was black with one white foot. It looked slick and wet, varnished, with an oversized head and withered body, like a human fetus. Chinook licked at it. I edged my hand closer, and she licked my hand and allowed me to touch the wet puppy. I lifted its tail but couldn't tell if it was male or female. I wrote down the time of birth and a description.

Forty-five minutes later, another was born, and then another a half hour later. "2:50—Black with white-tipped tail," I wrote. "3:20—Solid black."

"You are a wonderment, dear Lucy," I told her.

We waited another fifty minutes. "Is that it, Lucy?" I asked. "Three puppies?" In amplified wakefulness, I sat on the bed with her and the pups. Finally, at four-twenty, she began panting rapidly, and the rear of a pup appeared. The others had come head first.

Nothing happened. I began counting seconds. One thousand one, one thousand two. I didn't know why I was counting. At what number would anything be done? And by whom? Chinook tried to lick the half-expelled puppy.

"All right, all right, let's do something here," I said. "I know you're scared. I am too."

I took a towel from the whelping box.

"It'll be all right, it'll be all right now," I told her, and I grasped the half-born pup's body with the towel and slowly tugged it out.

A membrane covered its head, and Chinook seemed to take a long breath before she licked it off and began slowly cleaning the puppy. I was still shaking. I wrote: "4:25—Black with white fore-head stripe. Midwifed by Kitty."

After another half hour, I lay down with Chinook and slept for a couple of hours. Then she let me lift each puppy into the box. I put the bloody quilt and sheets in trash bags and scrubbed the mattress. The stain was ineradicable, and when the mattress dried, I turned it over.

When Daniel returned, I didn't tell him about the stain on our mattress, and he didn't say anything about the bedroom's smell of blood and humid birth. And I couldn't tell him about the night's shaking ecstasy.

We nicknamed the puppies: Bear, Monster, Plain Jane, and Little Girl. Chinook mothered them, first dutifully and then erratically. Her teats were inflamed and she'd try to climb out of the box with puppies hanging on. The puppies opened their almond eyes. We moved them to a box with higher sides. At night the puppies cried like human babies. Finally we ran a classified ad and allowed three puppies to be taken. We kept our Little Girl, the one I'd delivered.

At the edge of the burned jungle, high above the sea, was a cross made of pipes wired together and set in concrete. Behind the cross was the mound of a grave. I blew the soot from the scratchings on the cross pipe until I could read: RONNIE 1964–1983. Had Ronnie risen and thrown off his blackened sod and stepped to the cliff's edge, he'd have had a vast black-lead seascape to view. He'd have believed he was still among the shades.

I tried to picture a map of Tanô. I didn't know how deep the jungle was. I wanted to go south. After all, I couldn't go north without going far inland to get back around the harbor; and what was north anyway but the contaminated Air Force base and the hotel ruins? Taitano might still be on the other side of the harbor, too—though if he still had gas he might well have taken Rogelio south.

If I followed the cliff's edge south, eventually the land would descend to sea level and begin the slow turn around the southern end. But I couldn't remember where roads were, how many shallow bays were dented into the cliff, or how far it was from the harbor to the end of the island. It was windy, and the sea was seamed with long white-gray streaks, and if a typhoon was coming, I wanted to be inland.

I'd already driven, honking wildly, past the remains of the southern village, and no one had appeared to help me. So perhaps the people, if there were people, weren't in the south. Or perhaps I wouldn't find them or they wouldn't show themselves. Still, I thought they must be there. I'd seen the mass grave with the huge cross and its fluttering names of the dead. The southern part was less burned, too, and there might be coconuts, bananas, and breadfruit, if anyone dared eat them. The south had been the island fantasy, with people who believed in spirits, with palm-thatched huts, with barter of the day's catch for a woven hat.

All right, boys and girls, what's wrong with this picture?

It was funny. I was in the midst of the classic island fantasy. I hadn't received a bill for two weeks! The Island Power Authority hadn't sent any notices. I was paying no rent! I never had paid the outrageous new phone installation fee. Visa would never collect on the bright island-wear and new sandals I'd charged at Tina's Tropics. And there were no more paychecks, no more Friday rush to the principal's secretary, no more standing in line for forty minutes to deposit the check at the bank with all the other government employees. Money did not exist any longer. And wasn't that the fantasy? No cash, no credit. Just the person and what he could grow, catch, make. No more offices and El-trains and traffic and telephones and windowed envelopes in the mailbox and gold standard and petroleum products. No more dunning calls at the office, as Daniel had suffered when we'd been behind in payments, when he'd tried to maintain a phony civil voice so the others in the office wouldn't think he was a deadbeat. No more thousands a year deducted for the money-sucking government. Everybody left was bankrupt. Everybody left owed nothing.

It was funny.

The fantasy was to live off the land, just throwing the net in the lagoon, just sending a boy up the palm for the coconut, just plucking the bananas and the breadfruit. The fantasy was a thatched hut with no electricity and no plumbing, it was grass skirts and loincloths.

Of course I'd left Chicago for the imaginary island.

Weren't the tropical-island books—when there were books—always about newcomers to an island, tourists? Didn't the newcomers always leave once they'd discovered whatever heated truth they were running from?

Perhaps I would have returned, though not to Daniel or my mother or Chicago, once I'd learned that the island was a real place. I couldn't know, now.

In the south were people who knew how to survive typhoons, take what the land gave, bury their dead—and I needed them. But what's wrong with this picture, boys and girls?

Cimarron.

A cowboy never ate until he'd fed his horse, wasn't that true? I couldn't have people until I'd tried to find Cimarron. Perhaps I wanted the dog more than I wanted people. Or perhaps if humanity was measured by its treatment of idiots and animals, I was becoming human.

She might be dead by now—drowned trying to swim after me into the floating bodies in the harbor, or shot and eaten by Tai-tano, or attacked by boonie dogs. I couldn't go south, though, until I'd tried to find her.

I headed east, trying to stay just inside the jungle as much as possible. *Cimmie, Cimmie, Cimmie Lou*, I caught myself chanting, and the chant continued silently as I walked. *Cimmie, Cimmie, Cimmie Lee.* We hadn't given Chinook silly nicknames. After she'd had the puppies, she shed so much that she looked clipped and thin, and I'd called her Skinny Shinny. But the indignity offended Daniel and probably the dog herself. Cimarron had naturally become Cimmie, and Daniel had added Lou as her middle name. I made her Cimmie Lee after a poetry lesson with the tenth graders. We'd discussed simile, and I'd driven home singing foolishly, *Cimmie Lou, Cimmie Lee, how are you, how art thee?*

The jungle along the cliff was only rocks and thin burned trunks. I remembered that forest fires were necessary for something. *Cimmie, Cimmie, Cimmie Lou.* Faint, I held onto the black leather of a tree trunk and then walked on. *Cimmie, Cimmie, Cimmie Lee.* The wind threw bursts of black dust against me. I walked east. Oh, it is the east and Cimarron is the sun. Abruptly I sat on a rock and hung my head between my knees, afraid I would faint. Get the blood to the head, they always said. In junior high the girls would hold their breath until they fainted and fell against the lockers. Panting shallowly, I moved on.

I caught a glimpse of motion, something black leaping, but when I stared into the ruined jungle I saw that it was not the dog but dust devils spinning among the trunks.

As the land descended, the jungle began to thicken. I ducked the spiderwebs when I saw them. Among the soot-covered tangantangan I recognized the spread-fingered leaves of a papaya tree. The wind lifted the crown of leaves, and I thought I could see fruit, like testicles, high on the thin trunk. I shook the trunk and then hit my shoulder against it as hard as I could. I would have to examine the fruit before I ate it, I thought. And that was foolishness: what would irradiated papaya look like? I knew that I would eat it. I threw rocks at the fruit. The wind slammed the leaves against the trunk and the fruit, but nothing dropped.

The ground became sandy, and I stepped farther into the jungle for firmer ground. And there, beside the prop roots of a pandanus, was a heap of eyeglass lenses: a foot-wide, six-inch-deep heap of lenses. I kicked at it, uncovering all the clear lenses beneath the sooty top layer, kicking wildly and scattering the lenses until the ground looked like a black-sand sea bottom scattered with frozen jellyfish. I couldn't imagine why the lenses had been dumped in the jungle. I didn't know why I kicked them until I couldn't see with my own filmed eyes.

"I just wanted to call and say I loved the pictures you sent," Mom said. "I showed everybody at school. 'Here's my daughter and her new baby,' I said."

I laughed. I'd sent photos of me with Cimarron in my arms. It was January, and in the pictures the three-month-old dog had snow on her black muzzle.

"Well, that's not quite all," she said. "Your dad and I thought you ought to know. I'm going under the knife next week."

"No," I said. I laughed.

"That's not exactly the sort of reaction that tickles a mother's heart," she said.

"Oh I know," I said. "I'm sorry. Listen, the puppy is trying to eat my foot off. I've got to take her out." I laughed. "I'll call you back in a bit."

"Make it collect," she said.

The puppy tried to chase her mother around in the pen Daniel had built in the backyard, but the mother wasn't playing. I should have found out what kind of surgery at least. Probably she was going to have her varicose veins stripped again. Or have a bunionectomy. I couldn't believe there was such a thing but the librarian at school had had a bunionectomy. Or she was having a suspicious mole removed. But that wouldn't be surgery, though.

I leashed up the dogs and took them for a walk. Daniel came home and we had chili and deviled eggs for supper, and I loaded the dishwasher, which made such a racket that I graded some vocabulary quizzes until it wound down.

Finally I called her back.

"Well," she said. "I wondered if you were ever going to call. Don't you write me off yet." I knew that formal hurt voice, as if she were talking on the phone in a roomful of silent guests.

"I don't want to know," I said. "I know that's selfish. I can't believe there's anything the matter with you. You're my mother."

I could hear her crying. "Here's your father," she said.

There'd been some bleeding, he said. They'd done a colonoscopy. They didn't think the cancer had spread. They were going to take out part of her colon. She wouldn't have to wear a bag.

"Here's your mom," he said.

I wasn't crying. I could hear myself taking sudden little breaths, and I thought it might sound like crying to her. Daniel came and put his hands on my shoulders as they jumped.

"You can't imagine how hideous it was," she said. "I'm on my hands and knees the whole time and they stick this cattle prod all the way up." She made a sound that I thought was a laugh. "Not even having you hurt that much."

"And at least you got something out of that," I said. "*Ta-da.*"

We both laughed, and Daniel's hands rode my shoulders.

I said, "There wasn't anything out of it this time but a brown cattle prod."

"Not even that," she said. "I was so cleaned out that you could see through me."

She'd called Judy earlier, after she'd talked with me the first time. Judy was calm. "'Look, you were brave enough for the colonoscopy,' she told me, 'and so you're brave enough for it all.' How do you like that for sympathy?"

She didn't want either of us to come down while she was in the hospital. Judy needed to be home with her kids. I needed to stay at school. Dad would call us.

After school the next day I sent her a yellow nightgown and a crossword puzzle book. Dad could take the package to the hospital.

Judy called that evening. "We called the oncologist," she said. I wouldn't have thought of talking to the doctor myself. "You might as well know, it doesn't look good. It's probably spread. They won't know until they look."

"Do you remember how she used to wake us up every stupid morning?" I said. "Daylight in the swamp! Up and at 'em! God, we used to want to kill her."

"Take it easy," Judy said. "She's not dead yet. Listen, I've got a kid here that needs some attention. I've got to go."

In February, my parents drove up to visit for a weekend. Dad sat in the car with the Sunday paper while Mom and I did the art museum. Daniel was somewhere.

"I'm not going to be one of those old ladies who talks about her operations every time you sneeze," she said.

The paintings in the first room were large and dark, reclining women in umbrose drapes, spoiled Christs.

"They said they'd rarely seen anyone recover from surgery so quickly," she said. "They were amazed. I was up and staggering around practically right away. Pushing my clothes-pole-on-wheels, all these bags and tubes hanging from it."

In the next room were Degas dancers. Mom had framed three of the ballerinas for our bedroom. Judy hadn't ever liked them, and I quit liking them in high school. Ours had been framed in white. I still couldn't stand the pink slippers holding their feet like thin leather skin over bone. I couldn't stand their fluffy certainty.

"See that one bent over?" I said. "Judy and I used to pretend she was letting gas."

"So much for feminine role models," Mom said. "I thought I'd see if Judy wants them for Cassie. And by the by, there's a list in the cherry chest of who should get what."

Gauguin's jungle was polished and fervid, and I thought of my mother's cancer.

157

"I always did like Gauguin," she said. She pronounced it *Gow-gwin*.

"Listen," I said, "you don't need to be making lists."

We sat across from the Gauguin jungles.

"I just don't know," my mother said. "I don't know whether to prepare to live or prepare to die."

"Are you ever sorry you didn't continue with art?" I said.

She gestured at all the oils and watercolors with their plaques. "No," she said. "Oh sure. But let's face it: I was pretty good, but it was mostly potential. I didn't have the dedication."

"You did," I said. "But it went to your kids. That was your art."

She nodded. Neither of us said if her kids were Judy and I or the sixth graders.

Finally we saw the traveling exhibit, Picasso ceramics. "That's how I feel after chemo," she said, pointing at a distorted face on a dish. "Like someone who's been cut on the bias."

In a glass case were a dozen pottery vases, all painted with skewed faces and shapes.

I said, "Will you just look at the women on those jugs?"

We laughed so hard that she had to hold onto my shoulder, and the afternoon ladies, as well as the art students, glared and we staggered out to Dad sitting in the driver's seat.

"At the risk of sounding profound," I said on the way home, "I suggest that preparing to live and preparing to die are the same."

"You girls want to stop at Baskin-Robbins?" Dad said.

"Your father doesn't want to talk about it," Mom said.

Before the next surgery three months later, after Daniel had kicked Warren and then returned to me, Judy flew down from Michigan to O'Hare. She spent the night in our guest room. Daniel came home early and fixed us stir-fry beef, attentive to our incipient grief. The next day Judy and I would drive down to be with Mom and Dad. It was Easter break, and I could leave school for a week.

"We're not eating red meat anymore," Judy said. "You know this business is in the family."

Daniel abandoned his chopsticks for a fork. "But you can't go fanatic about it," he said. "No more hamburger? No more steak on the grill? No more prime rib?"

"Salads. Fresh vegetables. Steam them. Chicken and fish," Judy said.

"Everybody eats salads with bean sprouts nowadays," Daniel said. "You know what I think of eating bean sprouts? It's like going down on an alien."

I choked on my wine.

"Oh gross," Judy said. "That's what it is with Cassie all the time lately: 'Oh gross, Mom.'"

"Really, though, we have some great recipes we do," Daniel said, "and it seems like they're all rotten for us."

A marriage is redeemable, I thought, if the man still talks about "recipes we do."

"You can do a lot with turkey burger," Judy said.

"More wine, monsieur," I said.

"Get your own wine if you're going to call me names," Daniel said. "'Your sewer', indeed."

We drank too much wine and played a game of Scrabble which Daniel won. I made up the guest bed. "Don't let the bedbugs bite," I said, as Mom used to say before turning the light off.

"Don't," Judy said.

"It's all right to be hurting," I said. "You wouldn't be human if you weren't hurting."

"Spare me," Judy said. "Next you'll be telling me to give myself permission to feel bad. You'll be telling me to process my feelings. Besides, I never cry. I'm a cold fish, remember?"

I carried a glass of wine to our bedroom to share with Daniel.

"I love you," I said.

"Do you?" he said.

We took turns with the wine glass. We lay in the dark, body to body, and kissed until the puppy jumped on the bed. We laughed and pushed her off, and Daniel moved over me and into me as if we were lit by the cadmium yellow of the first time in Daniel's single room, and our matched thin bodies moved until the bed began to squeak.

"Oh no," I said. "Judy'll hear us."

"She's a big girl," Daniel said.

"It'll make her lonely," I said.

We spread the blanket on the floor. The dogs retreated to the other side of the bed at the human panting and release.

"My tailbone may never be the same," I said.

"I hope it will," he said sadly. "It's a lovely tailbone."

"I don't want to die," I said.

We pulled the bedspread and pillows to the floor.

"I want to live the rest of my life with you," I said. "I don't know if you can forgive me."

We lay facing each other, his arm over my hip. The tears wet my hair against the pillow. Daniel was sleep-breathing, his mouth open slightly, and when he exhaled he snored as if he were purring.

Unmoving blue wheat waved on the wallpaper of the inpatient waiting room.

Those waiting sat with magazines—*Bon Appétit, Modern Maturity, Educational Horizons.* No one paced in this waiting room. Most of the waiting were husbands, wives, sisters. Most of the waiting wore pantsuits. Most were getting old, were already old.

A woman with dark gray teased hair sat beside her brother-in-law popping her gum. She unwrapped another piece and stuffed it directly from the paper to her mouth; her cheeks alternately bulged between pops. I stared at her, hoping she would see my anguish and stop. I was nearly crying in irritation at the smacks and pops. Finally she asked the waiting room attendant, "Where's the restrooms at?"

A family group was holding a reunion in the corner, close to the wall where the blue wheat swayed against the white background of the wallpaper. They gossiped and laughed and discussed how well they had slept. They'd slept well, they told each other. All of them had slept well.

That morning in Mom's room, Judy and I had talked with her about her wedding while we waited for her pre-op shot. Then I rode the elevator with her down to the second floor, the surgical floor. The elevator opened at both ends and was long, long enough to accommodate gurneys. The previous night, we'd sat in her room while she read the spiritual booklet the minister had left and then a few pages of an Erma Bombeck collection. Finally her sleeping pill had taken effect. She slept well.

My sister dreamed that she was in another room down the hall from our mother, with a brain tumor. I didn't know if Dad dreamed. Sleeping on the couch so Judy and I could have the beds or so he wouldn't have to be in the double bed alone, he snored in sporadic grunts and snorts and pops. I didn't know if I dreamed.

Mom had brought a packet of notes along to the hospital and handed them to me before the pre-op shot in the morning. "You could read this nonsense while you're waiting," she said.

The notes were from principals and parents and children who had been her students. I'd seen many of them before. But I opened the manila envelope in the waiting room. Already I had waited four hours. Judy had taken our father home. "I'll call when they're taking her back to her room," I'd insisted. "No point in everybody sitting here."

The gum-chewer and the husband were called away. "They sent you here too soon," the waiting room attendant said.

The notes in the manila envelope had been sorted and rubber-banded together. The fattest bundle was from the kids.

Dear Mrs. Falkenburg, Your the best teacher I ever had ever ever. You gut us the gunny pig. Love, Sheila

Dear Mrs. Falkberg, I love you, love Ricky.

Dear Mrs. Balkenburger, You not tell on what I did. You my bes ferit teacher. Love, Norbert.

In the inpatient waiting room, the waiting sat lined up against the wall of tall blue wheat. They looked at magazines or they just sat, yawning. They knew they couldn't doze. They yawned as men before combat were said to yawn. They were not restless. One woman showed a page from *Reader's Digest* to another woman, identical to her but younger.

I almost wished I could show my mother my own packet of praises. But mine were only bundled in my head.

The parents' end-of-the-year notes said that their children had never had a better year. Mrs. Falkenburg is the only one who ever made Richard want to go to school. Mrs. Falkenburg is the only one they want for Carrie's brother when he gets to sixth grade, he is hyperactive but she will understand that and let him go to the boys' room when he says. Carrie says Mrs. Falkenburg is fair even to the Northside kids.

In the inpatient room, I was cold. I wore a sweater that Mom had bought me years ago because the label said *Kit*. The others in the waiting room wore short-sleeved or sleeveless blouses; it was spring in Illinois, hot already. But someone in the corner was wrapped in a rust blanket.

In the third packet, words slid around in the mush of principals' official recommendations and scrawled notes. Innovative. Above and beyond. Creative. Sensitive. Learning centers. Individual needs. Loved your design, Catherine!

Last night, when Judy had gone to call Dad to come pick us up at the hospital, Mom had quickly said, "Are you and Daniel doing all right?"

"Don't you worry about us," I said.

"You're having an affair, aren't you?" she said.

"No," I said.

She looked at me with her eyebrows raised. Judy returned and said that Dad would be waiting for us outside the front door. "I don't know why he can't come up here at least and say good night," she said.

"I was," I said to Mom. "But it's over now."

"Your father can't face all this," Mom said.

We kissed her on her unpowdered cheek.

"Don't let the bedbugs bite," Judy said.

In the waiting room, I read all her letters and notes, and then I merely sat, chilled in my *Kit* sweater, knowing both of us. I sat in the waiting room, swept and still as the blue wheat blown unmoving on the white wall.

9

I thought it must be noon. Rounding the harbor, I was at sea level again. Here everything had been burned. The sand was black, though it had been coarse tan before, and in patches it was smooth and hard as if it had been fired. Above the beach, the few ragged black fronds left on the coconut palms blew in one direction, poised, and blew back until they tore loose.

I went into the jungle of black palm shafts so that I could climb the rocks heaped behind the dive shop. I made my way sideways on all fours until I saw the building below. Then I sat still with my head leaning on the boulder beside me. Never before had I been able to sit so slack, so forbearing. I'd always been nervous, moving, impatient. Now I waited for ten minutes or for a half an hour or more — without a watch or a sun I couldn't tell — watching and listening for people or an abandoned dog. I might have dozed.

Finally I climbed down the rocks. Already Cimarron's feces had dried to powder. There was nothing fresh, though I'd hoped she'd return to the shop. To what would she home? If to anything? Maybe the quarantine center, where she'd spent most of her island time. I would have to check the beach where I'd left her. And then the quarantine center.

Inside the dive shop, in my cache beneath the boards, were one can of liver-flavored Alpo and one last can of Sprite. I pulled the tab on the soda and immediately it sprayed my face and my shirt. I put my mouth to the opening to catch as much as I could. The Sprite was almost too hot to drink. It sprayed up my nose, and I coughed and sneezed and drank.

After I'd peeked out the front and back doors to see if my noise had attracted anybody or maybe Cimarron, I hefted the Alpo can and thought about eating the liver-flavored chunks. *Kitty, Kitty, Kitty,* I heard Judy's voice chanting. *Does Kitty want its din-din?* Did I believe I wouldn't find my dog?

One bad time before Daniel finally left he'd said, "You know, I always hated your name. I never told you this. Now *Catherine,* that's fine. But *Kitty?* Sounds like you're some stuffed angora *thing* to be petted. And *Kit's* even worse. Like you're not even human. Something to be assembled. I used to think of this Visible Man model I had when I was a kid. The clear plastic body you put together with all the organs showing through? Then I quit thinking about it for a long time. Except now I can't help thinking about it again. The Wife Kit."

"Batteries not included," I'd said. I wasn't even crying.

"God forbid," he'd said. "Who knows what you'd have been with batteries."

Maybe with batteries, though, I'd have had the vital juice, I thought. In the Wife Kit, everything showed through the transparent skin—the liver, the intestines, the pancreas, the little heart all hard plastic, painted dull reds and browns. And she held her arms out slightly from her sides, palms forward ingenuously: what you see is what you get. It had taken Daniel years to see that the whole model was plastic.

Now that it didn't matter, I could feel the malleability of the organs inside the opaque skin.

And so I opened the can and dumped the Alpo chunks onto the dive-shop floor, where I'd fed the dog before. Though I might be wasting it: neither of us might eat it this way.

But this was the risk once the systole and diastole began functioning.

I left the back door propped open with a rock.

Near the breakwater the sand had been blown into drifts. I could find none of the footprints that Taitano and Rogelio and I must have made the day before. The old red pickup was gone. The wind scattered sand into the harbor as if to supersaturate the water. In another day the harbor would crystallize. The swamp of bloated bodies was gone, and I wondered if Taitano had shot them all until they sank. But he probably wouldn't waste his bullets that way, sinking the dead. They must have been carried out beyond the harbor. I thought of them catching seaweed and, bound and woven, floating to sea like a sargasso island.

I was afraid to call the dog, afraid of Taitano and of my own loud voice, but finally I cupped my hands beside my mouth and tried to call. My voice was weak and hoarse, and I cleared my throat, angry, and yelled again and again, turning in the sand to send the call in all directions.

I sat in the blowing sand to give Cimarron time to find me. At least I hadn't found her carcass on the beach. I knew that meant nothing, though. I held my hands over my eyes against the particles, expecting any moment to feel Cimarron's thin, tentative tongue on my face.

The sand collected around my hips like snow at the corner of a house. My bare forearms stung. I started to call one more time, but my voice came out thin and embarrassed.

Back at the dive shop, I opened the front door.

"Anybody home?" I said.

The Alpo was gone.

Abruptly I began crying. Out of the wind, my arms and face stinging from the sand, I bawled like a healthy child once an immediate pain had subsided.

Cimarron stepped past the rock holding the back door open and shambled to me, low, her ears back, her tail sweeping the wooden floor. I sat down on the floor, bawling, and then she was upon me, wildly licking my wet face, pawing me, and we rolled and wrestled on the dirty, liver-sticky floor.

"May I join the reunion?"

I looked up from the floor. A tall thin man stood at the open door. Cimarron pawed at my arm and yawned, a whine rising in the yawn to a squeak as she snapped her mouth shut. I stroked her ears lightly. The man stepped inside. He smiled at me and at the dog on the floor. I felt saved.

"Can't have a reunion without a union first," I said. I patted the floor beside me, and he ambled over. "I'm Catherine," I said, and I heard the inflection of surprise in my voice at my mother's name.

"And I am Samuel Flood," he said. He sounded surprised, too.

"And now we have found each other." I felt as if I were reading lines. I had found my dog and this man had found me, and I felt myself delicately extricated, as if I might rise and peer down at the burned island and the little fat men twitching in circles and all the bodies of all the people. I was sad and distant as an angel at what we had done.

"I *have* seen you before," he said.

"Where? I don't remember you, I'm sorry to say. At school?"

He was pale and lean, with thick dark hair. He was clean shaven. His face seemed slightly small, perfectly suited to his body—he looked somehow pure, bewildered, and yet certain, like a hermit rejoining people. I certainly would have noticed Samuel Flood at school.

"I've been looking for you, Catherine," he said. His speech had a faint Southern slowness.

"Looking for me? What does that mean?" I thought of Taitano and his gun, the swim through the dead and across the black harbor. I choked. "I wish you'd found me a little sooner," I said.

He raised his eyebrows, and I heard the accusation in my voice.

"Oh, I know it's not your fault," I said. "You didn't know I needed rescuing."

"Maybe I was looking for someone who could rescue herself," he said. "Weaklings aren't going to make it in this world."

I had an image of sick kittens dropped into a burlap sack. I heard Judy's taunting: *See the poor little kitty, does the kitty wants its sandbox?*

"They'll make it if they get some help," I said. "That's what groups are for. Families. Society. All that." Why was I arguing with the man? For a civilization that had protected no one? Or only because Kitty was a weakling?

"We're finished with all that," Samuel said. "This is a new world."

"That's for sure," I said bitterly. "That is for goddamned sure." Finally I would not have to hold all the grief alone. A funeral was a communal project, with casseroles and old stories. A solitary mourner was only a sentimental image—a beloved dog howling at the master's grave. I couldn't hold a wake for the world by myself.

"I want to know all about you," I told Samuel. "Where you grew up and how you got here. How you survived."

"We haven't survived yet, my lady," he said.

"I know it. There's a typhoon coming." I didn't want to mention food. Hunger might be for weaklings.

"I know there's a typhoon coming. My name's Flood, remember?" He smiled. "And this here is no place to be. That storm is going to walk right down the harbor to your hidey-hole."

"How'd you know I've been hiding here?"

In his thermal shirt and camouflage pants, with his slow formal voice, Samuel Flood seemed like a tent evangelist at divinity school, like a sharecropper's son turned environmental lawyer, like a fiddler who'd ended up at Juilliard. I was sorry I'd asked the accusing question. I was afraid only that he'd abandon me.

"You sure are a suspicious lady," he said. "But that's good. As your reward—wait here a second."

He stepped outside and then returned with a canvas backpack. He pulled out two high-energy protein bars. I tore the foil wrapper—too eagerly, I feared—and quickly ate my bar while Samuel chewed methodically.

"You can have another one later," he said. "We'll have to ration but we won't go hungry. We all stuffed ourselves before. Just like we devoured too much of everything. Now we have to retrain our systems. We've had enough greed."

Cimarron was licking the foil.

"That's not a good guard dog," Samuel said. "It'll do her good to have to forage. If she makes it, maybe I can train her."

Probably he was right, I thought. The days of pets were over. Then, with her chin on the floor, she rolled her brown eyes up at me, and I thought, No, no, this is my Cimarron. I'd always been able to manipulate men, and now I'd have Samuel Flood to work on. We would save each other.

"What were you thinking about doing?" he said. "About the typhoon."

"I am Stormicus," I intoned, holding up my arms. I felt giddy in my relief. "I am the goddess of typhoons." I laughed. Would the goddess cancel the typhoon or call it to finish the job?

"What were you planning to do about the typhoon?" he repeated patiently.

"What is this, a test?"

"You got it, my lady," he said, but gently, smiling.

"Well then, I'd say we need solid shelter. And it ought to be inland." He was right: we had to plan to survive. I was glad he hadn't witnessed my wandering and my inept escapes. "The animal quarantine building might be good. It's concrete, and it's about mid-island. I know it's still standing."

"That's on the Strip, isn't it? The old airstrip? Good idea. Good thinking."

I grinned foolishly, like Cimarron showing her tongue and black lips when I praised her.

Samuel clapped his hands and stood. "I don't think we have a whole lot of time here. From what I'm told. So let's get organized. We need to stock the facility with food and water and some, ah, other useful items that I just happen to have tucked away."

Outside, a rusty three-speed bike with a broken cable leaned against the wall. He handed me a string of plastic milk cartons.

"Bring whatever water you can find. I'll have filters and halazone, and we can boil it, too."

"Wait," I said. "You're not going to leave me, are you?"

"My lady can make it," he said. "I'll get us some rations and meet you there."

I wasn't sure if he meant that I was his lady or that I would be his lady if I proved worthy. For an instant I was angry.

"How do you expect me to carry all these cartons when they're full?"

"You'll figure something out," he said and straddled the bike.

"Sam, wait," I said.

"My daddy called me Sam," he said. "My ma called me Sammy. Well, they're dead. Now I am Samuel."

"Well, Samuel," I said nervously, "I just wanted to say that I'm glad you found me."

After the surgery, Dad and Judy and I met with the oncologist and the surgeon. We were in some other anonymous doctor's office, with books and a hanging diploma but no photos of wife or squinting little girl on the clean desk, no wildly scribbled calendar or gold We're-Proud-of-You-Son pen set.

It had spread, they said. Uterus. Gallbladder. Duodenum. Liver. They'd done a hysterectomy. What could be done had been done. There would be more chemotherapy. There would be direct liver perfusions.

How long? Judy finally asked.

They crossed their legs in the anonymous office. They couldn't say.

Don't tell her, we said. She'll just give up.

They wouldn't lie, they said. But they wouldn't volunteer anything.

Dad was weeping silently. He brought out a large brown plaid handkerchief. How long? he said.

It's impossible to say, the surgeon said.

You'll be lucky to see the summer through, the other one said.

Judy and I stayed a week. We took turns sitting with her. We learned to unkink the tubes when the machine buzzed. Mom was stupefied with pain and painkillers. Every time I relieved Judy, I looked at the waxwork body on the bed and thought, You let her die.

She woke. "Don't want you here," she said, "see me like—"

"All right," I said. "I know."

"Go," she said.

"All right," I said. "You just hibernate for a little while."

I sat on the other side of the curtain where she wouldn't see me when she woke.

In two days she wanted us to fix her hair. I handed Judy the dry shampoo and the brush. I couldn't bear to touch her head.

"Can you believe it?" she said. "For the first time in my life everybody wants me to eat. And I can't get a thing down."

"That's irony for you," I said.

"But you will," Judy said. "Pretty soon you will."

"This is so hard on your father," she said.

"It's not exactly a piece of cake for you," I said.

"Don't say 'cake,'" she said.

We all laughed hopelessly.

Finally Judy said, "There's something you ought to know. We want to tell you before they do."

I stared at her. "Hey now," I said, warning her: Don't defeat her now. I thought that Mom was nearly sleeping again.

"I know this is going to upset you," Judy said. "But it's really not so bad."

Mom's eyes had closed.

"They did a hysterectomy," Judy said.

Mom laughed with her eyes closed. "That hurts," she said and opened her eyes.

"I thought it would depress you," Judy said.

"I'm sixty years old," Mom said. "I've been through menopause. You think I'm going to be depressed that I can't have any more babies?"

"Well, I thought . . ." Judy said.

In the hospital, Mom spent hours watching television, and Judy and I watched with her. No matter what else we were in the middle of watching at eight P.M., she aimed the control at the screen and changed it to "M*A*S*H." Every night she watched "M*A*S*H," and at last at home, she'd doze on the couch but awaken for the nightly rerun of Hawkeye laughing at death.

She never asked the doctors or us: how bad? how long?

She wrote us her usual letters—full of gossip, a bit self-deprecating—but they came three or four times a week instead of once. She'd toss in comments about chemotherapy, mouth sores, nausea, depression, the bunting she'd bought for a baby shower, a cousin's runaway son, the spinach casserole she'd made for Dad though she couldn't get any down, the problems the substitute teacher was having with her sixth graders. Everything was equally incidental, and I did not believe any of it would ever change.

When I called, she cried and then we'd gossip about their neighbors' bizarre habits, and then she'd cry. If Dad had to answer the phone, he'd quickly hand it over to her.

The next letter had been typed with carbon paper. I got the blue carbon copy.

May 3

Dear Girls,

Dad and I think you should know that things are not going as well for me healthwise as we'd like. Although not rising drastically, the C.E.A. test has gone up the past two blood tests. Prior to that it had been dropping each time. In addition one of the liver-function tests (I don't know which one) shows quite a dramatic change upwards. I have been having quite a bit of pain and/or feeling uncomfortable. Next Thursday I go into the clinic for liver scan, X-rays, etc. and a reevaluation by the doctor. I guess I feel I need to keep fighting, futile or not. I'll let you know the results. Try not to worry. I'm doing enough of that for all of us! I just hope I can get my act together and not weep away the rest of my life.

After yesterday's crushing appointment, I geared myself up with tranquilizers and went to the game with Dad. That was good therapy, even if we were beaten.

What's my purpose I wonder? But, heck, no, I'm not giving up yet. Just reevaluating purposes.

Well, until we know more, let's not be too down.

Love,

Mom

I filled the four plastic jugs with water from the rinse barrel. Later I could tell Samuel about Hidden Pond, where we'd have a good source. Maybe after the typhoon we should build our shelter above the pond. I remembered a treehouse Judy and I had tried to build in the peach tree. After nailing two boards across the branches, we quit until we could figure out how to make the walls. I used to climb up and sit on the shelf and read among the blossoms in the spring until one year, when I was twelve, the tree was infested with peach-bark beetles. My trying to build a shelter at Hidden Pond was as silly as our effort at a treehouse. Even if I managed to cut palm branches, I didn't know how the islanders had used them to construct huts.

But now I didn't have to plan my own survival. Now I was with Samuel Flood.

I found a thick branch behind the dive shop. I wrapped a piece of the torn beach towel around the center and hung two milk cartons at each end. Wearing my yoke, I started inland, thinking that Samuel would be pleased with my ingenuity.

Then I stopped. The yoke was the obvious, not an ingenious, solution.

The typhoon was going to walk right down the harbor to the dive shop, Samuel had said. What had I forgotten? I lifted the yoke over my head and set the jugs down and returned to the dive shop. The cache was empty, the air mattresses had been stabbed, and the books had been torn apart.

Outside, though, I'd hidden dive gear in the rock heap. I loaded the mask, snorkel, dead flashlight, and gloves into the gear bag that had been lining my hole under the floorboards. When we could return to real tropical life, I could dive in a lagoon for lobster. I could steam shellfish on the beach for Samuel.

I strapped the dive knife to my calf. This was the woman he wanted. He would never have to know what I had been.

Cimarron and I headed inland toward the quarantine center. The clouds were thick black, edged with luminescent gray, and they rolled like smoke from an oil fire. Surely a storm was at hand.

At the sign to Pedro's Wake, we stopped and I lifted off my yoke. Cimarron lay beside the post, panting and grinning up at me. The paint on the *r* and the *W* had dripped when the words were new. Now the *W* moved and I jumped back. The *W* resumed its position, and the *a* and the *k* and then the *e* crawled. "Jesus," I said. The dog pulled in her long tongue and stared at me.

"Oh never mind," I told her. "Fear not. This isn't anything supernatural. Look: it's just a gecko crawling on the sign. Nothing but a silly little lizard on poor old Pedro's sign."

Cimarron let out her tongue and resumed panting.

Poor old Pedro, I thought. Poor old dead Pedro. I thought of him in a woven palm-leaf hat that was still pale green and that smelled like hay. I pictured him dancing at his daughter's fandango, first with his daughter, then with his fat wife, then with his wife's sisters one by one. He would load up a plate with a slab of skin and pink meat cut from the spitted pig, with kelaguen and bland red rice and buttered pan de leche and lumpia and unburied kimchee. He'd have another beer and dance with another sister-in-law. And then I saw him draped over a donkey, though there had been no donkeys on the island, the woven hat, brittle and split, falling and then fallen from his hanging head, and the donkey bearing him to his wake.

I could barely make out Jesse S.'s words: I AM ALIVE.

The dog crouched and growled.

A lean shape was crossing the road, switchbacking toward me as if the blacktop were steep, or as if he were a slow-motion soldier dodging bullets.

I knew right away that it wasn't tall Samuel or Anthony Joseph Taitano or poor fat Rogelio. I watched him and I watched the gecko traversing the sign for Pedro's Wake.

Cimarron growled deep in her throat.

"Cool it," I said and put my hand on her head. "Let's wait and see just a minute here."

The gecko flipped around to the back of the sign.

A small man in an island-wear shirt and baggy pants stepped up to the sign. The flowers on the shirt were wrinkled and filthy, as if the man had tried to wash the shirt without soap, wring it out, and dry it in the sunless morning. He looked Japanese. I wondered how long he'd been watching me. I wondered if he'd heard me talking to the dog.

He pointed to the sign and looked at me.

"Pedro's Wake," I said.

He jabbed his forefinger at the sign as if he were shooting it.

"I don't understand," I said. "It says Pedro's Wake. It's just an old sign. Whoever Pedro was, he died long before any of the rest. And maybe it's just as well, wouldn't you say?"

He said something in Japanese.

Cimarron was waving her fat tail straight out.

"*Konnichi wa*," I said, and the man smiled, much like a dog's imitation of a human smile. I held out my hand. He glanced at the dog and then stepped forward to shake my hand weakly. Close, he smelled like mulch.

I saw him turn his face slightly. His eyes closed for an instant.

"I know I must stink," I said. I waved my hand in front of my smelly body and made a face.

He laughed a cardboard laugh and waved his hand before his own body.

"Kitty," I said and pointed to my chest. "Kitty Manning." Now I was Kitty again.

"Norio Onoda," he said. He pulled his shirt out and fluttered it. I didn't know if he'd said his own name or "stinks to high heaven," but I repeated, "Norio Onoda." He laughed and fluttered his dirty flowered shirt until I thought he was hysterical, and I began laughing, too, until I had to lean on the sign to Pedro's Wake. Cimarron raised her nose and pursed her lips and howled, and the Japanese man and I laughed in gusts. From afar, we must sound like a pack of coyotes, I thought.

"A pack of coyotes," I said to the Japanese man, and tipped my head back and pursed my lips.

He laughed and then subsided into hitches and sobs.

176

"I'm so glad there are good people left," I told him. "Come on. I'll take you to Samuel."

When the six o'clock news reported that customs investigators had seized a cargo of capacitors bound for Iraq, Daniel said, surprised, "I would have been there."

"Where?" I said. "You didn't tell me you were supposed to go to Iraq."

"No, I meant Heathrow. I would have been at Heathrow when they made those arrests. Not that that means anything." He laughed sheepishly, sorry he'd mentioned it.

We both knew he could lie with impunity now that he'd caught me on the floor with Warren.

"Why didn't you go?" I asked. I had no right to question him about anything more than what time he wanted dinner. "Are you staying home because of me?"

He looked steadily at me, disappointed. We'd tacitly agreed to avoid mentioning his going, his staying.

"What, to keep my eye on you?" he said.

A capacitor is capable of storing five thousand volts, the newscaster said. Fed into a tiny kryton, it could be used to trigger a nuclear explosion.

"I didn't mean that," I said. I felt as guilty and miserable as a scolded dog.

"I was supposed to go to Turkey," Daniel said. "Some spread on Black Sea refineries. I would have had a layover at Heathrow, that's all."

The sting netted four arrests, the newscaster said.

"I'm glad you didn't go," I said. "That part of the world is still scary. I wish they'd never send you over there ever, ever again." I was close to tears.

He put his hands on my shoulders and shook me gently. "Hey now," he said. "Hey. Turkey would have been all right, anyway."

"No, it wouldn't," I said. "You yourself said those Middle Easterners are fanatics. Men even kill their own wives and mothers and daughters." I remembered then that men killed their women who committed adultery, and I rushed on. "What if someone fanatic gets his mitts on nuclear weapons?"

An Israeli minister was saying they were very, very worried. "But what is the point in talking about it? If we are going to do something to them, we should naturally keep it secret."

Secrets, secrets, I thought. What good's adultery if it's not secret? What good's a preemptive strike if it's not a secret?

"I stayed for two reasons," Daniel said. "I declined a trip to the Black Sea because I thought it'd be a good time to stay home. I mean, your mother and all. That's what I told them at work, and it wasn't just an excuse."

"What else?" I said. I was finished with men, but he'd never be sure, and I supposed we both knew we could never return to the secret days.

"I'm getting scared." He gestured toward the television, which had moved on to a local gang's ritual murder. "I'm going to get out of *PetroWorld* as soon as I can figure out what the hell else to do. If we have any smarts at all, we'll both be heading somewhere safe."

"I love you, you know," I said. I didn't know where we could be safe, together or apart.

"And I have loved you," he said.

"Your father's rented a hospital bed," my mother said. "So I'm all set up here in the family room, with the TV and the phone."

"Now you can stay up with the big folks," I said. I tried to laugh. I didn't mention her last letter.

"It's funny," she said. "You know, I finally feel like one of the big folks. My whole life I've felt like a big kid. Now here I am on my deathbed, all grown up."

I held the receiver away from my ear. I almost set it carefully on the cradle, so gently she'd hear no click.

"It's just a figure of speech," she said. "Kitty? You there?"

She told me that the principal and a group of teachers had been over earlier. They'd presented her with a school bell, engraved with her name and the years she'd taught.

"Didn't I tell you I decided to retire? A group of mothers went to the principal and wanted to get me to stay another year so their kids could have me. Ah well."

"Leave 'em wanting more," I said. I was trying not to hang up. "It's almost the end of the year, anyway."

"I remember a PTA meeting I went to in high school. My mother was on a committee to plan a retirement ceremony for this old-maid teacher who was being forced to retire, and they wanted as many of the kids as possible to be there. They got her up there and made a spiel about her devotion. Then they gave her an umbrella."

"An umbrella?" I said.

"A black umbrella. She just went berserk. She'd never had anything but teaching, and they took that away and gave her an umbrella. They had to call an ambulance."

"I'm coming down this weekend," I said. "Maybe I can cut out early on Friday. Last hour's only study hall, anyway."

"Well then, we'll go shopping," she said. "I've got to buy birthday presents for Cassie and Jason."

"I'm sorry I didn't give you any grandchildren," I said.

"I've made a list for your father," she said. "Everybody's birthdays and anniversaries. It's in the cherry chest. Top drawer. You make sure he has it."

"Yes," I said. Now I was afraid *she'd* hang up.

"I always thought you were the maternal one," she said.

"And Judy was the cold fish," I said.

"But she's a great mother, isn't she?"

"Disgustingly perfect," I said.

"Well, she didn't come by that naturally," she said.

"Oh, she did," I said. "You were a fine, fine mother. We never for a second doubted we were loved."

She was crying.

"Here's your dad," she said.

"No," I said. "Don't give me to him. Don't hang up."

"My mouth is like raw hamburger," she said. "I can't eat. I've lost over twenty pounds. 'Good thing I had all that reserve,' I told the doctor."

"Remember how I used to call you in the middle of the night to come cover me up?" I said.

"No," she said.

"I used to kick off my covers on purpose. Then I'd yell 'Mama, Daddy cover me up.' And you always did."

"I don't remember that."

I held my breath as if the sobs were hiccups.

"My mouth hurts too much to talk," she said. "I'll see you this weekend. Carson's is having a sale. Maybe we'll get you a spring outfit, what do you say?"

The sobs rose, peristaltic.

"I say I love you," I said. I set down the receiver so softly that she'd never hear a click.

Judy called Thursday after school. I'd just taken a chicken from its plastic bag and was going to cut it up. I carried the pink-yellow chicken to the phone so the dogs wouldn't get it.

"You should have been expecting this," Judy said. "She died this afternoon."

Chinook and Cimarron jumped for the chicken. I held it by one footless leg. The plucked skin stretched from the thigh and back to the leg with no flesh under it, only pale yellow nodules of fat. Cimarron barked at the chicken and then threatened me in her low voice.

"Tell me," I said.

"We all knew it was coming," Judy said. "Dad couldn't stop crying when he called. The funeral will be Sunday. I'm flying down tomorrow morning."

"No," I said. "Tell me how she died."

"*How* she died? She had cancer, you idiot, what did you think?"

"No, I mean—no, wait. The dogs are going crazy trying to get the chicken."

I set the dead chicken in the refrigerator, and when I returned to the phone Judy was weeping.

"Dad took her in this morning for more tests. They were going to give her another transfusion. She kept throwing up blood. Dad said she thought it was the red Jell-O she'd had. I can't stand this, Kitty."

"I know," I said. I sat down on the kitchen floor. My bones felt long, and the ligaments stretched like old elastic. Cimarron kept licking my wet face.

"Dad was with her," Judy said. "He said she just couldn't breathe. She said, 'Help me,' and that was it."

"He's going to need you," I said. "Couldn't you fly down tonight?"

Neither of us said that I could drive down in three hours.

"Maybe," Judy said. I could hear her blowing her nose. "Maybe I better. Mitch and the kids can fly down tomorrow."

I retrieved the cold dead chicken and cut it up, feeling for the joints with my thumb and cutting through them.

Later Daniel timidly ate the cooked chicken.

"Oh go ahead, eat," I said. "There's nothing blasphemous about eating while you're still alive."

"I'm sorry, Kitty," he said again.

"Oh don't say that. As if you're some distant relative or something."

He'd tried to hold me when he came home.

"I'll get the car gassed up for you tonight," he said.

Daniel was flying to Alaska on Saturday for a series about the pipeline. Neither of us suggested that he stay in Illinois for the funeral.

I pulled the skin off my chicken breast and threw it to the dogs. Sure enough, there in the furrows of flesh, beneath the slick membrane, were the glistening tumors of fat.

The mail came early in the morning before I left, and there was her last letter. She wrote about the red flowers the church people had brought over. She said she was sorry she hadn't gotten everything sorted before she went to the hospital Thursday. Still, she didn't plan on staying there long and she might want her craft stuff next summer. "If I can rally," she wrote.

Dad had written a note at the bottom: "Your mother's going through the valley."

When I arrived at noon, Dad and Judy had already chosen a coffin and arranged for a viewing at the funeral home.

"It's a modern coffin," Judy said. "She'd approve."

"Modern?" I said. "What, does it have a built-in microwave or something? A cellular phone?"

Judy started crying. "You know what I mean," she said.

Dad had ordered dozens of white gladiolas. "She came into this world with white gladiolas," he said. "When she was born, her father filled the hotel with white gladiolas."

"I didn't know that," I said. "She never told me that story."

"Now she's going out with white gladiolas," Dad said.

Judy and I took her clothes to the funeral home. She'd told Judy she wanted to be buried in her good cream-colored suit.

"Why didn't she tell me?" I said.

We packed underpants, a good bra, pantyhose, and shoes.

"You never thought she was really going to die," Judy said.

I never knew if she was really wearing all those clothes in her sleek modern coffin.

At the house, the casseroles and the pies were arriving, all the dishes labeled on the bottom with names written on masking tape.

The stiff hugs and the tears and the platitudes were commencing. The minister came to discuss the service, and we argued over whether Mom had preferred "as we forgive our debtors" or "as we forgive those who trespass against us." I remembered "debtors" from childhood. Debtors were more easily forgiven than trespassers. Debtors could hardly help themselves.

When everyone had left at last, Judy and I set out the casseroles and the salads, and the three of us picked from the buffet.

"Funeral food," Dad said.

"We've got to start a list," Judy said. "Who brought what. We'll have to write thank-you's."

We cried onto our plates, we ate at her table, we watched the news, we loaded the dishwasher. We were efficient and lazy in our insensibility.

"I hate to ask you this," Judy said. "But what are you going to wear?"

A fresh flock of mourners were at the door. Dad handed me a wad of twenty-dollar bills. "You two go to that sale at Carson's. She wanted to buy you a new outfit anyway." He was weeping when he answered the door.

The shopping center seemed darkened and nearly vacant, the empty stores, the dim mall, and the single shoppers all limned with shadow. Under Carson's virulent lights, we chose bright dresses. No black for our mother, we said. No one else was in the dressing room, and we left our separate booths to laugh and choke at the baggy, unbecoming dresses. We scratched like apes in underwear. We hunched over like bag ladies. We were hysterical.

The salesclerk stepped in. "Are you ladies doing all right?" she said.

"Yes, thanks," Judy said, chastened.

"We wouldn't be caught dead in these dresses," I said, and we covered our mouths and retreated, hysterical, to the booths.

At last we chose dresses: Judy's spring green and mine bright pink, and paid for them with Dad's money.

At the funeral home, Catherine Larson Falkenburg lay at the front of the parlor. The room was pale, the lights were soft, the carpet silenced the heels of earthly shoes. We'd picked Mitch and the children up at the airport and then driven to the funeral home for the viewing. We were to have time alone with her before the visitors were allowed in. Cassie and Jason clutched the plush-covered puppies that she had bought them. Judy and Mitch believed the children should say good-bye to Grandma, should see her dead beneath the soft lights, should know and grieve.

She didn't have a chest anymore. The cream suit was flat from neck to waist. Her hair was too flat to her head and the hairdo too square, as if she were wearing a cheap wig straight from the box. I saw the single whisker on her left jaw. I remembered that hair grew after death. Her face was her face. Her mouth was a bit disgusted.

Beside her head was a small white satin pillow, with GRANDMA glittering on a banner across it. Two yellow rosebuds were pinned to the pillow.

I turned to say to Judy that she might have told me, so I could have ordered something special, too, even if I hadn't given her grandchildren. I was going to whisper, Don't you think that's a bit sentimental? But Judy held her children's hands and walked them to the coffin.

In the bathroom I wept aloud, my mouth open against the stuffed toy Cassie had given me to hold. I leaned over the toilet but nothing came, and finally I powdered my face and returned to the parlor. Jason sat silently on Mitch's lap. Cassie was crying quietly, and I gave her the stuffed dog.

"I got him a little wet," I said. "I'm sorry about that."

The parlor was filling, and we mingled and were hugged. We wept for anyone: distant cousins, her students' parents. Anyone.

I did not look at her in her coffin again until the funeral service. Then, while the organ spoke to the bones and the church filled, the family filed to the chancel to attend her for the last time. We

184

were pure, we were envied in our grief. *How well they're taking it,* they were whispering. *You can tell the doctor gave them something to get through it.* Two fresh yellow rosebuds had been pinned to the Grandma pillow. Her hairdo was smoother, though still not right.

She lay there through her service, her mouth disgusted. We all asked to be forgiven our debts as we forgave our debtors. The organ played the "Ode to Joy."

There was no sure and certain faith in resurrection. She was of this world, and everything in this world shuddered with mortality. Neither Judy nor I had taken the tranquilizers, and we sat in our pew in our bright new dresses, weeping, ugly, unable to touch anyone. The children and their stuffed dogs, the throbbing organ, the human voices behind us, the sure and certain minister with the white sleeves falling away from his raised fleshless arms, the rotting rosebuds on her pillow, the debts and the debtors, the lovely thin words, oh, everything was malignant.

She would be transported only to Mount Hope Mausoleum, temperature-controlled in Illinois summers and wormless, but her hope had been only in believing that the blood was red Jell-O. Her face in her lovely modern coffin was her face. Her mouth was disgusted. Everything, the "Ode to Joy," the white gladiolas, our wet red faces, underpants on the dead, cakes and casseroles, my body and Daniel's beneath the cadmium yellow light, everything was malignant.

We stayed with Dad two more days. He and Mitch took Cassie and Jason to the Lake of the Woods while Judy and I worked on the thank-you's at Mom's dining room table. People were returning for their dishes, and we stopped writing notes long enough to transfer all the uneaten food to Mom's Tupperware and wash the dishes, carefully reattaching the masking tape labels. *How's your father coping?* they asked. *Thanks so much for the casserole,* we said.

We worked out two formulas for the notes, according to closeness of relationship or friendship. The familiar ones made us weep. The remote ones were easier. "Dear _____. Thank you very much for the _____. We really appreciated it. Your thoughtfulness means much to us at this time. Sincerely."

Dad and the kids returned from the park. Mitch had let them off and disappeared. Jason's shoes and pant legs were mucky.

"Oh sweetie," Judy said. "Let's get you cleaned up."

"No," Dad said. "I want you two to finish that job."

"We could use a breather," I said.

"No, you stay there until you get those done," he said.

"Hey, we'll get them done," I said. "This isn't exactly homework, and we're not exactly kids."

Judy shot me a look. "Well, we might as well keep at it," she said. "If you'll clean Jason up and keep an eye on my two sweeties."

We sat across from each other at the teak table. "There's no point," Judy said, low.

Soon Cassie was at the table. "Grandpa won't let us open Grandma's junk box," she said.

"Well, sweetheart, it's probably just too sad for Grandpa right now," Judy said. "Why don't you get him to read to you from your big book?"

"Cassie, you come on in here," Dad was calling. "You let your mother work."

Judy and I began proofreading each other's notes.

"Thank you for the delicious molded salad," I said. "I'd forgotten how much I loved miniature marshmallows."

"Thank you for the delicious casserole," Judy said. "Even though bacon is one of the worst things you can ingest and our mother died of colon cancer, we ate it heartily."

Jason was crying in the backyard, and Judy started to get up. "No, let Dad handle it," I said. "He needs it."

"Look at what you wrote," Judy said. "'Dear Mrs. Bernstein,

Thank you for the potato. We really appreciated your thoughtfulness.' Thank you for the potato!"

"I meant potato salad."

"Thank you for the potato!" Judy said.

We put our heads on the teak table, hysterical again. "Thank you for the potato!" we kept saying, weeping.

Jason crawled under the table to his mother's legs. "Grandpa is being mean," he said, crying.

Dad stormed into the dining room and jerked Jason out from under the table.

"Ow, Grandpa, you're hurting me," Jason said.

"What did I tell you about leaving your mother alone?" Dad said. He pulled Jason up by one arm and swatted him.

"We're really done anyway," I tried to say over Jason's crying.

"I want my mommy," he sobbed, and pulled away to run to her. "I want my grandma."

Judy held him. "I don't want you to ever hit him again," she said. She was crying with exaggerated hiccup sounds.

Everyone else went to bed early. Judy and I sat on the guest room bed and cried some more.

"We'd have to say I have everything I wanted, wouldn't we?" Judy said. "Mom said I did. Though she still thought I was a cold fish. Even with two kids. Maybe she was right. I don't know. Do you— You guys have been married even longer than we have. Does Daniel still turn you on? I hate to say it, but with Mitch it's duty." She laughed. "And the funny thing is, I think it's duty for him, too.

"Here I am with this great math degree and I couldn't even teach junior high school now. Teach, Christ. I was the only tutor in the Math Lab who could do finite. And now . . .

"The best time was when Cassie and Jason were babies. I used to rock them in that rocking chair Mom and Dad gave me, and I'd just sing away—'Oh Stewball was a Racehorse,' and 'Yesterday,' and 'Puff the Magic Dragon'—and you know I can't carry a tune in a basket, but babies don't care. That was the best time. And now they're always sleeping over at someone else's and I can just see it all. I've got a little while yet, but this mother business is basically over. I can't even have another baby—did I tell you Mitch had a vasectomy?"

"Don't look at me," I said. "I don't know anything right now." And though I was the older sister, I couldn't play the mother.

Judy and Mitch had Mom and Dad's room, with the kids on the floor. From the single bed of the guest room, I could hear my father on the couch snoring, now and then waking himself up. There was no resolution. We wept together and we wept separately, stopping to pose for a family photo or to return a dish or to escort a cousin to Mom's closet. "Catherine would have wanted me to have this suit," the cousin would say. "We didn't use to be the same size, but lately I've put on so much weight. Well, I just know she'd want me to have this turquoise pantsuit." Before Judy left, she did all the laundry, weeping at Mom's nightgown in the hamper, and she ironed Dad's shirts. Later, Dad did his own laundry and washed a tablecloth and his underwear and socks with something red.

I drove Judy and her family to the airport before heading back to Chicago, to my students, and to Daniel.

"We'll all survive," Judy said. "It's rough. But we have all those good memories and we'll survive. There's not much choice anyway, is there?"

"Thanks for the potato," I said.

10

Cimarron walked beside me just as if she'd been trained to heel, and Norio Onoda followed us. I wondered if Norio, no doubt a tourist, believed I knew where to hide in the storm. By pointing at the sky and waving our arms like palm fronds over our heads, we'd agreed that the typhoon was coming.

Norio said something, and I turned. He held a blood-swollen tick between his fingers for me to see and then threw it the way an unathletic girl tries to throw a softball overhand.

I flapped my arms and glided, then pointed my arm like a gun at the sky, and then flapped again, falling, wounded.

"The birds are gone," I said, "but the ticks are immortal." I plucked an imaginary tick from my hair and examined it for life.

"*Hai, hai,*" he said, and put his hand over his eyes.

He seemed of such gentle blood, not impotent but childlike, that I felt protective. If his ancestors had ever been samurai, the family had been broken in long ago. I recalled the World War II atrocities, the camp at the southern end of the island, beheadings and torture, the death march. What had that to do with this docile man covering his eyes to conceal the pain? With the surrender after the bombing of Nagasaki, Japan had renounced war forever. What had our histories, any old atrocities, to do with us now on Tanô?

The wind pulsed against us as we walked and then abruptly reversed itself and held us in place. Black palm fronds, torn loose, and a Pepsi cup and a torn trash bag flew by us. I wondered whom

Norio had come to the island with. Had he been on his honeymoon? He looked young, in his twenties, I guessed. Or he might have come with his aged parents. Or he and his wife might have brought their children to play in the shallow blue water, to pose for pictures beside the giant Colonel Sanders statue, to ride the tour bus to Two Lovers' Point and pull back, lock-kneed, at the cliff's edge, to buy carved water buffalo—made in the Philippines—and T-shirts and sharks' teeth and coconut shell pen-holders at the gift shops.

I didn't know any way to tell him about Samuel, about surviving.

"Did you have any children?" I asked. I pointed to him and then rocked my arms.

"*I-ie*," he said, shaking his head.

I couldn't think how to ask him if he'd been married. I didn't think Samuel had been married. Our pasts were irrelevant now, anyway.

The wind blew against us until we were walking in place, and then suddenly let us go, and I nearly fell. Norio gestured taking the yoke, but I shook my head.

Dead dogs littered the quarantine center's yard. Cimarron stayed at my side, quivering. The blood on the dirt ground was dark and rotten. Near the open gate, a swollen boonie dog lay with its neck chewed open. Maggots spilled like rice from the open neck. Norio and I held our hands over our mouths and noses. We couldn't stay here with the stench and the flies.

"Samuel Flood," I called.

At my voice, a dog began yelping from the side of the building, and Cimmie's ruff rose. A boonie dog appeared, yelping still, dragging a black terrier-type dog with it. They must have been mating, and now they were stuck, rear to rear. The terrier's rump was pulled up so that her back legs were off the ground, but she was silent.

"Stay here a minute," I told Norio, and pointed to the ground. I held my nose and ran past the stuck dogs and the dead dogs. Inside, the sacks of Purina had been torn open and the contents eaten. There was nothing for us here but concrete.

I heard Norio yell something. From the left of the yard, down the old airstrip, a small pack of dogs advanced. Norio had Cimarron by the collar and was pulling her away.

"*Yukkuri*," he said and gestured with his free hand, pushing palm down: slow, easy.

I moved slowly after him, out the gate and to the right down the old airstrip. Watching the dogs slink after us, I tripped on the yoke and the water cartons fell over. I could see Cimarron's ruff rise again in spikes. She pulled back toward me, or toward the pack, and Norio bent to smooth her head and throat. Two of the boonie dogs headed into the quarantine building's yard.

"We're safe," I called, and hurried after Norio. The animals were just a few dogs, after all, fighting the wind, looking for food and a hiding place, just as we were. I broke into a run.

Norio yelled then, and I turned. The three-legged shepherd led the pack after me. I could see the dogs' lips pulled back from their fangs. In panic, I ran for Norio and my own dog.

He stood still until I reached him, and then he caught me as I tried to run past him. He shoved my hand under Cimarron's collar and held my arm so tightly that I knew I'd have bruises. The pack slowed and began to separate into individual dogs. Their ears were back, and over the wind I could hear their snarls. Strings of saliva hung from their black lips.

Norio spoke placatingly, whether to me or to the dogs, I couldn't tell. He loosened his grip on my hand and pointed to the ground as I'd done to him earlier: stay. As the dogs spread to circle us, he clapped at them and then broke and sprinted toward the quarantine center. Instantly the pack was after him, yelping.

As he reached the gate, the shepherd and the largest boonie dog lunged and I saw him go down beneath them. Kamikaze, I thought. Cimarron jerked away and charged toward the pack.

191

"No, no, no," I screamed and ran after her.

Norio was up again, and I saw him kick the shepherd's remaining back leg. The dog collapsed, shaking his head, slinging ropes of yellow saliva into the wind. The largest boonie dog went for the neck.

With the rest of the pack after him, Norio ran for the trailer beside the building. I kicked my own dog back and pulled the chain-link gate closed, shutting in the dogs but also the man. Norio clapped and yelled ferociously at the dogs, and when they pulled back, he yanked the trailer's door open. Once he was inside, they charged the door, biting at the aluminum.

I remembered the small animals inside the trailer, cats and poodles dead in their toppled wire cages. Now Norio was trapped with them.

"Samuel," I yelled. "Help! Samuel!"

The boonie dogs gave up on the door, and when they joined the one already savaging the shepherd, Cimarron cringed and whined. The little black terrier was among them.

Before I could figure out how to kill the dogs, Norio appeared on the roof of the trailer. He must have climbed through the back window, I thought. Still, I might have to kill the dogs. I felt weak and domesticated myself. The dogs swarmed over the dead shepherd, pulling away meat, growling and snapping at each other. Norio held a finger to his lips. He crouched and then leapt over the fence. He rolled as he hit the ground outside the yard.

"Are you all right?" I said. "You? Okay?" I helped him up. His pants were torn and bloody in the rear. "I'm glad you didn't do a kamikaze on me," I said.

He must have understood the word, for he shook his head. He grinned and pointed to the seat of his pants. He touched the finger stripes on my arm.

"*Sumimasen,*" he said, shaking his head still.

"It's all right," I said. "I thank you." I put my hands together and bowed.

I looked up at the sound of clapping. There was Samuel, applauding our escape. He was wearing the backpack and a long leather sling.

"Oh, where were you? Didn't you hear me calling?" I was nearly crying as the adrenaline ebbed.

"But you didn't need me, did you?" he said. "Whoever your gook friend here is, he did fine. Just fine." He turned to Norio. "You done good," he said slowly.

"Don't call him a gook," I said.

"Yes, ma'am," Samuel said somberly. I couldn't tell if he was mocking me. "Anyway, I think he's a keeper."

I pointed to each and said their names.

"You—" Samuel said, pointing, "with—us." He put his hand on my shoulder.

The wind flapped Norio's flowered shirt and our hair, and we could hardly hear each other. Samuel was looking at the T-shirt blown against my chest.

"You weren't really here all the time, were you? Just watching us through all that?"

He lifted the sling over his head and extracted a long gun.

"What do you think?" he said.

His hand on my shoulder, when he'd claimed me, had been heavy, and I could still feel the press of his palm. Samuel was saving me.

"Now where do we go?" I said. "We can't stay here."

Samuel led us down the old runway until it merged with the cross-island road, which angled slightly south. The World War II airstrip was intact after all these years, but the new road was already buckled and split. Three times we passed stacks of bodies, clothed and desiccating. I wondered if Norio, too, thought of the grainy photos of the concentration camp bodies piled like firewood. These piles weren't as tidy. They looked as if they'd been heaped merely to comfort each other. I hoped we'd find those who had stacked the bodies. Samuel's new world would need people.

193

"How'd you come by the gun?" I yelled in the wind.

"It's a rifle," he said. "This is my rifle," he chanted, slapping the leather, "this is my gun." He grabbed his crotch. "This is for killing and this is for fun."

Norio looked at me, puzzled. I laughed and circled my forefinger by my ear: he's crazy. I was glad Samuel had a weapon. Later I'd tell him about Taitano's shiny gun and his idea of fun.

"Yeah, right," Samuel said. "Plenty of folks thought I was nuts. But I saw all this coming." He waved his arm at the blackened jungle and another pile of bodies. "They're croaked, and I was ready. Why do you think I'm here?"

I didn't know if he meant on the island or with me or among the living.

"One thing I did was order this baby from Montana. White Eye's Rifles. You'd think I'd have a .223, something like that, right?"

"Of course," I said. I knew nothing about weapons. The wind carried the words away from Samuel.

"What happens when you're out of ammo? Even if you locate some, it might not be the same caliber. No, this baby is for survival. You see here a .57-caliber Hawken. Handmade."

"What's the difference?"

He walked backwards, facing me. "Muzzle-loader. No ammo problems here. When I run out of bullets, I cast my own balls. Lead's everywhere—battery plates and wheel weights from all these vehicles, say. When I run out of black powder, I use smokeless powder from any shell." He held out his palms ingenuously.

He stepped into the wind and kissed my mouth quickly. His hair lashed my eye and the wind whipped away the tears.

"Oh, my lady," he said.

Soon after the fourth heap of bodies, we came to the ruins of a row of shops. I thought we must be about halfway across the island. The sign on one storefront said: RINSE 'N ROLL—SUDS YER DUDS. The rest of the shop had fallen and shattered, and the facade swayed in the wind. Hunks of concrete and gridded plaster and lengths of rebar were strewn across the road and into the burned jungle. I saw two imploded washing machines among the black trees.

Samuel headed around the shops.

A red truck lay on its side before the one remaining shop. For a moment I thought it was Taitano's pickup, but then I saw that it was new, a red so shiny it looked wet. The bumper sticker read: STOP CONTINENTAL DRIFT. I laughed and choked. There was no explaining to Norio. Who cared about causes now? And those who had might just as well have demonstrated against the implacable.

Cimmie's ears were high and quivering. Norio held his hands before him, palms down and fingers spread, ready to palpate the air. Then I heard something, too, a cry, the sound a shrunken baby might make. We moved slowly to the shop, stepping high with hunched backs like cartoon spies: sneak, sneak. The singed sign above the doorway announced LIM BONG LIQUORS. The baby bleated again. The windows were gone. I stepped in the open door, with Norio's hand gripping the end of my T-shirt, and we stood for a moment while the darkness grayed slowly. In all the dusk we might begin to imagine slow gray dawns, I thought. The baby bleated, and as I stooped, it stepped to me on four thin legs. I stroked its head, over the knobs of horn and down the thin neck.

"Look, it's a little goat," I told Norio. "*Baaa*," I said, more like an animal's sound than the goat's, I thought.

"*Bleeaah*," the goat answered.

"Quit that," I said. "We're probably going to roast you."

"*Bleeaah*," he said.

Cimarron was interested but quivering. The little goat spotted her, or smelled her, and stiff-legged, marched over and ducked his head under her, looking for teats.

From behind the checkout counter, someone spoke one clear word. "*Susus*," we heard, and then a whimper.

A nearly naked man lay against the counter, hunched over, his legs sprawled out. His clothes were scattered behind the counter, as if he'd torn them off in great heat. Norio pointed to his right leg. In the dim room it looked darker than the other, swollen as an overripe plum before it starts to shrivel. We could see a black wound on the calf, the flesh around it spread like fat lips.

"I don't suppose you're a doctor," I said to Norio. "Dok-tor?" Now I was speaking my father's pidgin.

He shook his head.

The man behind the counter was shivering almost convulsively. "*Susus*," he cried.

Norio shrugged at me. But I knew what *susus* were: Malcolm Yarrow had taught me some Chamorro words that the kids might try out on me.

"Tits," I said, which had been Malcolm's translation. I cupped my hands under my breasts and lifted.

He pointed at the little goat, and I got it right away: both the goat and the man needed the breast.

"Catherine!" Samuel was calling.

I stepped back into the wind. "There's someone in here," I said.

He put his hand to his ear. "You're going to have to learn to scout out a place before you go barging in," he said.

"Right," I said, and pulled him inside to the wounded man. "Meet the rest of our party."

Lim Bong's Liquors was one room. The shelves were on the floor, but the broken glass had been cleared and heaped outside the rear door. On a nail on the back wall hung a woman's pink sweater, and I draped it and his shirt over the wounded man.

Norio moved his fingers together in the air. I didn't get it. He cupped an imaginary little bowl in his left hand and dipped into it with imaginary chopsticks.

"I think he's hungry," I told Samuel.

"Secure the premises first," he said. I thought of Taitano's order to Rogelio. *Secure the area.*

We began searching the little shop, with both the dog and the goat following. In the back we found a large electric cooler with dozens of cans and bottles of beer floating inside. We scooped up handfuls of the water and drank. It tasted sour and slightly brackish, but we drank. I fed Cimmie from my cupped hands and I offered them to the goat, but he touched his nose to the water, sneezed, and refused to drink. Norio carried water to the shivering man behind the counter and managed to get a bit of it into his mouth.

Beside the cooler were stacked wooden crates full of bottles in packing popcorn. When I pulled out a bottle of gin, the goat tried to eat the Styrofoam stuck to it.

I slowly poured capful after capful of gin over the black wound on the man's leg. He didn't wince or moan, but only shivered silently.

"That's probably pointless," Samuel said. "But nobody's going to be drinking any more hard stuff, so you might as well dump it on him. Though—come to think of it—we might use it for barter."

Norio called something from behind the shop. First he pointed west. Low behind the wrought-iron tree trunks, the clouds had ripped, and for a few seconds we had the shifting of an aurora of green and orange and purple. Then the clouds sealed, and he pointed to a wooden crate beside the broken glass. Inside were cans of Spam, packages of ship's biscuits, white utility candles, and matches. This must have been Lim Bong's, or someone's, cache of emergency typhoon supplies.

"Great," Samuel said. "You—done—good."

In the dark and the wind we dragged in the crate and stacked it and the crates of liquor behind the counter. The two of them dragged the heavy cooler over so that it boxed in the area behind the counter, leaving a narrow passageway.

"Okay." Samuel clapped his hands and grinned. "This'll have to do it. Now you stay here with the kiddies. I need to fetch another load."

This man would always be leaving me, I thought. On the floor of the enclosure, the men and the animals and I must look to Samuel like children in a playpen.

After he left, we kept a candle lit for a short while with our hands around the flame, long enough to wind the key around a can of Spam and tear the cellophane from two packages of hard biscuits and pull the tabs off two cans of Budweiser. We passed the gelatined meat back and forth, and I thought it must be to the Japanese man like the Alpo had been to me. Cimarron licked the globs of gelatin that dropped until Norio opened another can and fed it to her. The goat only sneezed at it, but when we got to the ship's biscuits he drew his lips up and bit neatly.

In the little room we'd made, Norio and I watched the shivering man and fed the animals and had a moderate feast and drank Budweiser beer. Stop continental drift, I thought. Suck the missiles back into their silos. Stop Daniel from leaving me. Stop the typhoon. Or send mourners.

After the funeral, I drove home and went to school the next day and sprung the dogs from the kennel in the afternoon. Daniel stayed in Alaska four more days. My students were subdued, as if I were a carrier of death. When Daniel returned, we talked about the funeral and about Alaska, we made love, we slept in on Sunday morning and read the fat *Tribune*, and I forgot that I had to die, and I believed we would be all right.

My father sent a copy of the autopsy report a week later. I read it as if it were a student's paper, catching the errors.

Mrs. Falkenburg is a 61 year old female who was admitted from the Oncology Clinic with massive gastrointestinal hemorrhage. . . . Original carcinoma was Dukes C category discovered in January. At that time metastatic carcinoma of the liver was found and a second primary involving the sigmoid colon that had invaded through the wall with continuous extension into the uterus and abdominal wall. A lower anterior anastomosis was performed along with a hyster-ectomy. She was admitted on May 8 with melena and her hemoglobin was 7.9. She expired approximately 1 p.m. on the 8th secondary to massive gastrointestinal hemor-rhage.

I did not know why my father had sent the report, except to tell me that she had been a cadaver.

Patient is a well-developed, well-nourished white female ap-pearing younger than the stated age of 61 years. The breasts are soft, nipples everted. The abdomen is full and tam-ponadic. The genitalia is that of an adult female. The ex-tremities are unremarkable.

Judy called when she received her copy of the report. "Wouldn't she have loved that?" she said. "Younger than the stated age of sixty-one years?"

"Maybe not the 'well nourished' part, though," I said. Maybe not the instruments—which wouldn't even have to be sterile, I thought—maybe not the gloved hands and the unmasked faces dispassionately analyzing the flesh, cutting and taking notes and suturing to make it coffin-ready.

"I can't stand this, Kitty," Judy said.

An abdominal incision is made and the abdominal contents are examined with marked difficulty because of severe adhe-sions and the abdominal wall contains plaques of metastatic tumor. The stomach is markedly dilated and the small bowel and remaining colon contains blood. The spleen weighs 170 grams. The capsule is glistening. The liver weights 2430 grams. There is a yellow white tumor and many of the masses contain central necrosis. . . . The gallbladder contains yel-

lowish bile. The common duct is examined with great difficulty. . . . The stomach contains approximately 1500 cc of
fresh clotted blood. There is a large gastric ulcer that has
eroded ito the pancreas and appears to be the source of the
bleeding. This ulcer has raised edges. There is a kissing ulcer
measuring about 2 cm in diameter.

"You just hold on to the memories," I said to Judy. "You just keep
remembering."

"I only started to get along with her when I had the kids," she
said. "I just kept my trap shut before that."

"So what?" I said. "Did it matter? At least *you* kept your trap
shut."

"Yes, but it did matter," Judy said. "I remember all those dumb
begging notes we wrote her. My God but we were sorry kids.
Every month we were sorry."

If examining her was so difficult, I wanted to say, they didn't
have to do it. Daniel is going to leave, I wanted to say. What sorry
notes can I write?

"I can't stand it either," I said.

PROVISIONAL ANATOMIC CORELATION: Patient
had massive liver metastasis, adenocarcinoma of the colon.
Immediate cause of death was a sanquination secondary to
massive gastrointestinal hemorrhage.

She was absolutely dead. She was no sleeper in her underwear and
her cream suit. I could not bear the misspellings and grammatical
errors in her autopsy report. Some secretary had transcribed
"exsanguination" as "a sanquination." After Daniel left me for
good, I wrote to my father and to my sister about the new adventure of the island. She'd died of exsanguination. Daniel left me
Cimarron and took his own dog to Alaska, and during the hours
between Chicago and the island I remembered that I couldn't

stand it, and that after we'd entombed our mother I'd told Judy "Thanks for the potato," and that in my mother's dead body the spleen capsule was glistening and an ulcer was kissing, and that my father had dyed a tablecloth and his underwear pink. In the sleepless altitude above the Pacific Ocean and the clouds, I remembered Daniel lying with me on a narrow bed, incarnadine, my necrosis bleeding into all of us.

Inside Lim Bong's Liquors, in the enclosure we'd made, Norio and I flanked the other man. When he shivered, we pulled close. Cimarron slept at my side, and I could feel her twitching as she chased or was chased in her dreams. The goat collapsed his legs at our feet, and I reached down to touch his supple lips and the bumps of horn between his ears. With the storm beginning to take the island, I believed I felt the darkness on my skin as a fish must feel salt water.

I waited for Samuel Flood to come to me.

Later I woke when the man beside me flung his arms out. "No," he said. "Kill." He felt hot, but I didn't know what to do for the fever. "Jesse," he said. "No."

I felt his forehead, as a mother would. His face was wet. He began bucking silently, and Norio and I held him gently until the convulsions subsided and he shivered.

The wind alternately blew and sucked. Objects, rocks or buckets maybe, hit the concrete walls. Occasional spurts of rain sprayed our heads and our hunched shoulders.

Did you ever think this is natural? I wanted to ask Norio, but he could not understand me and I could not bear to hear my own voice in the moment's vacuum when the wind reversed direction. *Stop continental drift indeed. No nukes. Stop the war. Right. As easily stop the entire flux from birth to the end. There was only one current and only one destination. Whenever you disembarked, you arrived. Forget your Baedeker, your Fodor's. There was no wandering, there was no navigation. The current had you, and you had to go the way of all flesh.*

Samuel might be lost. And I knew that no one saved anyone, anyway.

Norio and the wounded man and Kitty and the dog and the goat were merging, tangling into a sargasso island, pulling the flocks of rain, the sanguine darkness, the continents to us. *My mother died and they all died and our old species died. As easily stop the entire flux: the tail dropped away, we breathed air, we looked into our brain, we were ashamed, we were towed into the spiral, we believed we could escape. But my mother died, and Daniel and all the others were carrion now, and holocaust had always been the end.* The rain was salty. I reached across the wounded man and felt Norio's wet face and carried his hand to my wet face. The wounded man absorbed our shaking. The island was coral, collective bodies, and in the jungles rotted carcasses of boar and rat snakes and tiny deer and geckos, and in the sea settled husks of crabs. So the creatures died. I didn't believe a Japanese man would weep. *It's natural,* I wanted to tell him. *So the species dies.* We wept with our hands on each other's face. We had been as lovely as the coral, as the geckos, and now we would settle with the ragged claws and the mammalian bodies, buried and unburied.

"No, no," the wounded man cried and flung his arms out. "*Susus*," he said. "Jesse," he said.

But we held him, converging like coral breathing water.

11

In my sleep I was watching Daniel take a pee. His limp underwear sagged over his flat buttocks. His left hand was on his hip,
with the fingers turned back. He was staring down. His right hand
gave the expert shake.

When the man next to me moved, I kept my eyes closed to hold
Daniel's familiar form. I pictured him not with longing or passion,
but the way Judy might have seen her children when they were
grown.

"What did the typhoon say to the palm tree?" the man said.

I opened my eyes but could see nothing in the dense blackness.

"You're awake," he said. "So what did the typhoon say to the
palm tree?"

"What?" I whispered.

"You'd better hang onto your nuts because this is going to be a
helluva blow job."

Now I could see his white underwear, as if it were weakly
phosphorescent. He'd taken off the shirt and the pink sweater.

"Are you all right?" I said. "You were . . ." I was going to say
he'd been out of his head. "You were feverish," I said.

"So how'd you get to old Limp Dong's joint?" he said. "Oh,
excuse me—I'm Jesse Santos. At memsahib's service."

"I'm Kit," I said. When he was silent, I whispered, "Kitty
Manning."

"Who's the dude?"

"Norio," I said. "I think he's Japanese. Is he awake over there? I figure he must have been a tourist."

I didn't say anything about Samuel. Had he even existed?

"What do you get when you cross an American and a Filipino?" Jesse said.

"I wouldn't know," I said. "I'd say this is hardly the time for jokes."

"You get a haole-pino," he said.

"Do you think the storm's over?" I said. I thought I felt the dark air shifting around us, but the wind had died.

"Shit no," he said. "Excuse my French."

"*Lanya*," I said.

"Not bad for a white lady," Jesse said.

Daniel had come back from Alaska with pictures of a black lake, of tidewater glaciers, crenelated, dirty blue, crawling into an ice-littered bay. He'd sent me a postcard of a sled-dog team. The dogs' tongues hung long from the sides of their mouths. Two of the dogs, grinning at the camera, looked very much like Chinook and Cimarron. Behind the dogs was a range of stippled blue-and-white mountains. "There's something here," he'd written. "I'll try to tell you about it when I get back. In the meanwhile, tell your father and Judy that I'm thinking about all of you. Yes, I love you."

Just as if I'd asked. I'd wondered if we could take the dogs and live near the blue-white mountains and forgive us our debtors.

I said, "Are you the one who left the message on the Pedro's Wake sign?"

"That was before my leg turned black on me," he said. "Stupid, stupid. I laid it open with a shovel. Can you believe that? Here I am always hollering at my kids to be careful. And I lay my leg open."

"What were you doing?" I said, not really listening, hearing *shovel* and *kids*, thinking of the silence of the Japanese man, thinking of the apparition named Samuel.

"What do you think?" Jesse said.

The wind blew something metallic against the rear of the shop, and flakes of rust flew in the window. Norio stirred and spoke. I wondered where Jesse Santos's kids were. I wondered if he'd been burying his kids when he laid his leg open with the shovel.

"You should have washed out that cut," I said, "before it got infected." I didn't know if the infection could kill him. If this were a movie, Norio and I would have to cut off the leg, and Jesse Santos would drink a gallon of bourbon and yell only once. I couldn't remember how they stopped the bleeding in the movies, but Samuel would know.

"Yes, Mother," Jesse said. "I certainly should have washed up. Sorry you weren't here to take me to the emergency room. Sorry there isn't an emergency room. Where's the Bactine when you need it?"

Norio was tapping Jesse's shoulder. "*Sumimasen,*" he said. I couldn't see his face but his voice sounded worried, and I thought he must have understood Jesse's bitterness.

"Shake hands with him," I said. I pointed to each. "Jesse. Norio."

"Is it morning?" Jesse said.

"Who knows?" I said. I didn't think I'd slept very long. "I don't think so."

"You ever seen one of these typhoons?"

"I've only been here . . ." I couldn't finish.

How long had I been on Tanô? I'd taught at the high school for two months. How many days had it been since Malcolm had taken me down to the *Tokai Maru?* Island survivors were supposed to keep a record—notch a tree or something—but this was the present only, as if the span of the island and the lapse of moments had thickened. Tides and stars and revolution were gone. Continents had powdered into the sky or calved like glaciers and disappeared into the black oceans.

"It doesn't matter," Jesse said. "Nobody home but us chickens anyway."

There was no time, no space, no flux. The island and the moment had condensed, as if by mistake, when everything else had evaporated.

"Is this the eye of the storm?" I asked Jesse.

"No way," he said. "Let me tell you about typhoons."

"Gnab gib," I said.

"Say what?"

"Gnab gib. I remember that from my astronomy class. The gravitational collapse of the universe. Big Bang backwards. Get it?"

"Yeah, well, you can call it that if you want," Jesse said.

Norio was tapping on Jesse's shoulder again.

"I think that bitter tone of voice worries him," I said.

"Hell yes, I'm bitter," Jesse said to Norio, but more gently. "This storm, it's all right. It's going to blow this island to China, sure. But you can't blame anybody for it. It's stupid civilized *human* fuckers that cremated my kids and all the rest." He shook his head. "It really is all gone, you know. My uncle was up at SAC and he heard the radio. He was a spook."

"A *spook?*"

"Crypto-communications," Jesse said, his voice puzzled at the need to state the obvious.

"Well, how should I know? I'm not military. I thought you meant one of those ghosts or whatever you call them. Taotao-mona."

Jesse was silent. My voice echoed for a moment, and then suddenly the wind rattled the door and Jesse jumped.

"Jesus Christ," he said. "For a second there, I thought we really had a taotaomona knocking on the door. And you know what, in a few hours this sucker's going to hit, and we'd better be ready." He tried to stand and grabbed the counter.

"You can't do it," I said. "Don't you fade out on us again. Anyway, this outfit needs a foreman, right? You just tell us what to do."

206

Jesse dropped to the floor. "If you're not military, then I bet I know what you are. You're a schoolteacher."

"Well, I can't help it," I said, hearing my mother's voice, and Daniel's sure, superior voice, too.

"All right, the idea is to block those windows," he said wearily. "Old Limp Dong's will flood and you'll be blown right out on your schoolmarm butt if we don't get those windows blocked."

Why hadn't Samuel known that? To him, survival meant rations and camouflage and a Hawken rifle. To Jesse, survival seemed to mean burying the dead and knowing the nature of the wind.

I gestured to the two windows and pantomimed nailing boards over them, and Norio rose. We began searching the room in the dark. We didn't need Samuel.

"Did your uncle the spook say if Illinois is gone?" I asked Jesse.

"Yes," he said.

Norio was working at the storeroom door at the back of the shop.

"Is Michigan gone?"

"It's all gone," Jesse said.

"How'd you find out all this?" I said, kicking at the fallen shelves on the floor. I'd known that my father and Judy were gone, that everything but this one overlooked island was gone, but I wanted to kick Jesse Santos.

"Look, I know how you feel," he said. "My wife and my kids were in L.A. It's all gone. It's *all* gone. Oh yeah, there are probably a few little pockets, like us. But it's gone."

"Is Alaska gone?"

Norio had the storeroom door off the hinges.

"My uncle got it with the nerve gas. He made it back home and my Auntie Luz said he was jerking and burning. Could hardly breathe. But he told her some of the tribes got together and hijacked Baghdad's bombs. They tried to bag Jerusalem."

"Kitty Manning," Norio called. He was shaking a small jar and

laughing. It was a baby food jar full of nails. He held up his palm—
wait—and went out the back door.

I put the jar in Jesse's hands. He shook out a few nails. "Not very
long ones," he said. His voice was shaking.

"Motives hardly matter, considering the outcome," I said, gesturing in the dark at the outcome: black sky, bodies, ashes. "But
why?"

"Only too simple," Jesse said. "Jerusalem's the number three
holy site. You know how all those boundaries got blurred in the
mess after the war. Anyway, Mecca and Medina are already
Moslem. So they want number three. So they go after Israel.
Simple. All the rest is collateral damage, as the military would
say."

"So then what? Israel hits back?"

"My uncle said that someone bombed Volgograd. They blamed
Israel, although I doubt it. That was probably a set-up. But once
you hit Russia, the United States gets dragged in, and it's all up."
He snapped his fingers. "The world zaps itself into oblivion."

"All in the name of religion," I said.

"Religion? Don't kid yourself. Religion has nothing to do with
it."

I thought of a holy man dousing his saffron robes with gasoline.

"After my uncle died, my auntie took his shoes off him and tried
to close his eyes and straighten him out, and pretty soon she's
twitching and crying that she's burning up, and then she's dead,
too." He was shaking. "Me, I'm freezing. Can you cover me up?"

I draped the shirt and the pink sweater over his chest again. His
skin was hot and damp.

"It wasn't religion," he said. "It was the whole organization of
the whole world. Everything depended on permanent prepara-
tions for war. If it didn't happen on purpose, it would've happened
by accident."

He sat up and flung the clothes off. "The U.S. alone accidentally
launched nuclear missiles at least four times. My uncle told me."

"That's hard to believe," I said. "We would have heard about it."

"I'm burning up," Jesse said. He waved his arms. "I'm freezing cold."

"Shhh, just lie back," I said.

"No!" he yelled suddenly. "I was just staying here. You did it."

For an instant, I thought Samuel had reappeared.

I heard Norio shut the back door. Jesse was out of his head again. Was it possible that all the while I'd been living my little life—analyzing and abiding my mother, looking for the sensation to connect me—the country was launching missiles? I thought of the gasoline-drenched monk changing his mind. All around him the faithful struck matches. I remembered reading a headline about "armstalks" and seeing arm stalks. We all knew about the hundreds of thousands of nuclear warheads in the world, the thousands of satellites, packing their loads like huge mayflies around the earth, the combat aircraft, the subs and the warships, and all the armed human fleets, the bases and the installations, the war games, the parades, defense budgets, arms makers and sellers and buyers, underground testing, the military-industrial complex. All the words had become background chatter, in the news but not really news, as we aimed the remote control and switched to a movie, as we steamed the spinach and broiled the skinless chicken and splurged on the super-deluxe pizza only once a month, as we skimmed the front page and read the horoscope and the funnies, as we shook our heads about political corruption and the greenhouse effect and other countries' spats that festered and erupted like boils, as we gathered clothes for a dead mother and wrote thank-you's for funeral casseroles, as we made our money and worried about paying off American Express and made our love, raked our brown leaves in the fall, walked the winter beach and watched the bright gray water toss chunks of ice.

"Kitty Manning," Norio said.

He had the door laid flat. He drew his finger across it and then began puncturing the imaginary line with a nail and rock. He handed me a nail and another rock, and I started pounding holes at the other end. When we had a line of punctures across the thin wood, he set the door on a pair of crates. He shrugged and smiled—here goes nothing—and jumped lightly onto the door. It cracked neatly on the dotted line.

Though I bent many nails trying to pound them in with my rock, I finally got a board nailed to the wooden frame of the front window. When Norio got the rear window boarded, the shop was totally dark. He lit a thick white candle. I wished that I could talk to him. He was too young to remember firebombed Tokyo. He had a round face with a small straight nose, black whiskers covered his chin, and the corners of his mouth dipped at exactly the same angle as his eyes. Perhaps he'd been taught that destroyed Hiroshima provided the face-saving reason for surrender. He looked dearly familiar, like someone I must have known in Chicago. He looked at my face in the candlelight, sadly, knowingly.

"*Ashita*," he said.

"*Ashita?*" I repeated.

"*Hai,*" he said, and smiled wryly.

The word was meant to be significant, or perhaps only some comfort. I knew it wasn't an object he could point to or an action he could demonstrate. What abstraction could he offer in the dimness of Lim Bong's boarded-up shop? What would he have been able to say except that this was what it all had come to, this immolation?

The little brown goat was stepping over the shelves on the floor, and Cimarron followed him, high-stepping too. The shop floor was littered with goat droppings.

"Come on, pups," I said. "We'd better do some yard duty while we can still get outside."

Dark winds whipped the trees in all directions. The dog and I squatted close to the wall. Rain hit us in splatting bursts.

Samuel stepped around the corner. "Let me get downstream," he said.

Quickly I pulled up my pants. "Caught in the act. How embarrassing."

He gave me his guileless smile and unbuttoned his camouflage pants. He urinated against the corner of the shop, then walked through the wind and marked the back corner. I followed him all around Lim Bong's. In the old world, men had always stopped on hikes to pee against trees, while women had ducked behind bushes only when they couldn't hold it until the trail-head outhouse. Perhaps in the new world, instinct would swell in us and consciousness shrink to an appendix. I watched Samuel tuck himself back in. We would have no need of shame. I wanted to pull him down to the ground behind the rattling shop and fling out my arms amidst the flying leaves and earth while he took me.

When I opened the door, the candle blew out behind Norio's cupped hand.

"Help," I said. "I can't see a thing." I reached for Samuel and got the waistband of his pants, and with my hand on Cimmie's back, I let her lead us to the counter. Jesse lay still. I put my hand on his face. His skin was heated and sweating.

"Don't get too attached to him," Samuel said.

"Shhh," I said, though Jesse didn't seem conscious. "You think he's not going to make it?" I whispered.

"If the leg doesn't make it, he's not going to make it."

"Even if we have to amputate, maybe we can find some antibiotics. Maybe we can get into the base hospital. We can save him."

Samuel was silent.

I was exhausted, but I didn't think Samuel would approve of my lying on the floor with Jesse and Norio.

"Should we try to get some sleep while we can?" I said. "Jesse said the storm is going to get a lot worse."

"Jesse said, Jesse said."

"Yeah, well, we're going to want Jesse Santos around. He *knows* this island. He *knows* these storms. He's spent his life here. You and I, we're just tourists."

I thought that Samuel was jealous, the way a man might wish he could catch chicken pox and crawl into bed next to his sick child and let his wife nurse them both.

"Over here," Samuel said, leading me to the corner opposite the enclosure. "Don't sit yet. I've got a poncho liner in my pack."

He spread a light nylon cloth and we sat, leaning side by side against the wall. He had the sheathed rifle against his leg. My arms and legs were rough with scabs, my lips were swollen and sore, and my head throbbed. I felt battered and weary, yet satisfied, as if I'd worked long and well. Now I would have to fight only the typhoon, and once we survived, we'd clear the debris and live.

"Tell me what we'll do after the storm's over," I said.

He had a delicate odor of brine—not sweat, but as if his essence were salt. I wondered if my senses were growing more acute in the dusk. Did testosterone have an odor?

I moved my head against his shoulder. His shirt felt as clean and soft as a baby's blanket. Rain hit the walls in bursts, and the wind rattled the boards. I pulled the poncho liner over my legs and stroked Cimarron. It was almost over.

"I told you I was looking for you," Samuel said. "I was expecting you. Now I have to see what the typhoon is going to do. I told you I am Flood. We'll see what's left."

I was half-asleep. "And then we go forth and multiply," I said.

He stiffened and then stroked my shoulder. "You got it, my lady."

I didn't tell him that I couldn't get pregnant. Before, I had been deficient, and I'd thought carnality would bring me to life. But no one's vitals could infuse me. Now I carried my own seed.

"Can we please name the first boy Pedro?" I said. Pedro would live his long life here, catching rock crabs, climbing thin trunks to the crown of palm leaves and tossing down the coconuts, and he would finally have his own wake and be carried along in the old planet's diurnal turning. All this was pure sentimentality, I knew, but I felt rocked by the storm, and I hardly tried to make sense of the rise and fall of Samuel's slow words.

"I named myself," he said. "Flood."

After technical school, he said, he put Tanô at the top of his dream sheet, and because not many actually requested the armpit of the Pacific, he'd done two years' duty here. He'd been a Corrosion Control Specialist.

"What's that?" I asked. "Sounds like a censor. Or thought police."

"*Thought* police? As in Commies and Fascists? Not hardly. It's just removing corrosion from metals—aluminum, titanium, like that. Painting, too. You have to know where to use latex or polyurethane or whatever." He shifted, and I opened my eyes. "We worked on all kinds of different weapons and systems. B-52Ds. KC-135s. F-16As. Minuteman II missiles. You name it."

I thought of the contorted yellow-and-orange splotched bodies on the base. "How'd you make it?" I said. "I saw the base got hit with chemical weapons." I closed my eyes against the image of Samuel's long body convulsing on the ground.

"Wasn't on the base," he said. "I was stationed here years ago. I only just came back. I was in Achung when it hit."

After he'd got out of the air force, he told me, he'd gone back home to Kentucky. "Ma drug me to church twice a week and Daddy got me to painting tractors. What a life. See, in the military, you just climb the ladder. Third class, second class, first class. Like grades in school. Eighth grade, ninth grade. And then when you get out there's no more ladder."

He was silent. "I'm listening," I said, though I was nearly asleep. I didn't care what he said. I only wanted the thrum of his voice against my cheek.

"All those jerks back home just plod around in their little circles. Buck bales for their daddies or get ragged on by the foreman at the factory for $5.08 an hour. Go drink beer or pick up some whore.

Hose down the pickup on a Sunday. Watch the game. What a life. Circles or a short ladder, it don't matter."

I wondered if I'd have had anything to do with Samuel before. In the new world, grammar wouldn't matter. I didn't think he'd had much education, but sometimes his language was oddly formal, as if he were reciting. I was sure that I would have felt the same compulsion to touch him before.

"The Baptists were the same thing," he said. "Once a month the preacher comes by to give you hell, and the rest of the time some biddy reads you a lesson from *The Messenger.* The whole idea is don't ask no questions, just pant for Heaven. I used to read the Bible, though. I used to read the Revelation. Over and over I read the Revelation. Man, that guy must have been using. A lamb with seven horns and seven eyes. A star with the name of Wormwood. Locusts with hair like a woman's and scorpion tails."

"Pretty weird stuff," I said.

"Yeah, but here's the thing. It's weird but I got thinking it was true. All those plagues were coming. All that fire and smoke. I kept reading it over and over. 'Alas, alas, for the great city, in one hour she has been laid waste.' All that blood and smoke and fire was God's judgment."

"I guess it did come true, too," I said. "But you can't blame God."

"No, it's because everybody is so wicked."

Samuel eased me down and pulled the poncho liner over me. The bloody rain beat on the wood, and the wind, heavy with smoke, reeled between the trees and our walls.

12

The first time Daniel left, it was the details of our life that I missed. After Daniel kicked Warren and walked out, the moaning man on the floor had become instantly repugnant.

"Drive me to the emergency room," he moaned.

"You'll live," I said. I couldn't imagine how I'd ever desired him. I sat on the double bed and gave him a half hour to recover. I wouldn't cry until he'd gone. "Get out," I said.

Once he'd staggered out the door, I strode from room to room crying with my mouth open, flinging my arms up and down in openhanded supplication. *What have you done, you fool, you idiot,* I said aloud, *what has stupid, corrupt Kitty done now?*

The rest of the day, I kept seeing the details of our life—the tin cookie jar we'd bought for the dogs' Milk-Bones, the slat that had fallen from the bed frame again, the Indian rug, our dusty turntable, the cup of pens on the kitchen counter. I walked from room to room caressing objects. The rest of the day and the evening, I kept remembering the details of the man—the way he'd reach around to tuck his favorite yellow shirt into his pants, the pair of dimples in his flat buttocks, his gesture of pushing back his hair. I thought of his skin against me at night. Already I missed his lean, fastidious body, his exacting ways, even his moods. I wanted him to sit in the dark backyard, sunk in a mood, so I could show him that I'd learned to let him be. In the dusk, I sat on the back step and wept. *You're as moody as my mother,* I'd told him, *but she at least had PMS as an excuse.* But I must have chosen him and perhaps abetted his

215

moodiness precisely because it was like my mother's. I thought then that I must have wanted uncertainty, that expectancy must have seemed more desirable than satisfaction.

Daniel returned the next day.

"I was wrong," I told him plaintively. Wrong to need to seduce, wrong to believe I knew Daniel so thoroughly, wrong to desecrate our union, wrong to deny the details and the satisfaction of our present life.

At school, Warren cornered me, intent on the story, ready to carry on now that Daniel had left me.

"Stay away from me," I said. "Your presence offends me."

"Hey," he said. "Hey, it wasn't my fault."

"I know, I know, I know it was all my own doing," I said. "But I loathe you."

Daniel and I didn't talk about my guilt or his forgiveness. We returned temporarily, shyly to our life.

Now that Daniel was dead, it was the intact man I missed. The details were gone or irrelevant. He was more than an aggregate of detail, more than a composition of what I thought I knew about him. I had ruined our marriage. I'd known Daniel only as much as he'd known me. He'd never have believed that I'd been faithless to my own integrity rather than to him. Faithless because I saw only my scattered selves. Before my mother died, she knew I loved her, and still there was no reconciliation of the loss. Daniel was himself incarnate. My grief was beyond the reminders and the poignancies of details. It did not matter that he looked good in that yellow shirt or that he had no patience for Mahler or that my thumbs had fit perfectly in his dimples when he lay on me. Daniel the embodiment of himself was dead, and the ruin and the grief dwelled incurably in me.

"What was it you found in Alaska?" I asked Daniel before he finally left.

"Oh, lots of great country," he said. "Country like you've never seen." He was on the floor, looking through the record albums.

"I know, but you said there was something there." I was light-headed with fear, as if I were breathing the Alaskan mountains' thin air.

"Oh, I don't know what I meant," he said. "I'm not sure I can tell you. It might be safe in Alaska."

He laughed lightly to pass it off, and returned to the records. I supposed I knew that he'd found something that would let him leave, now that my mother had died.

"Want to go to Alaska?" I asked Chinook. She cocked her head, and we both laughed. I did not ask him again what he'd found in Alaska, and I did not say that I knew he wanted to go. What was unnamed had no existence.

"Did I have this album before we got married?" he asked.

I stayed late on the final day of school to clean my desk for the summer. Now that they didn't have to be there, students kept coming into the classroom. I put them to work sorting books and asked them about their summer plans. They were casual and vague, as if the formless future needed mollifying. They supposed they'd have to find a job or something. They guessed they'd just hang out.

It was after six when I got home. Daniel's car was in the driveway. He'd left no note. The house was intact. But the puppy was yipping, and when I looked out the kitchen window and saw her chasing frantically around the pen by herself, I knew Daniel had taken his dog and left.

I brought the puppy in and fed her. "He shouldn't have let me think everything was all right," I told her. She lay in front of her dish, chomping nuggets. We'd always laughed at the way she lay down to eat. I'd known, I supposed, that all could not be forgiven, that the peace of the last three weeks had been solicitude for my grief and the virtue of having seen me through the dying and the relief of his decision.

That night I slept hard, woke in the early morning only when the puppy pawed me, and after I'd let her out, slept again until

217

mid-morning. During the short hot days I took the dog for numb walks and fed us both and stared at the television. When the phone rang, I stood in the backyard until it quit. I returned to the double bed early. My sleep was opaque and dense, too blind and close for any flickering memories or any shifting dreams. One day there was a registered letter, and I signed for it but I didn't read it.

I was still narcotized, staring at every page of the *Tribune* that still appeared on the front walk every day, when I saw an ad recruiting teachers for a Micronesian island. I couldn't go to Alaska. I hadn't believed anybody would launch missiles, but Daniel had tried for safety from bombs and perhaps from me, and an island might be my own safe place. I didn't even get out the atlas to find Tanô until I'd made the phone call and filled out the application and been called for the interview. I was still numb, but after all these years I knew how to pump the blood to the cheeks and a smile to the mouth, how to stand straight in the ironed body, how to simulate interest and hope, and so I examined the pictures of palm trees and beaches and laughing brown children, and I answered the questions, and I was hired.

"We'll arrange the flight," the man said. I wasn't sure if I'd have been able to follow through, even though there was nothing left to flee, if the tickets hadn't arrived. "We'll have someplace for you to stay. Apartments are expensive but there are families you could board with, or other teachers you could room with. Whatever's your pleasure, just let us know."

"I'll need the apartment," I said. I couldn't fake it all the time.

"There's only one thing," I said when he stood.

"Oh no," he said. "Here it comes. There's always something."

"I'm taking my dog."

"Is that all?" he said. "It's hardly ever that simple. Seems like everybody's got a motive for going. I'm glad your only problem is a dog. Sometimes I wonder why nobody wants to go just to live on a tropical island. A paid vacation."

"Well, I'm not running away from anything. Except maybe another Chicago winter."

He smiled. "The dog'll have to be quarantined for three months."

"What's the island like?" I said. See? I don't have motives, I'm not running.

"Let me take you out to dinner tonight," he said. "I'll tell you about it."

"Oh well, I'd better not," I said. "There isn't much time left." I hadn't really seen him. He was only the interviewer.

"I haven't even been there myself, anyway," he said.

On the long flight from Honolulu to the island, I began to emerge from the stupor, and details sprang up like the pricks of sensation as a deadened limb awakened. I didn't really see the man in the seat next to mine, but I saw the article in the flight magazine open on his tray: "Extra Virgin Olive Oils." I had a window seat, but I saw only a wash of blue and white, featureless below the plane. When I left my seat to go to the bathroom, I caught pricks of conversations.

"That's my dream—to set up a Middle East office for Burger King," a man said.

As I waited for a free cubicle, a woman said, "I don't even know the man." She was crying.

A man spoke: "And you bought a wedding dress?"

"Why do you think I'm so upset?" she said.

Back in my window seat, I still didn't see the man beside me, but I saw his unopened book: *Catechist Guide and Resource Book, Level II: Of Water and the Spirit*. Level I, the cover said, was *Be Born Again*. I didn't see the man but I heard his steady breathing, with glossy little pops as the breath cleared his lips. I slept and woke, numb and prickling, and the plane carried me straight into the sunrise. I imagined I could see meridian lines on the bright sea, great circles around the earth. We'd crossed the dateline, and skipped a day, and landed on the island tomorrow.

Tanô's air was so hot and moist it felt supersaturated, as if the sky might condense and run on the inside of its glass. The palm trees rose straight and held their fans high and still. I looked back at the Air Micronesia plane—Air Mike, the stewardess had said affectionately—to see if the freight was being unloaded, and then I followed the other passengers into the airport. We waited a long time for the single conveyor to move our baggage to us.

"It's back to island time again," some woman said.

"Pretty soon you'll be glad of it, too," another answered.

A little girl wearing a pink skirt and cowboy boots kept saying, "Mommy, look at me." Every couple minutes she said, "Mommy, look at me."

I hadn't brought much to the island, just some cotton clothes and my school materials. I'd boxed up our dishes and linens, our books and records, our leftover clothes—my winter sweaters and coats, Daniel's summer shorts and polo shirts—and left it all at Hap's Mini-Storage. I found that Daniel had taken some of the records and tapes, the good leash, and the file folder containing the official papers, including his passport and our marriage certificate. Had he taken it so he could file for divorce? Or so that I couldn't? He'd left the carton of all his issues of *PetroWorld*.

None of the bills came to the house after he left. Daniel was a man in charge of details. I arranged with a realtor to rent the house furnished and send the checks to Daniel at the *PetroWorld* office. Someone would forward them, I supposed. Had he thought I would live on in our house all summer while he tried to pay for his absence? I cleared out what he'd left in our account and packed up my dog and left everything else.

A tropical island was like hunger. The slick-paper photographs matched the fantasy—blue lagoons, silken waterfalls, natives in outriggers, long white beaches edged with palms, papaya, and passionfruit, bud-breasted girls in grass skirts, toucans in jungles

220

green beyond reality—just as the clean polished stomach imagined a still life of eggplant and onion, or a sideboard of thin meats, cheese, and croissants. Just as the smoothed skin imagined the strokes of the next man. While the mouth still watered, before the stomach began to devour itself, before the seduction, the slickpaper island was still attainable, still waited within the wash of blue. But then the limp vegetables and leftover fish were reheated and devoured, along with yesterday's drying, lard-frosted cake. Or even if the oiled skillet was heated until it popped a drop of water and the whisked eggs were poured in and bubbled and settled perfectly, before the omelet could be eaten it cooled and toughened, and the onions and mushrooms softened under the yellow grease, and the cheese grew a crust over its thick liquid flesh. The stomach was glutted, the body was cloyed with ejaculate.

On the island, the snakes years ago imported to eat the rats instead had devoured most of the birds. The reefs had been dynamited and the coarse-sand beaches were littered with disposable diapers. Everyone had donned T-shirts bearing mottoes or advertisements or flocked sunsets. And even without people, the shallow bay was full of black-spined sea urchins and the jungles were meshed with viscous webs. Only underwater did the body skate like a ray, only underwater did the blue angelfish and the rainbow parrot fish and the lionfish and the gorgonia and the brain coral embody themselves, only underwater did the flying blue fantasy survive the consummation. But on earth we waited tantalized on the beach, for the perfect red-gold sunset and the green flash, until the sky's lining devoured itself and the sea absorbed nothing, and we were left with appetite prolonged into pain. Or we photographed the beaches and tipped the rigged-up native dancers and glutted ourselves with tours and exotica until we were gorged. For humans there was no present, only anticipation or surfeit. All along, perhaps, this had been my deficiency. And so it must have been for all of us. Only creatures lived in the moment. Perhaps we began to remember Eden when we entered the amniotic sea, where all light was refracted for us; but on land we could only yearn for Eden or in the unrefracted glare consume it to death.

Most of the teachers at the high school were Chamorro, but many didn't have teaching certificates, and the government was recruiting stateside teachers. The few other haoles always ate lunch together, segregating themselves as imperialists always did, forming their own compound in the midst of the brown skins. They welcomed me in. I met David Harper, who didn't count with the haoles because he'd come to the island twenty years ago as a Peace Corps volunteer and married a Chamorra. He had three stylized dolphins tattooed on his arm.

"I've been here since before there was dirt," he said, grinning. "I've gone native." He said the words with mock horror.

I met Alexandria Lipscomb, a young woman with long very dark hair and bangs framing her fat face. She'd come the year before from Indiana to teach math. She was the sort of woman about whom everybody said, She'd be really pretty if she wasn't fat. I liked her crisp speech, but she always made self-deprecating remarks and noted her fat so often that I felt virtuous and slightly guilty. Her face was bright and self-conscious, and she smiled as if she were bravely holding back tears, and in her company I felt the pain of being in her body.

I learned that *haole* was a derogatory word on Hawaii, to describe a white non-Polynesian, and that it originally meant "without breath," but I was assured by the other haoles, the term was neutral on Tanô. Even Clarence, the black reading teacher from California, was a haole on this island.

The school was wood with tin roofing. All of the classrooms opened onto a center courtyard. Guards with walkie-talkies and nightsticks roamed the grounds and the courtyard. My room was whitewashed, with louvered windows, and black butterflies flew over our heads. When it rained, the students came in wearing turtleneck shirts. "It's so cold, *mees*," they'd say, and I'd turn off the fan that sat on an extra desk at the front of the room. Geckos ran and stopped, ran and stopped on the walls.

When the louvers were half-closed in the morning, the sunlight fell in sliced squares on the cement floor. Once when I was correcting an island lapse—adding an *s* to words like *furniture, scenery,* and *stuff*—a huge black lizard suddenly appeared in a square of light on the floor, and I jumped away. The kids laughed until I was embarrassed.

"*Hilatai*, miss," one boy said.

"Monitor lizard, miss," Juvy said. She was from the Philippines, and I'd learned her name right away because she might well have been the brightest student I'd ever had.

The narrow body and the long skinny tail on the floor was the shadow of a lizard crawling from window to window. It must have been three feet long. Its head was narrow as a snake's. Its toes were long and elegantly curved. As it crawled from window to window, I watched its shadow ripple on the classroom floor. The shadow of its forked tongue flicked out.

Of course in the beginning I'd meant to enlighten the natives. These kids listened to heavy metal on the ghetto blasters they bought at the Tick Tock next door to the school, they wore Budweiser T-shirts, and they could break-dance better than any Chicago kid. But I would introduce them to poetry and all the graces of English. They could keep their chests bare, I'd thought at first, but they would read Steinbeck.

"Hey, you're not a missionary," Alexandria told me.

Every second hour, I'd begin with a drill on pronunciation. "Says," I'd say. "Not *sāys*."

The second-hour boys would chant *sez* and snort at Rogelio Torres who still said *sāys*. But reading aloud or talking to each other, they all said *sāys*.

"Hey, miss," Frankie Reyes said, one second hour before the bell rang, "how do you get forty Cambodians into a shoe box?"

"We don't tell ethnic jokes in this classroom," I said.

"You tell them it'll float," Frankie said.

They called each other "dude" and "brown," but they were indulgent of me and ingenuous.

"My auntie had this coconut crab that was a strange color," one boy told me, "and peoples was afraid to eat it because it might be a taotaomona. So they gives it to this other brown and he cooks it and the next day he breaks out in real bad hives."

"Well, it could be a coincidence," I said. "Or maybe there was something wrong with that crab."

"No, it was a taotaomona," he said.

When Malcolm Yarrow drove me around the island, showing me the base at the north end and the thatched huts and the black-sand beach at the south, I asked him, "How can these people be Roman Catholic and still believe in ghosts and evil spirits? Tao-taomonas and all that."

"If a mother dies giving birth," Malcolm said, "the baby is draped in red to keep the mother from taking the baby with her. Sometimes the mother's seen watching, for years even, with her arms outstretched. She wants to take her child. I don't know."

"That's just primitive spook stuff," I'd said.

"I don't know," Malcolm said. "Well, my mother didn't die in childbirth, but she died when I was young. Maybe she wanted to take me too."

"No, she wanted you to live," I'd said glibly.

"My father was with I.B.M.," he said. "You know what that stands for? I've Been Moved. She probably just couldn't keep up long enough to snatch me."

"Or you wore lots of red," I said.

I hadn't really wanted to know Malcolm's story. If he'd had a vagrant, motherless childhood, then I'd had a mutable, insecure mother—who'd also had a mother who'd rejected her, maybe for

224

the permutations of her own mother. I'd wanted to live on the island clean, as if it were indelicate even to have had a past.

Outside my rooms at the Two Lovers' Apartments was a banana tree; in the evenings, grading papers at the table by the window, I'd listen to the wind flap the banana leaves like an awning. One Saturday morning the landlord chopped the tree down with his machete. It wasn't producing bananas, he said, but the new tree would. I thought he meant to plant another tree. But two hours later, a thin stalk had risen a half inch in the center of the chopped base. Every day the stalk rose several more inches.

"That's the way to live," I said to Malcolm. "Lop off the past and start again, all tender and new."

"Nobody comes to an island like this without a past," he said.

"What does that mean?" I said. "You want to know what an evil rotten person I was back in the world?"

He said, "Hey, I just meant everybody has some sort of past. That's all." He pointed to the pale shoot rising from the banana tree's old trunk. "That's just a tree. You English teachers are always looking for symbolism."

A month after school had begun, Alexandria Lipscomb came to my apartment. She'd walked from the house where she boarded.

"They put a bomb in my car," she said. Her face was red but she wasn't crying.

"A bomb? Who would put a bomb in your car?"

"I was taking the back road home and the car started sounding kind of funny, as if something was dragging underneath. So I stopped and got out. Luckily I stepped back, intending to look underneath. Then it blew up."

"But are you all right?" I asked. She'd lost her expression of vulnerable pain. She still enunciated carefully, but she sounded numb, and I wondered if she could be in shock.

"When did this happen? Let me take you to a doctor. Did you call the police?"

"Just drive me to the airport," she said.

The car had probably quit burning by now. She thought some of her students had done it. A group of boys was mad at her for giving them zeroes on a test. She'd caught them cheating. But it might have been anyone. She wasn't trusting anybody.

"At least stay here tonight," I said. "You can't fly out now, anyway." We all knew Air Mike's schedule.

"No," she said. "The Untalan family is gone right now, so first I want you to take me back to the house to pick up my luggage, and then take me to the airport. I'm getting out of here." Her face was very red, and she was shaking. "And don't you tell anyone until I'm gone."

"Alexandria, you're being paranoid," I said.

"Paranoid? Paranoia is a *delusion* that people are out to get you. I told you: they put a bomb in my car. They blew up my car and they meant to kill me."

I drove her to the house where she'd been rooming. We carried out her blue leather suitcases, moldy after a year in a closet, and then waited in the empty airport.

"You don't have to stay here," she said.

The flight left, or was scheduled to leave anyway, at six in the morning. She looked terrified in the flimsy, dim airport, and I stayed with her all night. We finally slid down in the low-backed seats and slept.

I couldn't believe any of the kids would try to kill Alexandria Lipscomb. If there was a bomb, it must have been placed in her car at random by someone who'd broken into the faculty parking lot to defy the gate guards. Alexandria escaped the island a month before Indiana and the rest of the country were bombed. I didn't believe any of my students would ever want to hurt me. Alexandria told me not to be a missionary, and I hadn't meant to be, no more than any teacher seeking to convert the students to the subject. I thought of Alexandria in Indiana, staying with her parents and jerking awake as her car exploded beside her again and again.

"She shouldn't have let them intimidate her," one of the Chamorro teachers said.

"There's been a nuclear war. You're in a bomb shelter," I told them, "and there's food, water, and air enough for only ten of you. Fifteen of you will have to go."

Then I'd assign parts: You're a fifty-seven-year-old doctor, you're a mechanic, you're the mechanic's wife, you're the mechanic's six-year-old retarded son, you're a nun. . . .

When I taught the speech unit, I used the role-playing exercise to ease students' fears of speaking to a group and to illustrate group dynamics.

The students would argue and consider and defend. One or two would always decide to sacrifice themselves for the group's survival. Once, after the group had all agreed and the losers were shown the shelter's exit, they realized they'd saved ten men and no women.

"Oh well, we don't deserve to carry on," one girl said, "if we're stupid enough to blow ourselves away."

"Yeah, but those poor guys," someone answered, "they won't have no fun at all."

I hadn't played the game with the island students, and I probably never would have. With all the factions and loyalties—the extended families, the village rivalries, the kids from Yap and Guam and Truk and the Philippines and China, the occasional military kid—the school's guards probably would have had to quell the group dynamics with their nightsticks. Even if Rogelio Torres had played a thirty-year-old doctor whose specialty was nuclear medicine, he would have been booted out of the bomb shelter because he was fat Rogelio Torres. Anyway, the island had already seemed a capsule, though the ones inside had been randomly chosen.

But in Chicago, the students played their assigned roles, and parents tried to save children, husbands refused to stay unless their wives were chosen, too. Sometimes nuns were excluded unless they agreed to bear children, prostitutes were saved while politicians and professors and a baby with AIDS were condemned, old people gave themselves up. The Chicago kids played their parts soberly, believing in the war; yet they left the classroom at the end of the period relieved that it had been a game—like the military's simulated real world exercise situation—and reassured by their thoughtful choices. If it happened, the right ones would survive.

Some people believed that talking about it would tempt God to make it happen, cross yourself, knock on wood, quit that or your face will freeze that way. But most of us believed that looking at the horrors would make it impossible. You can't hug children with nuclear arms, the bumper stickers said. So we discussed Ground Zero and watched the miniseries and read the survivalist paperbacks, almost as if they were reenactments that we must remember lest history repeat itself, but that we had somehow survived. The details became incantatory. The students left the classroom reassured—see, it was just a game. Wake up, honey, you were having a nightmare. It was just a bad dream. Now go back to sleep.

From the Two Lovers' Apartments, I could look east to the ocean. Before school started, before I'd bought the old brown car, before I'd met Malcolm Yarrow, I watched the ocean. I carried my kitchen chair outside to read and watch the ocean over the sword grass on the hill. The leaves of the grass were light green and sharp. Now and then a couple of boys with machetes cut it down. From the hill, the sea's color changed, but it was always pale—gray, metallic blue, white at midday, flower blue. Some hot days the sea and the sky merged, and sometimes the sea's convex meniscus made the horizon a white or a Prussian blue band.

Sometimes I covered my arms and legs and face with sunscreen and hiked down the dirt-coral path to the beach. Here the water was brighter, clear and hot turquoise within the reef, bright blue deepening to royal blue beyond the reef. I watched the waves curl and break as if they were fire. I've come out of the blue, I thought, and though no man watched me, I felt my weight and my substance as my feet pressed into the wet sand.

Or, I thought, I have vanished into the blue, and the hollow Kit Manning has lost her rattling self-consciousness and is filling with blue light. I was sweaty and dizzy in the heat.

At five o'clock I climbed back up the hill to the apartments. The moon in the blue sky was the same texture and the same distance as the sketches of clouds. The sky graduated from light blue at the horizon to bright backlit blue around the moon to deep blue at the zenith. The moon was gibbous and so thin that the blue sky showed through it. My mother and Daniel and the old sins were lost in the blue.

In the underwater pictures Malcolm took with his yellow Sea & Sea camera, I looked bug-eyed and white. My breasts were pushed together and flattened by the buoyancy compensator vest.

"I look like I've got a pair of flounders in my b.c.," I told Mal.

We'd ride out in an outboard. The spray was cold on my sunburned skin. Mal would drop the anchor onto the sand for a shallow reef dive or hook it onto a wreck. After the dive, we'd haul ourselves back into the boat and shed the heavy gear. We'd sit for a few minutes, adjusting to the air, and then we'd open the iced beer and cruise back with the salt water drying on our skin and gummy hair. Before and after the dives, I was a human creature, worrying that Mal would notice that I'd forgotten to shave my legs, enjoying the fatigue of the sun and the cold beer in my dry, salty mouth.

Underwater, though, after the initial panic of hitting the water and gulping air, I floated down head first, easily clearing my ears, and felt as if I'd grown pectoral fins like a stingray's. I flew along the bottom, close to the scroll coral, the crown-of-thorns starfish, the gorgonia and the sea fans, the fields of staghorn coral with the flocks of tiny cardinalfish whisking into the interlocked horns. I finned a little higher to avoid the fire coral. I somersaulted, I pulled Mal into a double somersault, I pulled down his trunks and flew away. I took a plastic bag out of my b.c. pocket and fed crackers and Vienna sausages to the butterflyfish, the blue chromis, the triggerfish, and the smiling blue tangs. Malcolm poked at a puffer until it inflated. I held it and looked into its orange eyes and let it float away.

In the harbor we wore gloves and sorted through the debris. We found a heavy white bowl and two thick handleless mugs. We took them up and chipped and scraped the coral off. They were World War II Navy dishes, Mal said. I used my mug for a pencil holder on my desk at school.

Inside the wrecks, the water was clear and coppery until one of us stirred up the silt. We floated down rusted ladders into holds. The hulls were crusted with coral like lichen. In the wheelhouse we'd often find a lionfish, a body of orange, black, and white stripes with a halo of striped feathery spines. Under one wreck a moray emerged, opened its narrow jaws at us, and slid back. Once we saw a shark motionless on the sandy bottom. I thrust my thumb up at Mal and started as smoothly as I could for the surface, but he grabbed my ankle and pulled me down. NURSE SHARK, he wrote on his slate.

"At least I wasn't the shark this time," I said later. I told Malcolm about the persistent remora that had attached itself to my belly when Daniel and I dove in Florida.

"I don't think I'd panic like that now," I said.

I might have come to love Malcolm Yarrow. Underwater, we were naked and guileless, only as sentient as porpoises. Sometimes underwater I felt corporeal, immersed in the continuum, simple as a lionfish.

13

I woke with tears on my face. Sweating and shivering, I lay sprawled on the poncho liner. The wind shook the doors in their frames. I lay still and listened to the voices.

"Man, I have got to piss like a racehorse," someone said. "What do you suppose that means, anyway? Piss like a racehorse."

"Ain't you ever seen a horse let go?" It was Samuel Flood's voice. The other had to be Jesse. I remembered his addition to the Pedro's Wake sign: *I am alive.*

"No, I haven't," Jesse said, his voice gentle. "But why a *race* horse, that's what I don't get."

"Who gives a flying fuck?"

My skin itched all over my body, but I lay still, spread-eagled. This was the way Samuel would have had me, I thought.

"How I am going to hit that hole?" Jesse said. He hadn't seen a horse because he belonged here. I heard my students say, How I am doing? I am getting an *A* in your class, miss? I was glad to hear the island rhythm in Jesse's voice.

I watched Norio go back and forth between the enclosure and the front door. He bent and sluiced something under the door. The smell of hot urine mixed with a fatty pink potted-meat smell, and I thought that Jesse must be peeing in the Spam cans.

"I'm the one who makes the floods around here," Samuel said. He burst into a high laugh that rose in yips as I imagined a hyena would have laughed.

"What's that mean? You make floods. You're a racehorse?"

231

I didn't know what Jesse did then, but I heard Norio giggle and Samuel say something in a low voice.

With the poncho liner over my numb shoulders, I leaned over the counter. The three men jumped and the little goat bleated.

"Je-sus, I thought you were a ghost," Jesse said. "Don't do that. Not until we're a little more used to the dead all around us, anyway."

"I'm not a ghost yet," I said.

Norio lit a candle and a stream of wind immediately put it out. He relit it and kept his palm cupped around it. Later we would have to worry about finding more matches or maybe keeping a constant fire.

"Later," I said. "I actually thought about later."

"I'm thinking about now," Samuel said. His voice had softened. The rough grammar and the growls were only for Jesse, it seemed. In the first flare of candlelight, he'd looked wild, but his face had melted in the dim light. "Come over here," he said.

A burst of rain hit the side of the building. Water leaked from the boarded windows. I climbed over the cooler, and the four of us sat, with the dog and the goat, in a circle around Norio's candle. We've practically got a manger here, I thought.

"This storm's no banana-bender," Jesse said. "But it won't be too bad. It'll blow some of the scum off. It'll shake a few bones. But I remember Pamela."

I'd already heard about Supertyphoon Pamela. Though the storm had hit fifteen years before, people talked about it as if it had been last year. At the peak, the winds ran at 173 mph for an hour. The eye was eight nautical miles in diameter. Jesse said he saw a tornado pick up a shack, hold it in the air for ten seconds, and throw it down. The sea came far inland and flooded out the southern villages.

"My auntie looked outside for a second and yells, 'My husband's Jeep is climbing up on top of my daughter's car!'"

Norio was watching Jesse as if he understood.

232

Afterwards, Jesse said, roads were all ripped up, everything was flooded, only one store had a generator, there was no electricity or water for two months. There were fishing boats sitting in the Chinese Park.

"Every day there were fights at the ice plant," he said. "Ice was rationed, and there were these long lines. People kept trying to cut in line and then they'd fight."

"I guess we won't have to worry about that this time," I said.

"I wouldn't have had to worry about it that time," Samuel said.

Jesse looked at him silently, benignly.

"They said I was a dreamer," Samuel Flood said. "I saw it coming, that's all. Everything was greed. Greed. You name it— everything that was wrong had its origin in greed. Pollution? Cuts back on profits if we have to dispose of all that factory waste, don't you know. Whole blasted earth's already a giant landfill anyway. Ships cruising for years with nobody who'll take their load of toxic shit. War? Same thing. Give us more, more, more of your oil, oil, oil, and take our democracy in return, want it or not. All those Arabs and Jews blowing each other up: it's my homeland, no it's *my* homeland. People can't even goddamnit stay married to each other for greed. 'Oh I'm so sorry honey-sweetheart,' Martha tells me, 'I just had to see what it'd be like with your old buddy Ronnie.' Everything comes down to greed."

I put my hand on his back and rubbed. "I know," I said. "I know."

"When I saw it coming, I got ready," Samuel said. "All the fools just kept on polishing up their pickups and saying, 'No, no, can't happen here, can't happen to us, why we ain't greedy. This is the U.S. of A.' But me, I remembered this armpit of the Pacific which no one would pay real serious attention to. So I ordered me a year's supply of rations and all the halazone you could want and shipped it to myself. Sent me the Hawken and some other stuff. I am ready, man." He looked belligerently at Jesse. "It's all here, all safe."

233

"Good for you, dude," Jesse said. "Good for you. No greed anywhere around here in evidence, no sir."

"Don't you get righteous, *dude*. If greed was lead, this hunk of rock'd be at the bottom of the Mariana Trench."

"Who blew up my kids and my wife? Who did that? It wasn't the browns on this island, I tell you that."

"You would have. If you'd been farther up the evolutionary scale."

"Some evolution," I said. "Shut up, you guys."

"My leg hurts like hell," Jesse said.

"Maybe that's a good sign," I said. "If it hurts it can't be dead."

I got the bottle of gin and poured more capfuls over the oozing wound.

He began chanting: "Who won the war? Are we all red? *He* don't care as long as he's fed. Oh baby, if it hurts it can't be dead."

Cimarron got up and began beating us with her tail, and Jesse said, "If you wag your tail any harder, you'll throw your ass out of joint."

The dog whined and I took her into the shop. I pointed to the floor. "It's okay," I said. She squatted, looking at me with her guilty eyes rolled back. "It can't be helped," I told her. "It's okay. If the goat can do it, so can you."

Soon it hardly mattered. Water flowed under the front door toward the rear, and then surged in under the back door until it was two inches deep. Rain spurted around the edges of the window boards. As the wind rushed against the shop and then abruptly rushed in another direction, currents swept around my ankles.

Lightning flashed through the cracks, and then the thunder boomed, followed by echoing detonations.

The front door burst open and slammed against the counter, and the adrenaline rushed in me at the report. Horizontal rain swept by the open door.

I heard Samuel calling something in the clamor. He forced the door closed and pushed me against it to hold it. The wind blasted against the door and then reversed direction. The suck pulled the door against the frame until the wood squealed. Samuel was back then, and he nailed a pair of shelf boards across the door.

"Are you all right?" I yelled to Jesse.

Water surged across the room, but the floor behind the counter sloped up, and so far the corner was dry. Jesse and Norio and the dog and the goat huddled against the wall, out of the torrent. Cimmie's ears were back, and so were the goat's, and they looked so much alike, two miserable, trembling animals flanking the men, that I laughed.

"When I die," Jesse yelled, "bury me upside down."

"You're not dying," I yelled back. "But why?"

"So the world can kiss my ass," Jesse yelled.

Norio and I picked up as many nails and pieces of broken baby food jar as we could before the wind could take them again. Samuel held the split door half over the window and Norio pounded it into the frame again with his coral rock. The wind still jolted it, and they hammered shelfboards over it vertically. I pointed to the back door and window, and though the wind hadn't been battering the rear as hard, we nailed more shelfboards over them.

"Goddamn it!" Jesse yelled. Norio and I climbed over the cooler into the compartment behind the counter. I held the dog and stroked the goat's head and side.

"This is not my fault," Jesse said. "None of this is my fault." He laughed, an acrid burlesque of a laugh. "My uncle was with the commander at a civil defense meeting. All the browns were almost disappointed to find out Tanô probably wouldn't be a primary target in a nuclear war."

"Christ," I said, "why would they be disappointed?"

"We weren't all that important." I thought he laughed again, but the thunder sounded, deep and full, and I wasn't sure.

Norio was patting Jesse's shoulder. "*Wakarimasen,*" he said.

"It's not your fault, either," Jesse told him.

The adrenaline was draining away, but I still felt somehow quickened with the typhoon distending around us.

"Is this the eye of the storm?" I asked.

"It's coming," Samuel said. "The flood is coming."

The candle was out but we huddled together behind the counter.

"They thought I was a dreamer," Samuel told us again. "But I read the Revelation and I knew it was coming."

The whole building lurched. The board blew off the window and slammed against the back wall, and the storm swooped into the room, swelling to occupy it with thunder and pumping rain and wind that gathered the Spam cans and the pink sweater and the jar of nails and the packing Styrofoam, eddied, and then drove against the back wall.

"Just reading the news ought to have been enough," I said. "We just didn't believe it could happen."

"I did," Samuel said. "I was told. I'm repainting this guy's Camaro, cherry red, and I hear this deep voice saying something, sounded like 'Blot, blot.' There's nobody from Daddy's garage to Taylorsville, but then I hear it again: 'Blot, blot.'"

"You were dripping paint," Jesse suggested. "Or the Camaro's engine was missing."

"Shut up, you crippled heathen wimp," Samuel said furiously. "You wouldn't know the voice of God if it was tuned into your ass in stereo."

I was glad Samuel couldn't see me in the dark. I was shaking with laughter and with dread. None of my men had been anything but themselves. I'd never known a fanatic.

"The trouble with a zealot," Jesse said, touching my knee in the dark, "is that they've got to have prey. It's no good hearing a voice if everybody else hears it, too."

"I went and found Martha and my boy over at Ronnie Foote's,"

Samuel said. "In spite of she'd dumped me and took my boy. I tell them what 'Blot, blot' meant. It's the Lord saying, 'I will blot out man, whom I have created, from the face of the ground, man and beasts and creeping things and birds of the air, for I am sorry that I have made them.' I looked it up and I've got it down. I *tell* her what's going to happen, and I *tell* her I'm supposed to take my wife and my sons and my sons' wives, and what does she say? 'You ain't got but one son and he's only eleven. If he's got a wife, he's keeping her out behind Ronnie's shed.' 'Shut up, Martha,' I tell her. 'One son'll have to do it. I've got me an ark, so you come on.' 'You're as full of shit as a Christmas turkey,' Martha says. That's what she tells me."

"So Tanô is your ark?" I said. To Jesse, it must have been a solid home, but sometimes to me the island felt insubstantial, an unattached piece of land that could sink or float away at any moment. I didn't really believe that Samuel had been elected.

"If God picked you," I said, "then how come the rest of us survived too?"

"Could be a reason," he said. "You might be the wife. Could be a mistake."

I shivered, and Jesse touched my knee again. I wished the four of us could put our arms around each other and listen to the voice and know we'd been chosen.

"God wouldn't make a mistake, though," Jesse said.

"Hell he wouldn't," Samuel said. "He admitted we were a mistake in the first place. We were wicked. But one way or another, He fixes his fuck-ups."

When the wind lurched and changed direction, I heard Norio moaning.

"He's asleep," Jesse said. "The Japanese don't snore. They moan."

"Poor man," I said. "At least we can talk to each other."

"Wasn't nobody I could talk to in Achung," Samuel said. "But that was the plan."

"What's Achung?" I remembered that he'd said he'd been there when the bombs were dropped.

"Good concrete walls," Samuel said.

"The prison," Jesse said.

Suddenly I was wet. My thighs and my buttocks were cold and wet.

"You were in prison? Why didn't you tell me you were in prison?"

"I was meant to be there," Samuel said. "Maybe you and you and you were accidents. We'll see. But I was meant to be there."

"What'd you do?"

"Nothing. Just shipped over some pistols. That's all. I already had the Hawken, safe and hidden. But I got to thinking it might not be enough. No doubt He got me to thinking. Got me caught and put behind concrete for a month so I could ponder and try to save a couple possible disciples and mostly be protected from His fire."

"What happened to the disciples?" I said.

"The whole place is just blasted. Except for my block. And some of those guys, like this Lujan I'd been talking to, bought the farm anyway. It's like they were heaved against the walls until they were jelly. I got down and breathed next to the floor, but Lujan kept saying, 'Mother Mary, save me, I'm penitent' over and over and screeching. Then that disciple bites the dust."

"I think your flood's here now," Jesse said. We were sitting in an inch of water.

"But look!" I said. The flood flickered and pulsed with tiny lights. I cupped water in my hands and let the phosphorescence stream away.

"The walls were cracked," Samuel said. "But I stayed. I breathed on the floor. The concrete saved me from the poison. I fasted. I saw a whirlwind. It was out to sea and it gathered up water and I knew it would hit. 'Wasn't the fire enough?' I say, and then I hear one clear word: *Flood.* I figure a flood would put out the fires and finish the job, too."

"Who were you before?" I asked.

"Sammy Dillman," he said, low. "But look." He raised a handful of glowing water and let it stream down his arm. "It is the flood come upon the earth."

Cimarron gave a tentative *ah-rup* bark then, and I thought I heard drumming against the back door. The dog growled low and began barking in her deep voice.

"I think there's somebody out there," I said.

The pounding on the door was too regular to be the storm. Samuel climbed over the cooler and I followed. The dog barked behind the barrier.

"Who's there?" I called at the back door. The pounding continued, and Samuel began pulling the boards away. What did I expect to hear, anyway? I'll huff and I'll puff?

When Samuel pulled the door back, three people nearly fell inside, and a wave a foot high rushed in. The burned jungle behind the shop was flooded. Norio was beside me, and together we shut the door against the force of the water. A woman was wailing. Water still flowed under the door. The water to our shins pulsed with phosphorescence. The woman wailed and the wind burst and recoiled against the walls. The doors squealed in their frames and the dog barked. For a moment before I went to the woman, I watched the iridescent lights pulse around my ankles.

In the murk I saw Norio shaking hands with two fat men. I put my arm around the woman's shoulders. She was shivering and her wails died to jerking sobs.

"All right, Cimarron," I called, "that's enough now."

I couldn't see more than the woman's outline. She was hunch-shouldered, bulky and loose as though she'd been solidly fat and recently been ill. Her clothes were soaked.

"I wish we had something dry for you to put on," I said.

239

She shrank under my arm and said something in my ear, but I couldn't understand in the roar of the storm.

"Let's get you to higher ground," I said, and led her toward the counter. "How did you find us? I'm so glad you found us." I was babbling. I thought of my solid mother, flat-chested in her modern coffin, her face slightly disgusted. The phosphorescence flickered in the water and on my legs.

One of the men jumped up on the cooler, awkward and graceful as a fat monkey, and disappeared behind the counter. Cimarron yiped once, shrill, and I ran over to the enclosure. The fat man stood and held his arm out. I could barely see him in the dark.

"Shake hands, *mees*," he said, and trying to look over the counter, I held out my hand.

There was a gun in his hand. I jerked my hand back.

"My God, did you shoot them?" I said. "My God, Samuel, help!"

He put his hand, his gun hand, to his ear: I can't hear you.

I thought then that I'd have heard gunshots even over the storm's howl, and I thought what a naive gesture that was, putting the gun hand to his ear, and I thought of jumping at him. But I couldn't find Samuel and I didn't think Norio knew what was happening, and the other fat man probably had a gun too. Maybe the wailing woman did too.

"What did you do to them?" I yelled, pausing between each word.

"Cold cock," he yelled and pantomimed hitting with the butt of the gun, politely eager to fill me in.

I wondered if he'd cold-cocked the goat as well. The man didn't stop me when I climbed over the cooler. Jesse was leaning against the wall with his head tipped and his mouth open. The floor behind the counter was flooded now. I put my head on Jesse's chest and felt his heart beat against my cheek. Cimarron lay with her face in the water. Her head was bleeding into the water. I got my hands under her wet body and heaved her up on top of the counter. I couldn't stand it. *If you're dead*, I said, *if you're dead* . . .

After all this, after all the bloated bodies, after all the burned jungle, after all the dying, after the cave nothing meant anything, I should be dead too. Nothing could save me. I rolled the heavy wet dog over and put my ear against her chest. I couldn't stand it. I muzzled her with one hand and opened her little front teeth with the other. With my mouth against her wet black lips, I blew. I pushed against her barrel chest. Her legs stuck out as if the joints didn't work.

Then a back leg kicked, and I rolled her on her side. She lay still and wet on the counter. I believed I could feel her side move.

"You're Anthony Joseph Taitano," I said furiously.

"Hey, I don't mean to kill it," he said.

The shop's side walls wrenched, and I felt very heavy. "Samuel!" I yelled. "Samuel Flood, help me." But I couldn't see him. I lifted my heavy right hand and chopped Taitano's wrist. The board from the front window burst past us. I thought Taitano dropped the gun, but I hardly cared. My escapes, the threats, and the rape were past, and I was beyond fear. I was furious and my body was so heavy I could hardly lift my knee, but I raised it and drove it into his groin. My plated knee met the fat flesh, and I felt sick, as if my knee had crashed into soft maggoty meat.

Norio and Rogelio Torres were beside us. Taitano was down in the water, lying on his side with his knees pulled up, and he kept turning his face up out of the water like a swimmer. Norio held the gun in both hands, straight-armed. Raindrops like nails flew horizontally through the window.

"Where's your gun?" I asked Rogelio, thinking that they might have had more than the one shiny gun.

"He gots it, miss," he said, pointing to Norio. "I never gots any gun my own self."

"Samuel?" I asked Norio. "Where's Samuel?"

He said something and swooped his hand toward the door.

The water chopped against Taitano's face and for an instant I wanted to step on his head. I was dizzy. I wanted to put my head between my knees but now my body felt too light to lean over. The boards from the back window burst off and shattered like old fiberglass against the front wall. Water rose in drops from the floor and was sucked out the window like a reverse rainfall.

Norio pushed Rogelio and me to the enclosure. We climbed in, and I hauled the limp dog down from the countertop and held her. I'd forgotten the woman, but she was squatting next to Jesse, rubbing his hands and arms. The little goat stood shaking in the water. Norio tore off all the boards and opened the doors and then joined us. I didn't know if he still had the gun. The doors slammed like shots until they burst off the hinges. We left Taitano on the floor.

I fought my way to the back doorway. "Samuel Flood!" I called again and again. He was gone. He'd decided I wasn't his wife. Or God had recalled him. He was gone.

Norio sat Rogelio on our crate of Lim Bong's typhoon supplies.

"Good choice," I said. I knew he couldn't understand me. "If you sat on it, you and that box could fly to the moon."

The old woman was chanting something, but I couldn't hear words. She's praying, I thought.

We all sat with our heads down as the walls lurched and shook, as the wind and the water rushed in and were sucked out. I pictured the wind and the rain swirled together into frothy whirl-winds that were sucked out like streaming ghosts.

And the dog hadn't moved, but suddenly I knew I was holding a live animal.

After the eye of the typhoon passed, the wind and rain continued for hours, but they felt weak and gentle. The water drained from the shop, and the air lightened. Silvery light seemed to rise from the ground so that the sky was a spectrum, dark above us, descending to grays and then to a shimmering band above the ground.

The shop's storeroom had been ripped off and the rear of the building was open and sagging. The crates of Lim Bong's liquor were gone, vanished as if they'd been airlifted out. One unbroken, full bottle of Smirnoff's vodka stood upright on the open concrete floor.

Most of the trees, burned and unburned alike, were down.

Cimarron was shaky, and she stayed right beside me as if she'd been trained to heel. The fur on the side of her head was stiff with dried blood. Whenever my hand was at my side, she licked it and took it with a soft mouth.

Jesse had revived. In the silvery light, his leg wound still looked red and purple, with fat lips and a brown scab growing between the lips. The old woman stayed behind the counter with him, now and then stroking his arm.

"Did you know her?" I asked Jesse. "Before?"

"No," he said. "Well, one Christmas she did a Nobenan Niño at my auntie's."

"Are you hungry?" I asked her. "We should all eat."

Her short hair, drying now, was dark with a sheen of red like rust, but her face was wrinkled. The skin on her face and arms and legs was mottled as if ragged patches of the brown had been peeled off. She wore a T-shirt that said *Chamorro Dude*; I remembered that Rogelio had been wearing one like it. Now he was bare-chested, and I was glad that he'd given his shirt to the old woman. She had three sagging rolls of flesh under the shirt. She wore baggy, dirty shorts, man's shorts with a zipper; they were light blue and had a pattern of white music staffs.

"She only speaks Chamorro," Jesse said.

She pointed to the gash on top of Jesse's head where Taitano had knocked him with the gun butt. She pointed to the side of my head. The water dripping from my hair was pink. The wound was oozing again.

I nodded. "He got us both," I said.

"Where's Saint Sammy?" Jesse asked.

"I can't figure it out," I said. "When they blew in, he blew out."

We found Taitano face up beside the cooler. His face was cut and dark bruises were appearing. One arm was dotted with purple-rimmed holes. Norio pantomimed hammering, and I got it: he'd been punctured by flying nails.

While he was semi-conscious, Norio and I sat him up and put him in the wet pink sweater. We'd found it outside, one arm showing under a fallen palm tree. We put it on him backwards, buttoned it up the back, pulled his arms behind him, and tied the ends of the sleeves together. It was a weak straitjacket, but he'd have to struggle to get out, and we could watch him.

We'd have to decide what to do with him. Later, if there were others on the island, we might return to jury trials. Now, maybe the victims should be the judges. I'd lost my rage, though. Disarmed, storm-battered, strait-jacketed in a wet sweater, he seemed harmless and pathetic. Still I thought about marching him to the animal quarantine center and shoving him in the yard with whatever boonie dogs had survived each other and the typhoon. I thought about letting Samuel execute him.

Rogelio sat slackly against the outside of the shop, oblivious to the rain.

"We're watching you, too," I said. "You behave yourself."

"I don't want to do it, miss," he said. "He let me do it."

"You mean he *made* you do it," I said.

"There's no school anymore, miss," he said.

I led him inside and we all ate Spam and ship's biscuits. The Budweiser must have been shaken as the wind hit the cooler, and when we opened the cans they sprayed foam. I told Rogelio to feed Taitano, who seemed numb but opened his mouth for the Spam.

"What's her name?" I asked Jesse. He asked the old woman in Chamorro.

"Josefa Fejeran," she said.

"She's a techa," Jesse said. He stopped a biscuit halfway to his mouth when she began stroking his arm.

"What's a techa?" I asked. She smiled and let go of Jesse's arm.

"She goes around to people's houses and leads prayers," he said. She spoke to me in Chamorro, and Jesse translated.

"Her grandmother was a techa, and her mother was also. She hoped her daughter would be one."

"What happened to your daughter?" I asked her. Everyone was dead, but I thought she wanted me to ask.

She flipped both hands.

"No translation needed," I said. "I'm sorry," I said and took her hand.

She shrugged and put a biscuit in her mouth.

"We should have her say a rosary," Jesse said.

I remembered the island's newspaper always full of old photographs, the faces hardly anything but blobs of newspaper ink, boxed among the ads for the Matuning Cockpit Sport-O-Dome and political candidates: "Vote for my daddy, Jesus Lujan Perez." Beneath the old photographs were birth and death dates and the "First Anniversary Rosary" announcement. The past tense didn't seem to exist in Chamorro English, but they honored death anniversaries with newspaper ads. Perhaps that wasn't a contradiction, though. Everything, even year-old death, existed in the present.

Josefa Fejeran was speaking and Jesse translated. "She says it's spooky to say a rosary for a funeral, but she had to be strong to learn to do it. Her mom said her grandmother's rosary and she said her mom's rosary."

She pointed to Norio.

"She says she won't say any rosary with him here," Jesse said.

"What's he got to do with it?" I said. "His family must be dead, too."

"'I remember my parents' nipa and bamboo house that they built,' she says, 'and the Japanese chased them out and took it.'"

"Does she mean the war?" I asked. "I mean, World War II?"

"They made us stand around a hole in the ground," Jesse translated. "They took these three men out of a car, a Japanese car, and made them kneel down over the hole. The Japanese soldiers kept trying their swords on the necks, like playing, cutting the neck a little bit, and the blood kept dripping into the hole."

"I don't want to hear this," I said. "My God, haven't we all seen enough by now?"

"One of the men yells out, we did nothing, we did not sin, and the Japanese kicks him. His head was not completely off his neck. They cut the other two heads off and they fell in the hole, but the one guy's head didn't separate."

I looked at Norio. He did not understand. The old woman wouldn't look at him.

"But then they ordered his head to be completely cut off and they kicked it in the hole. And then we had to go back to our work detail. They kept saying we were going to be the fertilizer of the earth."

The old woman wept with her head down.

"Does she think the Japanese did all this now?" I said.

Rogelio was dozing against the wall, and suddenly I was exhausted too. I'll never get off this hunk of rock, I thought. I went outside with the dog, and the old woman labored up and followed me. The rain had stopped at last. The white concrete shop was polka-dotted with bits of leaves.

Josefa pointed at my leg. My thighs below the torn-off pants and the inside of my knees were bloody. The blood was bright pink-red.

"What happened to me?" I asked her. Was I only now bleeding from the rape?

She held her arms in front of her to make a big belly, and then she shook her head and shrank the belly. I wasn't pregnant, she was saying.

I'd grown numb to my body. I'd made my body stone that couldn't be hurt. It was scraped, with scabbed-over abrasions, my arms and legs were covered with shallow cuts from leaves, my feet were puffy and white from the wet shoes, my hair was matted and ropy and blood-clotted. But I'd forgotten the body: shaved legs, clean teeth, trimmed nails, shampooed hair, the body powdered after a shower. And now here was my body returning.

"I don't suppose you have a spare Tampax," I said.

She understood the word and reached to the bottom of her long, baggy shorts. She tore the material three inches up the side and ripped a strip from around each leg. The dirty white music staffs held dirty white notes, and I saw that there were faded bits of lyrics under the staffs. When she turned, I saw *Dad-dy's rich* across one buttock. On the other side, *the cot-* ran into the pocket. *Ma is good* slanted off the side.

I took the torn strips and walked away. Behind the shop the land sloped down, and I began to run, a heavy, staggering run, waving the strips of blue cotton. I ran with the dog into the flood that had receded only partly down the slope. The gray water stretched until it sloped up into the sky. In the water, I danced heavily from foot to foot. "Sum-mer-time," I sang, reeling in the water and waving my streamers. The blood ran down my legs into the water. Cimarron charged into the water, barking wildly. "No fish jum-pin', and your mama is dead," I sang. Why had she appeared in that burlesque of clothing? I leapt and splashed and twirled like a cow in a tutu. As I spun, I saw all of them, even Jesse, lined up at the top of the black slope.

"Summertime an' the livin' is crazy," I sang, yelling it at them. "You want a show? Is that what you want?" I twirled and twirled, the grotesque blue streamers whirling, until I fell in the shallow flood, dizzy.

On each turn of the slope, I could see a figure farther down. "Go back," I yelled, pushing the figure away. "Go away."

When the land stopped spinning, they'd all disappeared. I took off the brown ripped-off trousers and my underpants and sat in the water. Rocks and sticks cut into my bare skin. I scrubbed the underpants between my hands and tried to sluice down my body. Finally I stood and put one of the cotton strips, folded, in my underwear and put the pants back on.

They were all sitting around the inside of the shop, pretending they hadn't witnessed my dance. "Oh, you're back," Jesse said. Rogelio was asleep again. The goat's legs were folded under and his eyes were closed. It was raining again.

"*Mees?*" Taitano said pleadingly. "I hear what the techa says. You know what? I lost my dad since I was ten years old. They kill my dad. My dad comes back from the work detail with skinned snakes and we cooks them and that's all we eat. Then they kill him."

"Yeah, it's a rough life," I said wearily.

"*Mees?* You can take this off?" He twisted in the pink straitjacket.

Norio was watching. I made a gun finger and looked at him questioningly. He patted his hip, though I could see he didn't have the gun in his pocket.

"I don't hurt anybody, *mees.* He says don't hurt you," Taitano said. "With this I can't even . . ." He tipped his head delicately.

"You're a creep," I said. Had Rogelio been trying to protect me? "You're a bully. You were going to kill my dog. You can just piss your pants."

"*Mees*, I am so sorry. All my village is kill. Until now I am crazy."

He was a pitiful fat man in a woman's pink sweater. He didn't have his gun, and I'd already defeated him, I thought.

I looked at the others. Jesse's eyes were closed. Norio shrugged.

I unbuttoned the back of the sweater and untied the sleeves. He

248

swung his arms to move the blood. *"Mees,* you aren't sorry," he said. "Now I am on your side."

"You behave yourself," I told him, "or I'll kick your nuts off this time." I felt strong enough to do it.

Taitano went outside and I gestured for Norio to watch him. Soon they were back in, their clothes wet again. It must have been mid-afternoon, I guessed, but everybody was settling down to sleep. I gestured to Norio: you, me, watch? I pointed to my eyes. He nodded and pointed to himself and held up one finger. First he would watch one hour. I smiled at him.

"You and I will never need to learn each other's language," I told him.

I woke with Cimarron licking my face. The room was dim, and outside the silvery band of light was narrow.

"Jesse," I said, shaking him awake, "where'd they go?" Even the little goat was gone.

He shook his head.

"I don't suppose Samuel came back," I said, and he shook his head. "All right, then I'll go look."

"You'll be in deep kimchee out there," he said. "You'd better stay here."

"So Anthony Joseph Taitano can come back for us?" I said the fancy name mockingly.

Jesse was up and hopping on one leg.

"Forget it," I said.

"Maybe you'd like to kick my nuts off, too," he said. But he was smiling.

I backed him against the wall and put my arms around him.

"Kitty Manning," he said. "Oh Kit Manning."

"Jesse S.," I said. "I'm glad you are alive. We're going to stay alive, I think. Samuel or no Samuel."

"That is not a sane man," he said.

"Nobody ever thinks fanatics are sane, at least in their own time. I'm not saying he really has a hotline to God. But he's a survivor. He can help us make it. We need him."

"Kitty, he's dangerous. We need him like we need a dose of radiation poisoning."

My gear bag was still behind the counter, and the mask and snorkel were still there, but the dive knife was not in its sheath. Taitano must have taken it, I thought.

"I'll be back," I said. I held the pink sweater to the dog's nose. "You're no bloodhound," I said. "But extraordinary times call for extraordinary transformations. Find them, girl. Find them."

I followed her down the road angling southwest. Downed trees were heaped like beaver dams. Brown coconut halves and blackened palm leaves and formless hunks of sheet metal were caught up in the heaps. The dog ran ahead and then waited for me to catch up. The road was blocked by an avalanche of mud. A car rested upright in the mud as if it were waiting for a light to change and then would drive on down the path of mud. In the jungle, where the flood was shallow, I found the footprints in the red-brown mud. They hadn't gone far past the mud flood. It was easy to follow the trail of mud clumps and prints.

I heard the woman's wailing. Beside the road was the wreckage of a house. Only one wall remained. I crept over the floor toward the wall. One section of the floor was covered with crayon scribbles. Part of a tiled shower stall remained. Debris had piled up on the outside of the wall. A strip of aluminum, with shards of glass sticking up, remained at the bottom of the window. I looked through the web of sticks and palm leaves against the window.

They had a smoky fire going.

A toilet sat in the yard. Josefa was leaning forward over the toilet tank. Taitano, with his shorts down around his ankles, was behind her. He had the gun in one hand; the other held Josefa's shoulder. Norio was down against a fallen tree, facing the toilet. His hands were behind him, tied, I supposed. The goat lay flat on the ground near the fire. His head was twisted around so the narrow face looked at the tail. The Smirnoff's vodka bottle lay on its side near the fire.

Taitano jerked his head—come here—at Rogelio, set the gun on the ground, and pulled the boy's shorts. Rogelio stepped out of them and stood beside the toilet, hands over his crotch, gray and naked except for his Nikes.

Taitano stepped back up to Josefa, and when she wailed he rapped her head on the toilet tank. He held her shoulders and began the old rhythm. In the smoky red light his face grimaced, and abruptly I remembered Warren on black satin sheets and the flickering of light from the television.

I stepped around the wall. I walked straight over to the toilet and picked up the gun from the muddy ground.

"*Mees!*" Taitano said. He grinned and kept up the rhythm against Josefa. "Here's one for you, boy," he said to Rogelio. "Maybe this time you gots hard chorizo."

I pointed the gun at his head. "Get away from her."

"I can't, *mees*," he said. I pictured him stuck like the dogs in the quarantine center's yard.

I pulled the trigger and nothing happened.

Norio called something, and then I remembered: Pull back the hammer. I shot again.

"Hold her," he told Rogelio, who uncertainly took his hands from his crotch and tried to hold my hands behind me.

"You said you were on my side," I said to Tatiano.

"I lie, *mees*. But I can't hurt you. Today there is never any bullet." To Rogelio he said, "Go on, brown, touch her."

In pleased surprise, Rogelio said, "Brown?" Finally he had been accepted. He was a Chamorro dude at last. He put one hand on my breast.

I jerked away and ran, the dog after me.

"You're a pussy," Taitano told Rogelio. "Good-bye, *mees*," he yelled.

There would be no more casual destruction. Preparing to live and preparing to die were *not* the same, I should have told my mother. For years I had carelessly played with destruction. And so had we all infinitely feared the death that we compulsively pursued. Behind the wall I yanked the biggest piece of glass from the window frame. Perhaps I should have tried to free Norio first, but the little brown goat was dead and Josefa was limp over the toilet tank, and I had already tried to shoot him.

I charged him. "Get him," I yelled to Cimarron. "Sic him." She ran at Rogelio, the growls breaking into deep barks.

I jumped on Taitano's back.

"*Lanya*," he said, exasperated. He tried to keep his balance against Josefa. He thought I was merely a nuisance. But I knew he was beyond redemption, and I knew there were no redeemers. Now I knew my own sins well and would judge and execute. Imprisoning him with the boonie dogs would be abdication.

"Help me, miss," Rogelio wailed. Cimarron had his leg in her mouth. She shook her head as if she could break the creature's neck. "Mister Flood," he called.

With my legs wrapped around Taitano, ride 'em horsie, I got my left hand in his hair and yanked his head back. This was the end to casual destruction. I reached around, everything working together, and pulled the glass smoothly across his throat. As if this were the performance for which I'd been practicing for years, I pressed harder at the Adam's apple, it was easy now that I was strong, and I pulled the glass smoothly in one stroke all the way up to the ear.

Dark blood spurted onto my arm and I let go of his hair. He sagged. As I dumped the body away from Josefa, I heard howling, and I shook my head. Was he howling from his cut throat? This had to be the end. The others, my dog, nothing could hurt them. I had killed a man. I, Kit Manning, had killed. This had to be the end.

Samuel leapt into the clearing, whirling and stomping and

whooping. I thought of my own hysterical dance in the flood behind Lim Bong's.

"God, Catherine, that was great!" He shook his head widely, as if it were too big or too heavy for his body, like a buffalo's.

Josefa was slumped over on the toilet seat, moaning, "Ai de mi, ai de mi." Cimarron was licking blood from Rogelio's leg. Norio's eyes were closed. He looked dead.

Samuel danced around the dying fire, stomping on the ashes and jumping back. Smoke and the smell of scorched cloth and the dark blood on the dirt filled me, and I bent over, sick and bloodless, thinking *malediction, malediction.*

"You are the one," Samuel said, lifting me, "you are my lady." He had spots of blood on his cheeks, as if he had nicked himself shaving, and spit frothed at the corners of his mouth. "You're ready now. Aren't you?"

I kicked loose. "You let me do that. You let me kill him." No, the Chamorro English was right. "You *made* me kill him," I said.

"You're with me," Samuel said.

"How long were you there? Why didn't you save us?"

"He said— He said I would have a wife on the ark. I had to see if you were the one."

"I killed a man," I said.

"You slew a man. You slew a beast. He stuck a gun up you. He'd have raped you if I'd let him. The Flood is the only one going to have you. You see? You see? I take care of my lady."

Everything was motionless. Norio still looked dead against the fallen tree. Josefa sat on the toilet with her face in her hands. The column of smoke from the fire solidified. I was a stone body, and a face—Samuel's face—watched through tangantangan leaves.

"You were there all the time."

"I have seen that you are righteous before me," he said.

This was not the end. There was no end. We *were* wicked, I thought, and I wanted to sink us all, all who remained, sink us in the black water.

For years I'd suffered a mild case of the human disease. Always my mother and I had felt deficient, and we'd tried to stuff our holes with sensation. I'd made Daniel leave. I'd killed our love. Tanô's people had been disappointed that they weren't important enough to be destroyed. They should feel important now, I thought, in their mass graves and firewood heaps, decomposing to humus in the jungle, bloating and bursting in the harbor.

Sam Dillman had *needed* corrosion. He had summoned the word *destruction* to his mind's gray chamber, and the word rebounded, shaking off rust until it shone and became God's voice. He had The Word. We needed to stuff The Word into our hollowness.

I knew what Samuel had to do now. He had to kill the others so that he and I could step onto dry land and begin again.

"Hey, I'm pretty good, aren't I?" I asked him. "That wasn't so hard."

I wondered how he would do the others. That wouldn't be difficult, either. Josefa was old and hurt, Norio was already tied up, Jesse couldn't walk with his wounded leg, and Rogelio was probably too slow to escape by himself.

Samuel put his arm across my shoulders, as if we were comrades. "It's a kick, isn't it?" he said. "A real jolt."

I wondered how many he'd killed before he found me, but I didn't want to panic the others by asking. Samuel would certainly level the rifle and shoot if they ran. Rogelio was the only one who understood English, though, and I thought we could talk around him.

"Why didn't you, uh, dispatch those two yourself?" I asked Samuel.

He grinned and jerked his head at the body. "We were in Achung. I was making him into a disciple after Lujan bought it. He found the kid noshing on a rotting dog and picked him up. Guess he'd kind of got used to kids. Anyway, I thought a couple of disciples might be useful for a while."

"And they were, weren't they?" I thought of his small, tight face at the window, watching Taitano attack me, testing to see if I was a survivor.

"They sure were." He almost danced to the blackened palms on the other side of the clearing where he'd left the rifle.

"You're not going to just—?" I made a gun finger.

"No point in expending any more rations."

"No, but . . . Remember who you are. What's the best method?"

He nodded and smiled. "Smart lady. One clever lady, you are. Flood's lady."

"I wonder what happened to my dive knife," I said. My voice sounded disingenuous even to my ears.

"I wouldn't know about that," he said. "Maybe the fallen disciple took it. You may never ever find it."

He wasn't quite taken in, I could see. And I was canny myself. In spite of all we had done and failed to do, I wouldn't have a hand in this final destruction.

"Okay!" Samuel called, clapping. "Everybody out of the pool!" He pulled me to him and whispered, "Or into it." He laughed the hyena yip again. And I remembered Taitano calling to me hidden in the rocks: *Everybody outta the pool.*

"Do you think you can walk?" I asked Josefa. I helped her up from the toilet seat and pulled her arm around my back.

"Right," Samuel said, loping on ahead. "Take her to the shop and wait there. I'll come back later for the gook. You, boy, you come with me."

Slowly, with the dog leading, we made our way back to the shop and Jesse. I kept listening for the shot.

"Anufat," Josefa said once, stopping to gesture with both hands at her side, as if she were trying to pack a wound. Then with her fist raising her lip, she made a long fang with her index finger.

"I don't understand," I said. "I don't know what you're saying." The darkness lifted a degree, or perhaps my eyes were adjusting.

I'd lost all sense of time. I didn't think I'd have the strength to save the others from Samuel.

"Maybe he won't really do it," I told Josefa. "Maybe Jesse can stop him."

When the shop was in dim sight, I thought I heard a yell.

"Jesse?" I said, inside. I led Josefa to our nest behind the counter and settled her down. "Jesse Santos. Where are you?"

In the typhoon box, I found a short candle and matches.

The room was empty. Beside Josefa on the wooden floor was a dark stain. She leaned over, sniffed, and touched her tongue to the stain. "Mejgâ," she said, nodding.

Although I knew the feeling was ridiculous, the room seemed full of live air, as if the inhabitant had been abducted, not killed.

"You can't stay here," I said. I helped her up again and grabbed the pink sweater and the gear bag. Outside, I picked the old woman up and carried her across the road and into the burned jungle. Behind a dam of branches and mud was the doorless hulk of a car, and I pushed her onto the seat and draped the sweater over her.

"Stay here," I said. "I'm going to get Norio." I hoped she understood his name.

"Iga," she said, sobbing and holding my hand.

Then I ran through the ruined jungle to the clearing, high-stepping through the mud and vaulting logs and debris just like Cimarron. He was still there.

"Norio, my dear," I said and lifted his head. His hair was sticky. "They hit you with the gun, too, didn't they? I'm so sorry I couldn't protect you."

He stirred and held his head up. I untied his hands and his feet. Cimarron sat panting lightly and watching us.

"Can you get up?" I gestured, palms up.

He stood and grabbed me as he started to fall. I held him as he shook out his arms and legs, and then walked him around the toilet, sitting alone in the clearing, and around the ashes of the fire.

"I need your help," I said. "I need to talk to you." I didn't know

256

how much of the scene in the clearing he'd witnessed. I took the sheath for the dive knife from the gear bag. "Empty," I said, shrugging. "Where is the knife? Did you see?"

He pointed to the ruins of the house and started over, staggering and catching his balance. He pulled the knife from a tangle of branches at the corner. With my fingers around the rubber handle, I imagined the thrust into Taitano's back, the jerk backward, and the heft of the knife as I reached around and sliced his throat.

If I'd had the knife, could I have done it? Could I use it on Samuel? I sheathed the knife and bent down to buckle it onto Norio's leg.

"All right, let's go do some heroics," I said.

We made our way silently to the slope below the dive shop. I held Cimmie's collar when we reached the edge of the flood. Norio pointed, and I thought I could see the shape of a man standing out in the water. He had them out there, Rogelio and Jesse.

I jabbed my chest. "Me," I whispered. "Go around." I made a half circle with my finger. "You go straight out." I pointed. Cut Jesse loose, I pantomimed.

I'd let him decide what to do with Rogelio: to save him if he could or let the flood take him. I spat in the dive mask and smeared the spittle around, fastened the snorkel to the strap, and put them on. I pulled on the rubberized dive gloves. The dog followed me along the edge of the water, and I didn't try to send her back. I felt unreal, squishing through the darkness, like a swamp creature with night vision. When we came to a row of palm trunks upright in the flood, we waded out. Soon the water was waist-deep, and Cimmie was paddling. I lowered myself and swam out, lifting my head now and then to check direction.

To the right I thought I saw Samuel's tall form rising from the water, and I sculled farther out until the bottom dropped away. I made a right angle until I was behind him. I wished I'd kept the knife.

The dog and I glided through the black water toward him. I

kept my white face in the water, only occasionally glancing up to see the shape swaying above the water. Through the faceplate, I began to see dense black patches that took the shapes of long sticks and waterlogged coconuts. A flat fish swooped by. As the water grew shallower, I saw a legged creature on the bottom, like a lobster with too many claws, and then a furry patch of spiny sea urchins.

I was shivering. Swimming in tennis shoes was difficult. The dog caught a mouthful of sea water and coughed. I held her up but her legs kept paddling.

Samuel was facing the shore. Someone moaned. His arms waved as if he were conducting. I could see two heads, like floating coconuts, in front of him. His voice carried over the water.

"Every living thing . . . I will blot out . . . from the face . . ."

Then I saw Norio, moving low in the water. Jesse's and Rogelio's necks were roped to a floating log.

"The waters prevailed," Samuel said.

Norio burst out of the water, yelling and splashing.

"What in the hell—?" Samuel yelled.

I swam as fast as I could, not trying to be quiet now. Cimarron bolted through the water beside me.

Samuel and Norio were down. Water flew up white around them.

I swam underwater past them to the bodies. Their legs floated, tied together, and their hands were tied behind them. I surfaced in front of them.

Samuel and Norio were thrashing like sharks in a frenzy. I saw a knife but I couldn't see who held it.

Rogelio whimpered, "Help, miss. I am being good."

Samuel rose from the water holding Norio upright to him. "Yes!" he yelled. "Then I saw a new heaven and a new earth!" He had the knife.

He hadn't seen me. I dove and skated along the bottom until I saw a black furry patch. I reached my gloved hand into the patch and extracted a sea urchin. Spines penetrated the glove, but, barely feeling the stinging, I held the creature and swam to Samuel.

The water was murky with churned-up mud. They were down again. With the sea urchin in my hand, I stood and yelled: "Samuel Flood, goddamn you, come here."

The thrashing stopped. As Samuel stood with the knife, I jumped at him. I jammed the sea urchin in his face. He screamed and brought the knife to his own eyes. He howled.

"See—no more," he yelled. "No more."

Maybe it was *no more sea.*

Spines were stuck in his cheeks and eyes. He tried to cut the spines away.

Norio pulled the knife from Samuel and cut Rogelio and Jesse loose. I saw gashes on Norio's chest. He slid Jesse into Rogelio's arms and gave a command that I couldn't understand. He pulled Samuel's arms behind him and handed me a rope. I put it around Samuel's neck.

"Lake of fire," Samuel yelled. "My lady, my lady." He shook his head fiercely.

"All right now," I said. "Rogelio, you get Jesse out of the water. You take care of Jesse. Cimarron, go!" I pointed to shore, though I knew dogs couldn't follow fingers pointed into the air.

Norio and I pulled Samuel into deeper water. He twisted in his ropes and shook his head.

"First earth has passed away," he said.

When we reached an upright palm tree, I tied the rope around the trunk so that the water lapped at his chin.

"Catherine?" Samuel said. "Why did you blind me? You were going to be my lady."

His eyes were oozing around the spines.

Norio gestured down, but I shook my head. The tides still prevailed, though we couldn't see the moon.

"I have a hidey-hole," Samuel said. "Rations. Ammo. I'll tell you."

"All right," I said. "Tell me."

The water was rising, nearly to his mouth already.

"Take you," Samuel said, shaking his head and spitting.

"No," I said. "No. The tide is going to take you. The water is going to take you. You are just what we all were, but you are our worst. You *wanted* the world to die. You are in love with destruction."

"Bunker," he said. "Food and light. Soap. Mirror."

As the water rose into his mouth, he choked and tried to tip his head back.

I was crying. Norio had his hand on my shoulder as if he thought I would change my mind.

Samuel was a haole, as I was, a civilized creature without breath, without spirit. I thought of Rogelio trying to stay alive by eating a rotting dog. We became the words we were given, or the words we chose. I could not save Samuel Flood. The water rose to his lips. I thought of him trying to shave his face in the bunker. The mirror showed a small face, looking out of cracked silver. I saw the human face watching through the leaves. The water rose, and the water bubbled white as he thrashed his head and expelled all his drowned spirit.

14

The whitewashed walls of Lim Bong's shop were speckled with bits of brown and green leaves for a day, and then the subsiding rain and wind cleaned them away.

Samuel had been an anufat, Josefa told us.

"What's that?" I asked Jesse.

"One of the aniti. Souls after death. He has a hole in his side stuffed with a bird's nest."

Josefa made a fang again.

"And he has a tooth six inches long," Jesse said. "She says you can't kill him. He'll live in a banyan tree and come back."

My right palm was cut from the glass, and my fingers were swollen from the sea urchin spines. My hand throbbed, but it was the pump of blood more than the pain that I felt. The embedded spines would soften and dissolve. All of us were cut or wounded, and we tended each other.

"What does 'iga' mean?" I asked Jesse.

"Daughter."

Jesse skinned the little goat with pieces of glass. The dive knife was gone, and I thought Norio must have lost it or dropped it in the flood. We cooked and ate the meat.

"I never eat dog, miss," Rogelio said. "I am never eating your dog."

"I know you wouldn't, Rogelio," I said.

We began to talk about surviving. Soon the wild pumpkin would return, Josefa said. I remembered the white blossoms and the dark green and orange squash. At first, we could eat the shoots, she said.

We would have to test the rainwater to see if it was poisonous, Jesse said.

Perhaps I could find Samuel's stash. We could use the food. He might have stocked medical supplies, too. I would throw the rifle and the guns out beyond the reef and hope the currents carried them to the Mariana Trench.

Josefa touched Norio's arm. She had decided to say a rosary after all.

"We're going to start learning each other's language," I said.

With no world to hide from or react to, with all the games gone, I thought, love would be different. Maybe we'd never have to split what was whole.

Rogelio and I used sticks and rocks and our hands to dig the graves.

"Human beings take care of the dead," I said. "We're still human."

I found a gecko egg washed against the shop. I broke the neck off the vodka bottle to make a jar and placed the egg inside.

Jesse said, "I'm so hungry I'll probably eat the little guy when he hatches. I'm so hungry, I'll eat a cockroach."

"There aren't any roaches left," I said. "At least I hope not."

"Oh yeah?" he said and turned his head away.

Then he faced us with a pair of cockroach antennae protruding, wriggling, from his mouth.

He showed us how he'd peeled the antennae from a twig. "I used to do that for my kids and tease them. 'Dad's weird,' they'd say."

Each of us had had an entire and separate life. I would remember that. I closed my eyes and saw my mother and Daniel and my sister and my father spin past until I let go and they fell in the wet cut grass. And then I twirled alone until, dizzy, I fell, a statue among them, and then we all rolled laughing in the grass and rose with grass speckled on our arms and legs.

The small white egg in the vodka jar shifted. "Oh my God," I said. "Oh my God, it's going to hatch and I'm going to see it this time." The shell split and the tiny gecko squirmed free. It ran right up the side of the glass and dropped to the floor and sprinted away.

I walked west down the slope behind the shop. The water had receded in the burned jungle. The ground was black and marshy, and the mud rose in my footprints.

There would be more typhoons, Josefa said. Times had changed. It didn't matter if it was typhoon month or not. If it wanted to come, it would come.

Marine Drive was foot-deep in sand. A trimaran rested upside down in the sand.

I walked down through the shallow flood. I remembered putting on a cotton ruffled bathing suit and swimming in the Illinois summer flood with my sister and Donnie and Carol Reynolds and Sally the deaf girl.

There was no beach yet. I sat on a rock and watched waterbugs skimming away as if they didn't know they were headed for the open sea. The chop farther out receded to swells around my rock. Each waterbug left a little wake.

I remembered diving with Daniel in Florida, and diving down to the Christ of the Abyss, a blue-green robed Christ with his arms out, his palms open, so still, he left no wake. Underwater, he was as alive as coral, and he needed no wake.

Josefa had taken the ragged skin of the little brown goat. She had Norio hammer it, stretched tight, onto a board.

The sky was still bulked with dark gray clouds, though the outlines of the mounds and towers were more distinct now. I thought that I hadn't been an adult—a grown-up, the children said—until my mother died, and perhaps the world couldn't grow into itself until it moved past death. Half of the sun appeared then, not from above the clouds but from below. It was low in the sky over the water, a dull matte orange like a harvest moon behind a screen. But we didn't move beyond death, I thought. That was

263

stupid. The dull orange sun glowed and flickered in the water like summer heat lightning. We could not live in the sea. Before, people on the island had stayed here, not lived. Now there was no Eden, because Eden was land, and because the unfallen were apes in gaudy island-wear. Eden could never be, because tempted Adam knew he'd fallen. He was awake. And he knew that finally he would cease to be awake, and that was all, and that was not enough for the pain and the loveliness of mothers singing in dark moving cars, of birth-stained mattresses, of winged skating through blue water, of yards and neighbors, of fathers shucking corn and watering the summer grass, of lying yellow and incandescent with our arms folded around each other like wings.

The matte orange sun fell beneath the water, and an aurora of orange and blue and purple and flashing green flickered on the surface, and then the towers of clouds descended. We would never rise from the island, and we knew that we would never rise, but we would live here in the meridian light, human and winged.